The Moonstone Duke

Moonstone Landing Series
Book 1

by
Meara Platt

Text by Meara Platt
Cover by Dar Albert

Dragonblade Publishing, Inc. is an imprint of Kathryn Le Veque Novels, Inc.
P.O. Box 23
Moreno Valley, CA 92556
ceo@dragonbladepublishing.com

Produced in the United States of America

First Edition May 2023
Trade Paperback Edition

ARE YOU SIGNED UP FOR DRAGONBLADE'S BLOG?

You'll get the latest news and information on exclusive giveaways, exclusive excerpts, coming releases, sales, free books, cover reveals and more.

Check out our complete list of authors, too!

No spam, no junk. That's a promise!

Sign Up Here

www.dragonbladepublishing.com

Dearest Reader;

Thank you for your support of a small press. At Dragonblade Publishing, we strive to bring you the highest quality Historical Romance from some of the best authors in the business. Without your support, there is no 'us', so we sincerely hope you adore these stories and find some new favorite authors along the way.

Happy Reading!

CEO, Dragonblade Publishing

Additional Dragonblade books by Author Meara Platt

The Moonstone Landing Series

Moonstone Landing (novella)
Moonstone Angel (novella)
The Moonstone Duke
The Moonstone Marquess
The Moonstone Major

The Book of Love Series

The Look of Love
The Touch of Love
The Taste of Love
The Song of Love
The Scent of Love
The Kiss of Love
The Chance of Love
The Gift of Love
The Heart of Love
The Hope of Love (novella)
The Promise of Love
The Wonder of Love
The Journey of Love
The Dream of Love (novella)
The Treasure of Love
The Dance of Love
The Miracle of Love
The Remembrance of Love (novella)

Dark Gardens Series

Garden of Shadows
Garden of Light
Garden of Dragons

Garden of Destiny
Garden of Angels

The Farthingale Series
If You Wished For Me (A Novella)

The Lyon's Den Series
Kiss of the Lyon
The Lyon's Surprise
Lyon in the Rough

Pirates of Britannia Series
Pearls of Fire

De Wolfe Pack: The Series
Nobody's Angel
Kiss an Angel
Bhrodi's Angel

Also from Meara Platt
Aislin
All I Want for Christmas

Chapter One

Moonstone Landing
Cornwall, England
July 1815

"BLAST IT, WESTON. Another one has gotten through," Cain St. Austell, Duke of Malvern, growled, his muscles straining and body plastered with sweat as he drew back on the reins of a team of oxen. He'd been guiding them while he and his workers hauled away a fallen oak. "Who is that woman and how did she get past my gates?"

"What woman, Your Grace?" his estate manager replied, squinting into the distance as he followed Cain's gaze. "Oh, her."

"Yes, her. Who is she?" He had fled London to avoid the Marriage Mart, but it seemed these young ladies were not held off by iron gates. They'd scaled his townhouse walls in London as well, some of them with surprising agility, and all with a reckless determination to be compromised by him.

The flighty fools were mistaken if they believed he could ever be forced into doing the supposedly honorable thing and marrying them.

No one could ever force him to do something he was not willing to do.

Cain shook his head in frustration.

He would have to marry someday, of course.

Not yet, however. He certainly was not going to be tricked or coerced into it. Nor was he fit company for any woman at the moment, and he did not mean because of his lack of proper attire. The war years had taken their toll on him. How could he be merry or even think of marriage when he had lost so many friends in battle?

Attending balls or idling the hours away in the comfort of a gentlemen's club was no relief for him and merely added to his anguish.

For this reason, while the *ton* elite were still celebrating Napoleon's demise at Waterloo, Cain had chosen to retreat to St. Austell Grange, the summer home his father had built almost a decade ago on the outskirts of the quiet seacoast village of Moonstone Landing.

The Grange was finer than any homes in the area, but parts had fallen into disrepair as his father's health failed. The work required to restore the grounds and structure to their original grandeur was turning out to be a blessing in disguise for him, giving him purpose and a chance to escape the hectic whirl of London.

A soft look came over Weston's face as he continued to squint into the distance at the young woman. "Weston? Stop mooning over her and tell me who she is."

"She isn't a trespasser, Your Grace."

"That's Lady Hen," one of his workers by the name of Mr. Jenkins remarked, and the comment met with nods of approval from the other hired hands working alongside him to haul the felled timber.

"Is that supposed to mean something to me? Lady or not, she does not belong here. What sort of name is Hen?"

"Lady Henley Killigrew," Weston clarified with a grin. "Her parents did not name her after a chicken."

"She's a good sort," Mr. Jenkins chimed in, which was met with more nods of approval from the other workers.

Was everyone besotted with this woman?

Even Cain's longtime retainer appeared quite taken with her—a surprising feat, since Charles Weston was almost fifty and usually as sour in disposition as he was.

"Get rid of her, Weston." He was in no humor to set his work aside and invite this young woman to tea. She must have heard he was here and wasted no time in surmounting his barricades in the hope of making his acquaintance.

Weston's eyes rounded in dismay as he stared down at himself. "Your Grace, look at me. I am hardly fit to approach her. You ought to do it, since she is your neighbor. She and her sisters reside at Moonstone Cottage."

Cain supposed it was not good form to chase away one's neighbor. "How am I more fit than you to greet her?"

The two of them, along with a team of workers and the oxen, had been clearing the old footpath to the beach, their shirts off and bodies sweating as they labored under the heat of the sun.

Cain enjoyed the grueling work, needing to exhaust himself daily in order to chase the demons from his soul. Indeed, he probably looked possessed by demons, since he had not shaved in over two weeks, nor had he allowed his valet to trim his hair. Added to the fact that he was a big man and had a surly disposition, he must appear like a heathen out of her worst nightmares.

Weston stared at the young woman and frowned. "We had better go to her. Am I seeing right? She looks unsteady on her feet. Do you think she might be hurt?"

Cain took a closer look at the girl as she approached and realized she was clutching her hand. "Blast," he muttered, tossing on his shirt. "Someone fetch Galahad for me."

Weston started toward her. "I'll go with you."

"No, stay here. I'll deal with her." Perhaps he ought to have allowed Weston along, but something drew Cain to this young woman. As he strode closer, he noticed blood spilling down her fingers.

He shook his head to fight off a sudden feeling of suffocation.

The sight of that crimson trail on her hand reminded him of the blood spilled on the battlefields. It stained her muslin gown, a pretty confection of pale green with embroidered pink roses that was now irrevocably ruined.

He shook his head again and forced his breaths to steady.

Who cares what she is wearing?

He quickly did up the ties of his work shirt as he strode toward her, although it would do little to make him more presentable. She was an unexpectedly pretty thing, he realized as he reached her side and was momentarily taken aback by the gentle beauty of her face.

Weston had mentioned the Killigrew sisters to him days ago, but Cain had assumed they were a trio of old biddies.

He ought to have paid closer attention when the man spoke of them.

Yes, this one was exceptionally pretty.

"May I help you, Lady Henley? Mr. Weston told me who you are. You seem to be in some distress. Let me see your hand."

She blushed as her gaze met his, and she backed off a step.

Well, he really was not fit company, with his work clothes damp and foul-smelling. But he'd quickly learned a duke would be forgiven anything, so he hoped not to offend her too badly by his appearance.

"I won't hurt you, but you are bleeding and it needs to be tended. One of the men has gone to fetch my horse. I'll give you a ride to the main house as soon as he retrieves it."

"Oh, yes. Thank you." She cast him a hesitant, but genuinely kind smile, and then turned to point in a southerly direction. "I was walking along the sand beach, got lost in my thoughts, and walked too far. By the time I realized what was happening, the tide had come in. I was not aware it would swallow up the Grange's part of the beach entirely. I found myself trapped by the advancing waves and barely managed to escape up some old, rickety steps that led me here."

She glanced down at her hand. "I cut myself on the splintered wood. I've bled a little and feel a bit lightheaded. Please do not trouble the duke, as I am obviously not fit company, nor would I ever presume to appear on his doorstep unannounced. But I would greatly appreciate something to drink."

Did she not realize who he was?

He took gentle hold of her hand to inspect it and then did a better job of tying the binding tight to stem the flow of blood. She had used a lacy handkerchief on it, hardly much of a binding, although he was pleased to note the bleeding had slowed to a trickle and was beginning to cake on her skin. "You need immediate tending."

Odd, she felt so soft and delicate to his touch.

Well, he had not touched a woman in a while.

"I shall see to it when I get home," she said, now staring with trepidation at Galahad, his enormous black Friesian stallion being led toward them. "Um, I would appreciate the loan of a horse, too. A gentle mare, please. I am not much of a horsewoman and could never handle one such as yours. My groundskeeper, Mr. Hawke, will return the borrowed horse within the hour. I just don't think I can make it home on my own two legs."

Cain studied her as she spoke. Her voice wrapped around him like a soft summer breeze. It was a cultured voice, not in the least high-pitched or whining.

Her hair was a vibrant tawny shade, not quite brown and not quite gold, but full and lustrous as the sun shone down upon her head.

Her eyes were a pale green that matched the color of her gown. There was a crystalline quality to them that gave her an ethereal appearance, as though stars shone in them.

Indeed, her eyes were spectacular. Her lips—

Those were irrelevant, he reminded himself.

But he liked the slight, sexy droop of her mouth at the corners.

"I'll escort you home after we've taken care of the nasty cut," he said.

"But I—"

"Will do as I say. You are in no condition to do anything on your own. I'll have refreshments brought to us while I tend you." He took her by the arm and led her to Galahad, who could be a temperamental beast at times and did not look pleased to have been brought here from the shady hedgerow he had been tethered to and where he was contentedly munching on leaves. He snorted at Cain to mark his displeasure.

"Behave, you devil."

He dismissed Mr. Jenkins with a word of gratitude and told him to put the men back to work. The man nodded and immediately left to do Cain's bidding.

Lady Henley gaped at his horse. "Um…are you sure I ought to be riding him?"

"He's well trained. He won't toss you off."

She met his gaze, her lips puckering in uncertainty—which was quite ironic, for in this moment he was quite certain he was going to kiss her before they parted company.

"I'll walk. But would you mind escorting me? Will the duke be put out that I am taking you away from your work? I will explain it to him—"

"The duke?" He realized she still had no idea who he was. Of course, why should she? Although a horse of Galahad's quality should have given her a clue. However, Cain looked like a barbarian and was out here toiling in the fields like a common laborer. Nor did he have a gentleman's hands, for his had been roughened in battle and worsened from farm work.

"No, the duke won't be put out," he replied.

He took a moment to enjoy the unexpected anonymity.

She would learn his identity soon enough, for Weston, that old warhorse, was staring at them, and Cain expected he would join them at any moment. Until then, it felt odd—in a good way—to be spoken to as a person instead of being fawned over or eyed as prey for the parson's trap.

"Mr. Weston and I were about to take a break from our

work," he continued. "You are not interfering at all. We happened to be clearing a path to the beach. Fixing those stairs was next on our list of repairs. I am sorry we did not get to it sooner. Nor do I have a clean handkerchief to offer for your hand."

He saw Weston now striding toward them, his limp immediately recognizable. Cain knew he would have little more time with the girl before she was formally introduced to him and turned into a fluttering goose. "Forgive my attire. We weren't dressed for company."

She cast him a surprisingly engaging smile. "I am the interloper. Please, no apology necessary, Mr.... Um...are you Mr. Weston's assistant?" She shook her head almost immediately. "No, that does not seem right. He appears to be awaiting your orders."

Blast.

Had she guessed already?

"You say you are repairing the path and stairs to the duke's beach. Are you an architect, by any chance?"

"Something like that."

Weston was almost upon them now.

Despite his desire to be left alone, Cain had not lost all sense of propriety and did not feel right in having the man show him up to be a liar. "In truth," he said with a sigh, "nothing like that, Lady Henley. I happen to be Malvern himself."

She regarded him doubtfully. "You are the duke?"

He nodded.

"The Duke of Malvern?" She shook her head and laughed. "Well, if that is true and you are not having me on, then may I say it is most refreshing to meet you. Your father was a lovely man and always so kind to us. But the gossip rags have made you out to be this paragon of elite society, and I was certain you would be an insufferable clot."

He could not help but grin.

"Well, it is a pleasure to make your acquaintance."

He waited for the calculating look to appear in her eyes, but her expression never altered. Either that, or he was slipping in his ability to detect greed and deceit.

His estate manager now reached them. "Lady Henley, what happened? Are you all right?"

"She will be, Weston. I am taking her back to the house and will summon you if I require assistance. You may return to your duties. There's still work to be done in the fields."

The old man frowned at him. "Jenkins and his boys can finish the task."

Cain arched an eyebrow in warning. "They will finish under your supervision. Lady Henley does not need a nursemaid."

In truth, Cain liked his estate manager, who had been with the St. Austell family for decades and was as honest and faithful as anyone he'd ever met. But he did not want him underfoot while he dealt with this young woman. Nor did he need the man jumping in to protect her at every turn.

"As ever, I am at your command, Your Grace." Weston shot back a warning glance as he walked away.

Cain returned his attention to this Killigrew neighbor of his. He understood why Weston was so peeved at his dismissal. She was remarkably pretty, even though looking a bit pale at the moment.

She must be in pain too, he realized, and admonished himself for dawdling.

He steadied Galahad, preparing the frisky steed for Lady Henley's light weight, then reached out for her. She was not looking at him, lost in her thoughts once again.

"Lady Henley, let's get you to the Grange before you bleed to death."

She turned to him and laughed lightly. "Goodness, I hope I am not that badly injured. But I will admit, it does hurt a little."

"I'm sorry. I should have seen to those steps the moment I arrived here and noticed their poor condition."

"It is not your fault. How could you possibly know I'd get

myself into this coil?" She still had not turned into a gushing ninny, batting her eyes at him or tossing him coquettish smiles.

Nor did she appear to be plotting to entrap him.

In truth, her mind did not appear to be on him at all.

It was refreshing and at the same time irritating.

No, infuriating.

Why was she not interested in him?

Was her heart given to another man?

And why did he suddenly care?

Chapter Two

CAIN PLACED HIS hands around Lady Henley's waist and lifted her onto the saddle. Warmth flooded him the moment he touched her. "His name is Galahad. He can be a little contrary at times. Can you hold on to him with only the one hand?"

"I'll try." She did not look at all comfortable in the saddle. "He is enormous."

"Friesians are bred for battle." He placed his hands around her waist again to settle her more securely.

He'd held women before.

Lady Henley was no one special.

Of course, his body seemed to believe quite the opposite.

He released her a bit too hastily, inadvertently jerking on Galahad's reins.

Lady Henley gasped as the horse lurched forward. "Stop! I cannot seem to get a grip on—"

Cain caught her in his arms as she tumbled off.

Her cheeks were now bright points of red, her embarrassment obvious as she tried to squirm out of his grasp. "I had better walk."

He refused to set her down. "Don't be ridiculous. You are in no condition."

"But—"

"Stop struggling or you'll fall again." He placed her back in the saddle and mounted behind her, which earned him a gasp of indignation. He ignored it. "This is purely for the purpose of getting you safely back to my house. I will not have you trampled because you cannot keep your balance on my horse. Rest your head against my shoulder, Lady Henley. Tensing will only make you feel worse, and I would rather not have you casting up your accounts all over me."

Not that anyone would notice, since he already looked like a beggar off the streets.

To his surprise, she stopped resisting and eased against him.

Good—he hated feigned prudery.

He quickly got her to the Grange and carried her to the gazebo, which was nestled in a corner of his garden. It overlooked the water, and there was a refreshingly light breeze present at this hour of the day. His father had built this garden niche as a place for the family to take tea in the afternoons as they watched the sun set over the water.

Indeed, it must be nearing four o'clock now, he surmised by the angle of the sun. The light would remain for hours yet, since this was summer and darkness never fell before ten o'clock in the evening.

Still, the colors of the sky as the sun began its descent were beautiful.

There was a sitting area in the gazebo, cushioned benches along the sides and a wrought-iron table with matching chairs around it in the center. "Sit," he ordered her, helping her into one of those chairs. "I'll be right back."

He startled his staff by walking into the kitchen and demanding clean cloths, bindings, a jug of water, and bottle of brandy. "Mrs. Chiltern," he said to his housekeeper, "I'll also need lemonade and some cakes brought out to the gazebo immediately. Enough for two."

"For two, Your Grace?"

"Yes, for me and the young lady who needs these bandages and brandy."

He strode back out with his supplies, hoping Lady Henley had not run off. Well, she would not have gotten far if she had tried. The girl must have walked a good distance in the heat to get from Moonstone Cottage to here, then afterward to make her way into his park while injured. That exertion would exhaust even an experienced soldier.

Her eyes were closed and her head lay propped on her uninjured hand when he returned, so he quietly set his supplies on the decorative table and knelt beside her. "Lady Henley, how are you feeling?"

She lifted her head and blinked her eyes open. "I am fine. Just needed a moment's rest."

Those eyes of hers were stunning.

Her smile was soft and rather beautiful.

Yes, he was going to taste those lips before they parted ways.

"Hold out your hand." He drew a chair close to hers and settled in it to face her. "I'm sure you've caught a splinter or two. I'll be as gentle as possible drawing them out. But first, I must wash the area of the wound and then cleanse it with this brandy. It will sting quite a bit."

She nodded. "Do whatever you must. My hand is already sore."

He was surprised by how stoic she was when he applied the spirits to her palm and then dug out the splinters. She kept her eyes closed the entire time, which allowed him to stare at her features.

She had a remarkably lovely face. There was also something utterly beguiling about her body.

He bound her hand properly and then set her ruined handkerchief and the dirty cloths aside. "Done, Lady Henley. You may open your eyes. Ah, the refreshments have arrived. Have something to settle your stomach, and then I shall take you home."

"Thank you, Your Grace. I am so sorry to have put you out. I should have paid closer attention to where I was walking on the beach."

"What distracted you?"

She gave a light grunt. "Do you really want to know?"

He nodded. "I wouldn't have asked otherwise."

"Very well," she said, taking his breath away with another of her smiles. "Men."

He arched an eyebrow, trying to appear casual as fire surged through him. Was there another man in her life? Someone other than him? Not that he wanted her or had any right to her.

Well, that wasn't quite right.

He wanted her.

Hellfire.

He did not care for this at all. "Men? In general? Or is there someone specific?"

"Specifically my father's weasel of a cousin. But you needn't listen to my woes."

"Not at all, Lady Henley. Perhaps I can be of help."

She cast him an engaging smile. "Thank you, but I will figure it out on my own."

"Are you certain? You almost drowned and then almost bled to death. Seems to me this problem of yours is troubling you greatly. Do you not need to confide in someone?" He had no idea why he was pressing the matter or why his insides were exploding in possessive torment.

He was not about to court her. He just wanted to kiss her.

Perhaps he was undone because she had not yet asked him for help, nor did she appear to have the slightest intention of doing so.

People always sought something from him. Why not this girl?

But she merely sipped her lemonade and nibbled at a slice of poppy cake.

"Lady Henley, are we to just sit here in silence and stare at each other? I think the time would be used more productively if we discussed your dilemma."

"But I hardly know you."

"Sometimes, it is easier to talk a thing out with a stranger than to confide in your loved ones."

"That is true." She pursed her lips as though mulling over the suggestion and then gave a curt nod. "Please, you cannot mention it to my sisters. I do not want them to worry."

He had not met her sisters and was never in the habit of repeating what was told to him in confidence. "I give you my word of honor."

"Thank you." She let out the breath she had been holding. "You may put a halt to this conversation at any time. It is not my intention to pile my burdens onto your shoulders."

He smiled. "Consider me warned. Go on, tell me."

"Are you well versed in business affairs? I know many noblemen leave such matters to their estate managers, men such as your very capable Mr. Weston."

"I am well versed. I trust Mr. Weston, for he is one of those rare men of substance, smart and honest. But now that I am back from the Continent, all important decisions will be made through me."

She took another sip of her lemonade. "Well, I was considering consulting Mr. Weston. But for this matter, perhaps you are the better source. He would likely have sought you out for advice anyway."

"What is troubling you?"

"My father, Robert Killigrew, was the Earl of Stoke. Upon his death, his cousin inherited the entailed lands and title. But my father left us well cared for, having set up a trust fund for me and my sisters, Phoebe and Chloe."

"Is this how you came to be at Moonstone Cottage? Was it a part of this trust?"

"Moonstone Cottage was left to us by my father's sister, Lady Henleigh Killigrew. It is ours outright, thank goodness. That grasping weasel of a cousin cannot get his hands on it, although I would not put it past him to try. I am named after my aunt, by the way. The spelling is different. I am H-E-N-L-E-Y and she is…was…H-E-N-L-E-I-G-H."

"One of my workers referred to you as Lady Hen."

She laughed lightly. "That is what everyone used to call my aunt and what they call me now. However, I assure you, I do not cluck, nor do my feathers ruffle easily. But as I was saying, after my father died we were no longer welcome in our childhood home. It was a lovely townhouse in Mayfair. The new earl and his wife kicked us out the day after we buried my father. They would have done it sooner, except they were afraid of earning the ire of society's powerful patronesses. We did not care, really. We loved coming to Moonstone Landing to visit over the years and expected to live at the cottage when the time came."

A streak of sunlight shone upon her as she smiled up at him, bringing out the gold and brown highlights in her hair. "It used to be haunted, did you know? Have you heard about our ghost?" she asked with a sparkle of mirth in her eyes. "He has not made an appearance in quite a while, but I think he is still with us. Well, that is another story."

"Tell me more about this weasel cousin of yours." He knew where this conversation was heading and wanted her to continue.

"While affairs were put in order, my father's solicitor, Mr. Garrick, looked after our trust. He is a kind man and was most reliable in sending us our monthly stipends. I've read the trust and know this is what was clearly stated, that we should each be given a generous allowance. I also know how much principal was set aside for us, and therefore have a good idea of what income should be coming to us monthly."

He pursed his lips in irritation, not at Lady Henley, but at this cousin who was the new earl. "And the payments have now dwindled?"

She nodded. "He has stopped them completely. We have received not so much as a ha'penny in the months since he's taken over trusteeship duties. I've written to him about it and have had no response. I've also written to the bank manager and got back a curt letter, bordering on rude. I think I will have to go to London and find out what is going on. But what am I to do once there? I do not think the earl or the bank manager will see me."

"You need a benefactor to intercede."

"I thought about contacting the Earl of Ashbrook, who has been a dear friend of my father's for many years. However, he is not in the best of health."

"I know him," Cain said. "He is a good man, but not up to the task. Don't bother Ashbrook."

"But I don't know who else to ask. Most of my father's friends are dead or not in good health. The other members of our family are as much at the mercy of our weasel cousin as we are. This matter will turn ugly, and I don't know anyone else well enough to impose this task upon them."

"You haven't asked me."

She ignored the comment, her magnificent eyes fixed on him as she continued. "My father left us quite well off, but I suspect the earl is… Oh, now he will accuse me of slander. I dare not say what I think he is doing with our funds. But the longer this goes on, the less likely my sisters and I will see any of our inheritance."

Cain hated men like this new Earl of Stoke. He'd spent years on the Continent fighting Napoleon to protect England from the little despot, and yet such tyrants still existed in the form of men like Stoke. He'd probably paid others to fight in his place while he continued to live his lavish life without a care for anyone else.

To allow this cousin to now cheat these innocent young women infuriated Cain. "I am due in London next week. Permit me to look into the matter for you."

She frowned at him. "I did not confide in you to rope you into this mess."

"Perhaps I am bored and would enjoy tossing a few punches."

Her eyes widened in surprise.

They really were beautiful eyes, the sort a man could wake up to every morning.

"Well, you do look like someone never to cross. A bit scary, really," she said, but her smile was soft and sweet, and she did not look particularly frightened of him. "You could knock him out cold with one blow. But his wife…"

He frowned. "I would never hurt a woman."

"Oh, you misunderstand. I did not think you ever would. You may look like a beast, but you were ever so gentle when tending my wound." She glanced at her bandaged hand. "No, I was merely allowing my wicked thoughts to wander. She has the nastiest disposition and is no doubt the one urging my cousin to cheat us. One cannot be in her company without wanting to throttle her. You will think me shockingly bloodthirsty, but I was imagining my satisfaction in hauling back and punching her myself, solidly in the nose."

"You are hardly bloodthirsty. You could not frighten a fly." He slapped his hands on his thighs. "That settles it. I shall speak to the bank manager. If he gives me any trouble, I will go directly to his board of directors."

"You can do this? Oh, I suppose because you are the Duke of Malvern and he will be afraid to offend you."

He leaned forward and growled softly. "Officious little prigs like him get my blood boiling. I will see him sacked without references if he dares defy me."

"How marvelous of you! I wish I had that power." She shook her head. "I would never really hurt him, for I'm sure he must have a family reliant on his wages. But it would be fun to scare him—"

"This is why you would be inept at getting results. He would sense your softness and put you off. But I am not soft," he said with a quiet growl.

She blushed as her gaze quickly darted to his body. "Indeed, you are not."

Ah, she'd noticed.

"Your Grace, your kindness only makes me feel worse. How can I drag you into our family affairs? If it were just for myself, I would not accept."

"But you have your sisters to think about."

She nodded. "I would do anything for them. I even considered marrying for the sake of claiming our funds. The terms of the trust require each of our shares to be distributed to us upon our marriage. Phoebe and Chloe are still too young, but I thought if I found a good, honest man, at least we'd have my share for all of us to live on."

"Have you found such a man?"

She winced. "No, not yet."

Relief inexplicably washed over him.

"The thing is, it cannot be just anyone. He must be someone with significant clout, someone a judge would take seriously when we petition to have my father's cousin removed as trustee. Someone who can make judges and bank managers jump to attention when he demands a full accounting. But he must also be someone who would have my complete trust."

"That is no easy thing to find."

"I am well aware." She rolled her eyes. "I refused several offers of marriage in my first Season—my only Season—because those men were merely after my trust fund and did not care at all about me. I always thought I would marry for love, and have not quite come to terms with having to marry for convenience. Well, I don't suppose it is convenient for me or my intended husband. Marriage of necessity is a better term for it. But I think I must go to London and see what can be done before I sacrifice myself at the altar."

"Lady Henley, you would be wasting your time trying to fix this on your own. Let me help."

"I've known you all of ten minutes and now feel as though I've bullied you into—"

He laughed. "You? Bullied me? Have you not noticed that I am a full head taller than you and probably twice your weight? My fists are three times the size of yours."

She grinned. "More like four. Your hands are big."

"And I am not afraid to use them on little weasels, whether

they be earls or bank managers. If the earl has cheated you, then he will restore every last farthing or face my wrath."

Her eyes sparkled as she laughed. "I would give anything to see him squashed."

Lord, this girl was exquisite.

"Even marry me?"

Chapter Three

HENLEY HAD JUST lifted her glass to take a sip and now spilled the lemonade all over herself. "What?"

She shot to her feet, ignoring the sticky liquid now oozing down the front of her gown. She needed to dart back home before this day got even more bizarre.

Had this gorgeous beast of a man just asked her to marry him?

He appeared mildly amused by her fluttering.

"Marry you? You are speaking hypothetically, of course. Are you not?"

He grinned as he rose and drew her to his side, one big arm circling her waist to keep her from bolting. "Did it sound like a hypothetical to you?"

"No…it… Blessed saints, I think I've hit my head and am hallucinating. Have you gone completely mad? Or did you say this to ruffle my feathers? Well, consider this hen duly ruffled."

"I said it because I meant it." He grabbed one of the clean cloths he'd brought out earlier. "Stop wriggling while I pat the spill dry."

"I don't know why you are bothering. My gown is already ruined." She tried to tug out of his grasp, but even though his hold was light and gentle, she could not escape him. "Not even Mrs. Hawke, my wizard of a housekeeper, will be able to remove the blood and lemonade from the muslin, no matter how often she boils the fabric." She pushed at him again.

He emitted a soft warning growl. "Blast it, Hen. Stop fighting me. I am not mad, but perhaps you are. I do not know of any other woman in her right mind who would run from me. Is my offer so offensive?"

She stopped struggling and turned to stare at him.

To study him closely.

He was handsome…if one looked past his gruff exterior. He looked like a big golden bear, one with intelligent brown eyes, and he certainly knew how to hold a woman in his arms. There was something quite exquisite about his muscles, and she hadn't been trying all that hard to wriggle away from him. "No, it is not offensive at all. But…is there something wrong with you, Your Grace?"

He emitted a hearty chuckle. "Not a thing wrong with me other than needing a bath. Is this what has put you off?"

"No, not at all. But I fear you have been out in the sun too long. I do not know of any man in his right mind," she said, tossing his words back at him, "who would offer to marry someone they've known for all of ten minutes. Is this your idea of a cruel jest? Are you making fun of me? I assure you, I do not appreciate your humor."

"No, Hen." He cast her a surprisingly sober look. "May I call you that? I am completely serious."

She shook her head. "How can you be?" She glanced around, desperate for Mr. Weston to make a timely appearance.

In truth, she would be screaming at the top of her lungs for him now if not for the fact that he often spoke of the duke in glowing terms.

"Your Grace, I am not suitable for you."

"Why do you think we do not suit?"

"Um…because…" She tried to ignore her body's response to being held in his arms. Well, he wasn't embracing her but merely restraining her. "You cannot be serious. Isn't it obvious? My sisters and I are merely castaway gentility now. What would you want with the likes of us?"

"Sit down and let us discuss this as adults. Speaking of which, how old are you?"

"Twenty, not old enough to marry without consent of my guardian, who happens to be the odious weasel cousin of mine."

He made a grumbling sound and motioned for her to resume her seat. "He won't dare refuse my offer. I'll circumvent him if he tries. All the more reason for you to marry me. You are in need of a savior, are you not?"

She nodded. "But not a husband."

"What do you not like about me?"

The question surprised her. Had she not been an obvious, fluttering goose around him? The man was stunning. He had to know it. "This is not about you, but purely about the short time I've known you."

"Then my looks are acceptable to you?"

Another surprising question. "Your Grace, are you having me on? You are the handsomest man I have ever met. You are no doubt irresistible to all women. I'm sure you've left a trail of swooning debutantes between London and our cozy village."

"Then it is not my looks or odor that offends you?"

Dear heaven, nothing about him offended her.

Apparently, she was partial to rugged men who growled like bears. She'd had no idea until this moment, which probably explained why she had not found any of the young lords who preened and strutted like peacocks about London to her liking. "Mr. Weston speaks quite highly of you. So did your father. My sisters and I adored him. He was such a lovely man."

"Thank you. He and I were always close, even though we did not always see eye to eye on a subject."

"Such as your going off to war. He always worried about you. But I've read the newspaper accounts and am familiar with your heroic exploits on the field of battle. You have also been kind to me in the few minutes we've had the opportunity to chat."

"Then where is the problem?"

She cleared her throat because this man was being awfully dense. "As I said, does it not bother you that you have known me for all of ten minutes?"

"I believe it has been longer than that now." His lips twitched at the corners and then curved into a surprisingly appealing smile. "Closer to an hour, I would estimate."

"That's right, not even an hour yet," she reminded him. "Are all military men this rash to act?"

He folded his arms over his chest. "I would prefer to think of myself as decisive, not rash. Do you not think you are a fine catch?"

"Of course I am. But what I think of myself is entirely beside the point." She cleared her throat again, hoping to take another approach. "Let us speak hypothetically for a moment."

"That word again," he muttered. "Why? My offer is real, Hen."

"Stop saying that. And now you are grinning at me. Stop it. This discussion is as much for your own good as it is for mine. If a man such yourself were truly interested in me…what would marriage to you entail? What demands would you place on me in return for securing my inheritance and that of my sisters?"

By his silence, she knew he had not thought this part through at all. "Aha! See? You don't know."

Which was all the more reason not to humor this absurd offer of marriage. Well, not really absurd, but more an answer to her prayers. The thought had assuredly crossed her mind, and perhaps her straying onto his property, although inadvertent, was not completely happenstance. Before ever meeting him, she had contemplated knocking at his door and asking him to marry her. But only as a last, desperate act.

She had also plotted scenarios in her head.

Encountering him by chance in Moonstone Landing.

Inviting him to tea.

Good afternoon, Your Grace. I am your neighbor, Lady Henley

Killigrew, and I would very much like to invite you to tea…and me. Would you mind terribly taking me on as your wife?

None of it was necessary now that he'd done the unthinkable and proposed himself.

How could he do such a thing when he did not know her?

Yet how could she pass up an offer from this duke?

Not to mention St. Austell Grange was a magnificent home overlooking the sea. It was three times the size of Moonstone Cottage and had a landscaped garden that ranked among the loveliest in England.

They stood staring at each other in the elegant gazebo, the scent of honeysuckle along its lattices filling the air and blending with the salt of the breeze off the water. Her breath caught with a silent ache, for she could see herself as mistress of this manor.

This was what her years of training and education had molded her to be—not only a wife and mother, but someone with the wherewithal to be a leader in the community, to see to the well-being of the villagers, and do her best to preserve the family's legacy.

His eyes were alight with seeming interest as he studied her. "What would you want our marriage to be, Hen?"

"Oh, no. You are turning the tables on me. Do not respond to my question with one of your own." She regarded him thoughtfully. "But since you ask, I would want a love marriage, something that cannot be accomplished in five minutes' acquaintance."

He folded his arms across his massive chest. "It has been almost an hour's acquaintance by now."

"Stop mocking me. My question is serious. Are you a rake?"

He cast her a devilish grin. "Do I look like one?"

She pursed her lips in irritation. "You are doing it to me again. Stop answering my questions with ones of your own."

He sighed and leaned closer. "I am not a rake. But women are attracted to me, and I will not deny that finding one to warm my bed has never been a problem for me. Knowing that I would someday inherit the Malvern dukedom certainly made me more appealing to these women. I am not so deluded as to believe they liked me for myself."

Now she felt bad for him. "I'm sure many of them did."

"I assure you, they were only thinking of my title and the material goods that came with it."

"Is this what you think of me? It cannot be easy for you to trust people when so many will befriend you only to use you. Which is what makes your offer all the more confusing. If you are serious about this…then why me? Am I not using you just as any other toady who strives to wrestle a favor from you?"

"Did you come here for this purpose?"

"No." She brushed back a stray curl that had fallen onto her brow. The breeze was strengthening, a reminder the hour was growing late and she really ought to get home. "Although I will not deny part of the reason I almost drowned was because I was lost in thoughts of you. To be honest, I was working up the courage to propose to you."

He laughed. "I should have kept my mouth shut and let you do it. That would have been interesting."

"It wasn't going to happen today. Perhaps not ever. I was only going to ask you if I were desperate and had run out of all other possibilities. Do I look like I came prepared to dazzle you?" She glanced at her ruined gown and bandaged hand.

"Do you intend to cheat me or lie to me?"

Her eyes rounded in surprise. "Of course not! I never would!"

"Then where is the problem? Seems to me I've made a wise decision."

She wanted to shake sense into this bear of a man who had the power to make her dreams come true. "Please, take me home." She turned to leave and took a stumbling step.

He sighed and put his arm around her. "Hen, I'm sorry. I am not mocking you or trying to overset you."

She shook her head. "I am not blaming you, just utterly confused at the moment. I am a bit dizzy. I don't know if it is because of the loss of blood or this unbelievable conversation. Perhaps a little of both."

Her hand was throbbing painfully. How could she think straight when she was in pain?

She looked up at him, irritated to find herself attracted to this man who looked as though he'd been lost in the mountains for weeks. He ought to smell like the oxen he'd been guiding, but beneath the scent of male heat—something she found surprisingly arousing—there was also a trace of sandalwood, which signified he'd actually washed this morning.

Her heart was doing little somersaults as she stood beside him.

He took her by the shoulders and gently turned her to face him. "I will take you back home now, but there is one more thing I want you to think upon. I would be a faithful husband if this is what you want, a true marriage. Whether our union arose from necessity or after years of courtship, if I am willing to comply with your terms, then what does it matter how long we've known each other? We can make of this marriage whatever we wish. Just give it thought. Talk it over with your sisters."

She gaped at him like a stunned peahen.

To go to London betrothed to him would open every door for her. The offer was almost too tempting to resist. Almost…but she had to proceed carefully or risk ending up trapped in a loveless marriage to a man who would take all of her inheritance and then cast her and her sisters off to one of his remote holdings.

He seemed to understand exactly what she was thinking. "Hen, I would never do anything to hurt you or your sisters."

"Even if you decided you did not like me? Do you understand my concern?"

"I do. I will be clear about it in the betrothal contract. You need never worry about being treated badly."

"And what of you? You would be stuck with me forever."

The comment must have stirred something within him, for an unrecognizable look sprang in his eyes. He raked a hand through his hair and groaned. "Stuck with you? Is this how you think I would ever view you? You have the smile of an angel and eyes made of starlight. Being with you would drag me back from the brink of hell. Why do you think I fled London?"

"Was it not to avoid the Marriage Mart?"

He cast her a wry smile. "No, I always expected to do my duty and marry someday. I just needed it to be on my own terms."

"What terms? You've just proposed to me, a trespassing stranger. Should you not give this matter a little more thought?"

"No. Hen, you are clearly not a dimwitted woman. Can you not understand?"

She placed a hand to his cheek, an impulsive gesture. But she'd heard the pain in his voice and could not resist. She gave his cheek a light, caressing stroke and felt the rasp of his beard against her palm. "This is about the war, is it not?"

He said nothing, but she saw the haunted look in his eyes, his hurt so raw and open.

"How stupid of me not to realize how badly these years have damaged you. But you seem able to hide it well."

"Not from myself."

She felt the depth of his ache in this admission. "I thought I was the one who needed you."

He took gentle hold of her hand and turned it to kiss her palm. "Perhaps we need each other. Do you understand now why I had to come to Moonstone Landing?"

She nodded. "You found the frivolity of London life unbearable. The cheer. The glitter. The acclaim for your acts of valor."

"The lavish ease of it just did me in. How can I laugh, have everything I wish for drop at my feet, when so many of my friends were lost in battle? Their hopes and dreams were shattered, their families never to be the same again, and I am here with all life has to offer. I cannot tell you how many women climbed over my townhouse wall to get at me."

"No, not at you, but at the Duke of Malvern. This is what hurt you most. After everything you had endured and sacrificed, they saw not the man you were but merely an object to capture."

He kissed her palm again, allowing her to see the pain in his eyes, but she also noticed something darker and drew in a breath.

"I think you have returned home angry and unsettled. Is this why you are offering drastic measures to aid in my cause? My cousin's behavior has inflamed your sense of honor, and you want to pound this weasel who represents the worst in humankind to dust."

He gave her another wry smile. "I am not angry, Hen."

"Then what is the abyss you are so afraid of falling into? Does it hurt you too much to talk about it?" She waited in silence for him to respond and then continued when he said nothing. "You needn't explain it to me. I understand what you are going through, your anger and your grieving."

She drew her hand away. "My cousin is my battle to fight, not yours. Especially not yours if you intend to unleash all your suppressed rage on him. I will not have you doing something you will regret."

She turned away to look off toward the sea, but he drew her back to face him, resting his hands lightly on her shoulders again. "He took advantage of his status to buy his way out of service in the army, did he not? This is what men like him do. Now he would steal from his own family, treat you like the scrapings on his boots. You cannot allow him to get away with it."

"I don't intend to. But I will not drag you down in this fight." The labor she saw him doing in the fields, clearing timber and guiding the oxen, was backbreaking work. She realized he was not doing it because those trees needed to be cleared, but because he needed to exhaust himself in order to sleep at night.

His fingers tensed on her shoulders.

"My sisters and I have helped out at the military infirmary in Moonstone Landing," she said. "We've seen the desperation in some of these men, the quiet seething of hopelessness and anger. These are men who have lost their bearings and cannot find their way home with any clarity. The war years have changed them, and they no longer fit into their old lives."

"And you see this same look in my eyes?"

She nodded. "I recognize it in you not only because of those men, but also because this is what I am going through at the moment. Oh, I've hardly suffered as you must have done. But I will admit to feeling beaten down. I almost drowned because I was so caught up in trying to find a solution to my cousin's perfidy."

"Then marry me, Hen. It is the only way for both of us to win."

She shook her head. "No. I will not enter into a marriage based on anger. Yours for the injustice of war and mine for the injustice of a weasel cousin. If you are still inclined to help me, I will gladly take you up on your offer because I have to think of my sisters. But I will put a stop to your helping me if I notice it is adding to your pain. The last thing I ever wish to do is hurt you. Agreed? We start out as one friend helping another and see what develops from there."

"If this is all I am to have of you…then for the moment, agreed." He cupped her face in his hands and gave her a feather-soft kiss. He barely brushed her lips with his own, but she felt it to the depths of her soul. "There," he said in a whisper, "our bargain is now sealed."

She had never been kissed before, never had a man's lips on hers.

Nor had a man ever run his thumb gently along the line of her jaw.

They stood so close, she felt the warmth of his breath upon her cheek.

His mouth remained achingly close to hers.

She closed her eyes to savor the moment.

When she opened them again, he was staring at her. Could he tell this was her first kiss? Her heart beat frantically and she could not seem to settle it.

"Blessed saints." He released her and ran a hand through his thick mane of hair. "Hen, I'm sorry. I did not realize…I did not think. Have you never been kissed before?"

Chapter Four

CAIN STARED AT the lovely girl, unable to believe how sweet her lips had felt on his. The touch of heaven—this was what had immediately come into his mind the moment he pressed his mouth to hers and felt the plump give of her lips. Was she real? Could he trust his own senses?

"Tell me, Hen. Has no one ever kissed you?"

Henley stared at him, her own senses obviously reeling. "You unwittingly handed me my first. Was it not obvious?"

He groaned. "You are too good to be true. Come on, let me take you home before I decide to lock you away in a tower room and never let you go."

Her eyes widened.

"I am jesting. I may look like a beast, but I will never do anything to hurt you. I give you my oath."

He led her to the stable where Galahad had remained saddled in wait for them. The groom trotted him out and held the reins while Cain lifted her up.

A now familiar flood of heat seared through him, as it seemed to do every time he touched the girl. He took the reins from the lad and mounted behind Hen.

She wriggled and turned slightly to look at him. "Your Grace, is there not another horse I can use for myself?"

He had a stable full of them, but he was not ready to let go of her.

"Quiet, Hen." He snapped the reins lightly, and they rode off at a gentle lope. "Since we are to be in close company for a while, you need not be formal when addressing me. You have my permission to call me Cain whenever we are not in the presence of others."

To his surprise, she did not protest, nor did she tense when he wrapped his arms around her to keep her securely in his grip.

How many times had he placed his arms around a woman? Too many to count, and yet not one of them had ever stirred his soul the way Hen did. Perhaps it was the magical way her body seemed to fit his. She was not a small woman, but he was a big man. Yet her soft curves perfectly molded to his hard frame.

How was he to convince her they were right for each other?

He hardly believed it himself.

When they were far enough from the stable not to be overheard by his grooms, he resumed their earlier conversation. "If you will not consider an actual marriage, then consider agreeing to a fake betrothal. It will give me more leverage when dealing with anyone involved in your cousin's plans to cheat you. Don't give me an answer to this idea now. We'll talk further when I call on you tomorrow."

"You needn't take time from your busy day to—"

"Hen, stop. It is not a chore for me. *You* are not a chore for me." Whether she wished to accept it or not, he was committed to helping her. "Nor will I ignore that you were injured on my property."

"You do not owe me a thing for that. I was the trespasser. But you are welcome to join us for tea. Tomorrow at four o'clock?"

He nodded. "I will be there."

They rode in silence a while longer before she shifted again and looked back at him. "When exactly do you intend to leave for London?"

He grinned. "I'd go tomorrow if I could. But as I mentioned, it will have to wait the week before I can sufficiently tie up affairs here. If you had a chaperone, I could take you along with me in my carriage. It is new and quite elegant. You'd be far more comfortable in it than in a hired private coach. Or…hell…you aren't considering riding a public mail coach, are you?"

She stiffened and cast him a defiant glance. "I would not rule it out if the private coach was too expensive."

"Put it out of your head at once." The girl was a newborn lamb. Soft and luscious. Although she was not helpless, for she'd shown remarkable endurance as he cleansed her wound and dug out those splinters. Not a cry out of her. Nor could it have been an easy feat to rescue herself from the oncoming tide.

Still, she hadn't the muscles to fight off unwanted attention, and this girl was going to catch the eye of every breathing male riding the common coach. "It is not safe for you. I'll ask in town for someone suitable to chaperone you, and then you'll both ride with me. Do you know where you will stay once you reach London?"

"With the Earl of Ashbrook and his wife, I expect. I've already written to them and should have their response within a day or two. Lady Anissa is diligent in her correspondence."

"I know where they live. It isn't far from my residence. I'll give you my direction tomorrow. If you need anything while you are in London, just send word to me there."

She smiled up at him. "Everyone knows where you live. The Duke of Malvern's home is one of the finest in London."

He let out a chuckle. "And still you will not marry me?"

She knew he was merely teasing her and laughed along with him, a sparkling trill that floated on the breeze. "I may change my mind upon closer viewing. Will you give me a tour of your London home while we are there?"

"Warming to the idea of a fake betrothal? It will not hurt your cause if I am seen as eager to marry you."

Which, Lord help him, he seemed to be.

It was one thing to be slammed by desire. It was quite another to be slammed by desire and immediately want to marry the girl. He hadn't even bedded her. Their kiss had been ridiculously chaste. What was it about Lady Hen that made her different from all the others?

Perhaps it was best if one of them used common sense and slowed down this…whatever this was. He could make no sense of what was happening to him, only that the numb organ he called a heart had sprung to life upon his meeting Hen and would not quiet down.

She frowned lightly. "Not a betrothal yet, but merely a courtship. Perhaps this will be enough to bring my cousin around and make him abide by the terms of the trust."

"I understand your reluctance, but I do not think a mere courtship will be enough to scare him. Betrothal is the better route."

"*Fake* betrothal," she insisted, "and I have not agreed to it yet."

He nodded. "Yes, fake…until you decide to make it real."

It was not long before they reached Moonstone Cottage.

The door flew open, and two young women who could only be her sisters rushed out the moment they saw Galahad trot into the courtyard.

"Oh dear," Hen muttered, obviously preparing herself for the thousand questions they were going to ask, especially when they noticed her hand was bound and her gown stained with blood.

Not to mention their curiosity about him. It was not every day a young woman arrived home in the arms of a duke.

"Please say nothing about our conversation regarding my cousin," she said, her tone slightly desperate.

"I gave you my oath, Hen. I shall not break it."

"Thank you. And try not to behave as though we are betrothed, for we are not. Nor are we *fake* betrothed yet."

He grinned, but certainly understood her concerns.

A betrothal was no small step. If everyone believed they planned to marry, she could not break it off without his cooperation. Even if he did cooperate, she might still be considered ruined, since betrothed couples were permitted certain marital liberties, and everyone would assume he had taken every advantage.

He had acquired a bit of a reputation in his younger days. No one would believe her if she claimed he hadn't touched her.

It did not help that his body already ached for her.

If he compromised her, she would be forced to go through with a wedding. Despite his own mindless leap in that direction, he had no intention of coercing her to such an end. If she married him, he wanted it to be on her own terms and a choice freely made.

She still had doubts about him, because she did not know him at all, and he looked like a bear caught roaming in the forest.

If he was displeased in the marriage, he could ship her off anywhere he wanted, place her in one of his remote holdings, and she would have no say about it. He would retain complete control over her and the wealth she brought to the marriage. Who was to say he could be relied upon to be fair with her and her sisters? What was to stop him from taking her funds and shirking his duties toward her?

He would never behave so cruelly, of course. But these had to be the questions swirling in her mind. He understood why she needed to be careful.

Her sisters surrounded her as soon as he helped her down.

Mr. Hawke ran over to take Galahad's reins and lead him to the stable, but Cain stopped him. "Good day, Mr. Hawke. I won't be staying. Leave Galahad with me."

"As ye wish, Yer Grace. I'm at yer service should ye require anything for that fine beast." Hawke returned to his duties as soon as Cain dismissed him.

"Hen! Hen!" Phoebe and Chloe now shouted in unison while Hen remained beside him. His presence certainly raised even more questions about her absence. But their relief at seeing her was palpable and joyous.

He shared a smile with Hen as her sisters continued to bob up and down, and now both were chattering at her, giving her not a moment to get a word in edgewise. The younger girl had a head of red-tinged curls several shades darker than Hen's golden curls, and the other had a mass of dark hair. He knew the youngest had to be Chloe, and the dark-haired one, the middle sister, could only be Phoebe.

They knocked Hen backward in their enthusiasm to hug her.

She fell against him and tried to apologize as he steadied her. But her voice was soft and her sisters were a pair of noisy magpies, so she merely shook her head and cast him a mirthful glance.

"Thank goodness you're home! We thought you had drowned! What happened?" Phoebe cried.

Chloe noticed the blood on Hen's gown. "You're hurt! We knew something awful must have happened to you."

"No, Chloe. I am fine. Your Grace, may I introduce my sisters to you? Oh dear. Chloe, stop wailing."

"I cannot help it." Chloe threw her arms around Hen's neck and would not let go. "I'm so glad you're safe. I was sure we'd lost you."

Phoebe was wringing her hands beside them.

Hen once again attempted an introduction. "The Duke of Malvern was kind enough to tend to my injured hand and bring me home. It is just splinters, nothing more serious. Chloe, do stop crying and take a moment to greet him."

"All right… Good afternoon, Your Grace. Thank you for bringing our sister back to us. I'm twelve," the girl said, sniffling as she reluctantly released her grip on Hen and curtsied.

"And this is Phoebe," Hen said, glancing at their middle sister. "Forgive me—as she is seventeen, I ought to have introduced her first, but Chloe can be quite persistent."

At least Phoebe had the presence of mind to behave with more decorum. "A pleasure, Your Grace. Would you join us for tea?"

He shook his head. "Another time. I'm sure you have lots of

questions for your sister." He turned to Hen. "I'll stop by tomorrow to look in on you. Summon me at any time of the day or night if you develop a fever."

She pursed her lips, looking as though she wanted to tell him to stop coddling her, that she was quite capable of managing for herself.

He supposed she was, but this was a new and marvelous thing to him, this caring for someone else.

"Thank you. I will."

"Then I'll be off." He mounted Galahad with a casual ease and galloped off to St. Austell Grange.

He had not known this woman two hours ago. How could she possibly make such an impact on his heart?

A heart that had given him nothing but anguish throughout the war years and his return to London. Death and bloodshed in battle, and shallow frivolity once home. So many people had accosted him in the few weeks since his return from the Continent, throwing themselves in his path. Demanding all of him. Grabbing all they could.

Scheming to grab more.

Hen was a gift, although she did not see herself as any different from those grasping at him. But she was nothing like that lot, and this was why he wanted to help her. This was why he wanted her.

She was sunlight.

She was starlight.

She brought hope into his life again.

His big Friesian ate up the ground beneath his feet, and they were soon back at the Grange, riding through its massive wrought-iron gates. Weston and his men were no longer by the wooded area. They must have finished for the day.

He looked forward to resuming their tasks tomorrow, the first of which was to start repairs on those cliff steps.

Hen would have drowned had she not been able to latch on to that broken timber. Thank goodness it held, or she might have tumbled down the cliff.

He gave silent thanks for whatever force had kept her safe and brought her to him.

But these feelings she aroused in him were most confusing.

He needed to sort them out, and ought to have been grateful to her for refusing his offer of marriage. Had any of his friends ever come to him claiming they had fallen in love at first sight and proposed to a woman they hardly knew, he would have knocked them out cold.

Yet here he was, behaving exactly this way.

Weston was waiting for him in his study when he strode in. "How is Lady Henley?"

Cain motioned for him to take a seat. "She is fine. Nothing more than a few splinters, which are now safely removed and her hand properly cleansed and bound. Her sisters were worried, of course. Care for a drink? I am in need of one."

He strode to his cabinet and poured him and Weston brandies. "We really must fix those stairs. Lady Henley could have been seriously hurt or trapped in the rising tide and drowned. I've seen too much death already, Weston. I don't think I could have handled hers. It tears me up inside knowing how close she came to disaster."

Weston nodded thoughtfully as Cain handed him the glass. "You like her, don't you? I thought you would. Her sisters are nice girls, too."

"Yes, Phoebe and Chloe. I ought to have listened more closely when you spoke of these Killigrew neighbors. Lady Henley is a mother hen to them. Her name is appropriate. Lady Hen. And her sisters are little more than baby chicks."

Weston laughed.

Cain took a sip of his brandy and grinned. "All right, just say it."

"What?" Weston arched an eyebrow. "That she's a good sort? I told you so."

Cain snorted.

"What?" Weston stared at him a long moment. "Gad, you like her. I mean, really like her."

"What if I do?"

His old friend laughed. "You've been moping about the Grange and hardly fit company for anyone, then she comes along and suddenly…dare I say it? You are smitten."

"I wouldn't take things that far."

"Your eyes are alight and you are chirpy as a bird."

Cain responded this time with a growl. "I am going to kick your arse from here to Dover if you dare refer to me as chirpy again."

Weston leaned forward and regarded him thoughtfully. "Fine, then I shall call this impact she has had on you something else. Life saving? Soul searing?"

"You are getting carried away. Although, I will admit, she is someone…"

"Special?"

"Different from the others, for certain."

"How does she compare to Lady Alexandra?"

Cain sank into his chair and took a healthy swallow of his brandy. "Do not mention her name in my house."

"Go ahead and sack me for my impertinence if you must, but I will not have you toying with Lady Henley's affections if your heart is still bound to—"

"Damn it, Weston. Do you think I would use the girl as a trinket? Besides, what business is it of yours if I do?"

"Those Killigrew sisters are among the finest ladies you will ever meet. Lady Henley in particular. She has a sweet, trusting heart, and I will not see her hurt by you. I care for her, not as you think… I am old enough to be her father, possibly even her grandfather. But I look at those girls and cannot help but think of all I missed out on by never marrying and knowing the joys of raising children. Now that they have lost their parents, they have no one but a distant cousin to look after them. Frankly, I think he is more of a danger than a help to them."

Cain set his glass aside. "What have you noticed?"

"Other than the worry etched on Lady Hen's face whenever I happen to see her coming out of the bank? It does not take a brilliant mind to figure out something is terribly wrong. These girls are not frivolous spendthrifts. I happened to mention the Earl of Stoke when speaking to her recently, and she immediately tensed. Something is going on. I want to offer my help, but what can a mere estate manager do? The man would shove me aside as though picking a flea off his waistcoat."

"He will not shove me aside," Cain said, deciding to tell Weston of his plans. "She has confided in me, and I have agreed to help her."

Weston looked disappointed. "She confided in you? But she hardly knows you."

"This is precisely the reason I got her to open up to me, because I was a stranger to her…and it did not hurt that I am her neighbor and a duke. But I'll tell you something, Weston. I never felt closer to a woman while I heard her speak. It wasn't the proximity. She touched something in my soul. Do not ask me to explain it, for I have no idea what happened to me today. But I know that I must help her. My feelings for Lady Alexandra have not a thing to do with it. I am long over her."

"You are?" Weston appeared astounded.

"She was a boyhood infatuation. I hadn't seen her or thought of her in years. My happening to run into her in London last month had nothing to do with my decision to come here."

Weston stared into the dark amber liquid in his glass. "I hope so. Tread carefully with Lady Hen, will you? I fear you have the power to hurt her far worse than this new Earl of Stoke ever could."

Cain rose to put an end to their conversation. "Duly noted. I'll see you in the morning. Let Mrs. Chiltern know I'd like supper sent up for me in my chamber. I have a bit of work to do and would prefer not to be disturbed."

"Very well, Your Grace."

Cain watched Weston leave the study and quietly close the door behind him. Only then did he sink back in his chair and bury his head in his hands. Was it possible the man was right and he'd never gotten over Alexandra?

Was this why he'd grabbed hold of Hen and behaved like that?

No, it could not be. Besides, Alexandra was married and out of his reach.

Not that he wanted to reach her even if she were free again. Their time had come and gone. He was no longer a boy fresh out of his first term at Oxford. Nor was Alexandra ever the angel he had imagined.

Were there some unrealized, lingering feelings for his old love that made him behave as he had toward Hen? How else could he explain his ridiculous proposal of marriage to this girl he hardly knew?

He ought to be relieved she had rejected him.

In truth, he did not feel relieved at all.

If anything, he wanted to carry Hen off to the nearest minister and have their wedding ceremony done and over. It would not happen, of course. He did not have a license. She was not old enough to give her consent. But at the age of twenty, she was only a few months off from that all-important age of consent.

He'd marry her sooner in Scotland if he had to.

He'd marry her again in England when she came of age, if necessary.

She was no child, but he needed to protect her.

This feeling in his soul could not be ignored.

He would not press her on accepting his offer of marriage, not yet. But he surely would if it was the only way to make certain her trust fund was put in safe hands.

His hands. For he knew no other way to protect her.

He was eager to see her tomorrow.

Were his feelings for her real?

Or completely imagined?

Chapter Five

HEN'S SISTERS STARTED tossing questions at her the moment the duke—she was not about to call him Cain—had passed through their gate and disappeared onto the road.

"Tell us everything," Phoebe demanded, locking arms with her. "Shall I make you some tea? Let's get you out of that gown. Oh, it is quite ruined. And it was one of your prettiest, too. I'm sure the duke must have appreciated the way you looked in it."

"I doubt he noticed anything other than the blood on my hand."

Chloe was still sniffling. "What happened? How did you hurt yourself? You were gone a very long time. We searched for you and could not find you on the beach. We thought a wave had swept you out to sea. Don't ever scare us like that again."

"I'm so sorry, Chloe. I will be more careful from now on." Hen led them upstairs and proceeded to tell them about her adventure while they helped her change out of her damaged garments, for the stain had worked its way through the muslin and into the linen of her chemise as well.

Her sisters listened, enraptured as she told them about the oncoming tide and how she'd clawed her way up the perilously splintered steps. However, she did not mention their cousin's possible embezzlement of their trust funds or the duke's marriage proposal.

How could she when she hardly believed it herself?

Phoebe frowned when she finished the recounting. "What had you so worried that you did not notice the tide coming in and got yourself trapped on the beach?"

"Just things in general," Hen answered evasively.

"It is our cousin, isn't it? Do you think we have not noticed your visits to the local bank or the anxious way you await the post?"

Hen sighed. "I was never good at hiding my feelings, was I?"

Chloe settled on her bed. "No, you show everything. Tell us about the duke. Do you like him?"

Hen shrugged. "He was very nice to me."

Phoebe gave her backside a playful swat. "Just how nice? Did he kiss you?"

"What a question to ask!" But Hen blushed furiously.

"Oh my! He did kiss you! How did it feel? Splendid and transporting?" Phoebe's grin was full of mischief. "He looks like a beast. I was tempted to run in and grab a rifle when I first caught sight of him. But then I noticed you looked quite cozy in his arms. I'm glad I decided not to shoot him."

Hen laughed, put at ease by her sister's teasing. "I did not look cozy. I was tired from my ordeal, that's all. And he did not exactly kiss me, not how you think."

"How many ways are there to kiss a person? Ha! You are blushing again. Oh, Hen. You do like him!" Phoebe examined the gown her sister had now taken off. "Do you think he might help us with our cousin?"

Hen nodded. "He has already offered. Annoyingly insistent about it, I might add."

Relief washed over both her sisters, something she immediately noticed, since they were no better at hiding their feelings than she was.

"Thank goodness," Phoebe mumbled, her voice a ragged whisper. "I hope you took him up on the offer."

"I did, Phoebe. Do not fret about our situation. Nor you,

Chloe. He will secure a proper chaperone for me, and we are to go to London together next week. I intend to stay with Lord and Lady Ashbrook, of course. But the duke will call on me while I am there. I've invited him for tea tomorrow so we can discuss our plans."

Chloe clapped her hands. "Excellent. He does not look like a man to cross. I think he looks like a big, wild bear. Our cousin, that slimy coward, ought to quake in his boots when he sets eyes on him. That horrid man deserves a good comeuppance."

Phoebe set the gown over a chair. "Should we all go to London? I would hate to miss out on the fun when the duke traps him in his big paws."

"Honestly, Phoebe. He has nice hands. And no, you are not coming with me." Hen gave a determined shake of her head. "I don't want you anywhere near that weasel. Stay here at Moonstone Cottage, where you will both be out of his reach while the duke and I deal with him. Ugh, I cannot stand to think of him as the Earl of Stoke. Papa was an excellent earl and everyone loved him. Cousin Willis is the lowest form of life."

Chloe put a handkerchief to her eyes and dabbed her tears. "I cannot wait to hear what happens in London. But what can we do if the duke does not bring Cousin Willis around?"

"Drastic action would be required," Phoebe said, done assisting Hen with her clothes and now settling at the foot of her bed. "We'd have to convince the duke to marry our Hen. It would be the only way. Do you think he would consider it? Any chance at all? He seemed quite solicitous of you, but is it only because you almost bled to death on his beach?"

Hen remained silent.

Phoebe's eyes widened. "Blessed saints! Hen…? No, it cannot be. Has he asked you to marry him?"

Hen wanted to deny it, but the words caught in her throat because she could never lie to her sisters.

She could not even nod her head.

"He was in jest," she finally managed to squeak, her breath

still trapped in her lungs. "A jest. Nothing more."

But she knew it was not. She felt it in her bones. She'd felt his sincerity in her soul.

"I turned him down, of course."

Phoebe groaned, fell back on the bed, and stared up at its blue damask canopy overhead. "Oh, what a nitwit thing to do! He was the answer to our prayers. How could you refuse him? Do you think he might ask you again? You have to accept him."

"Yes, Hen. You must," Chloe said with equal vehemence.

Phoebe nodded. "We are not saying this to save ourselves. Well, partly for that reason, of course. But we saw the two of you together. You...*fit*. He must have sensed this himself, or he would never have offered for you, not even in jest. Dukes are very careful about such things."

"Well, he wasn't. He hadn't known me more than an hour before he blurted that ridiculous proposal. Who does that?"

"A man who knows what he wants," Chloe chimed in.

Hen came to her side. "But that's just it, sweetling. I don't think he knows what he wants. He is restless and uncomfortable in his own skin. He is not the man he was before heading off to war and is still searching for the man he ought to be. Nothing feels right to him yet."

"Except for you," Phoebe said. "This is what he recognized on instinct. But you spurned him."

Why were Hen's sisters making this so difficult for her? She was already worried she'd made a terrible mistake, and they were only adding to her misery. "I talked sense into him. It isn't at all the same thing. Anyway, there is nothing to be done about it now. We shall see him tomorrow for tea and consider what happens then."

Phoebe patted her hand. "You are right. I spoke out of turn. Who in their right mind would ever trust such an offer? He might be our neighbor, but he's still a stranger. We only knew his father, but he's gone now, and who is to say the son is as nice?"

Chloe giggled. "I wonder what he'd do if you poked him? Do

you think he would bite?"

Hen rolled her eyes. "For pity's sake, he is not a bear." She pulled her young sister off the bed. "Come on, let's have supper, and then I am going to turn in early. We'll see if the duke shows up tomorrow or comes to his senses and completely forgets about me."

"No! He couldn't possibly forget you." Chloe launched herself into Hen's arms. "If he does, then I will dismiss him from my thoughts as the greatest fool ever to exist."

Phoebe laughed. "I second that opinion. I wonder what Aunt Henleigh and her sea captain, Brioc, think about him. Shall we try to summon back our ghosts and find out?"

"Or lure Cousin Willis out here and have Brioc chase him into the sea," Chloe said with glee.

"Nonsense—now we are all just getting silly." Hen scooted her sisters downstairs, and they had a picnic supper in their garden because the evening was too beautiful to spend indoors. They had light fare, a potato pottage into which they dunked fresh bread as they watched the vivid pink and lilac streaks darken upon the sky.

Later that evening, when they had all retired to their bedchambers, Hen walked out onto her small balcony to look up at the stars. Her chamber had belonged to the sea captain ghost, Brioc Arundel, at one time, then became her Aunt Henleigh's bedchamber when she bought the haunted Moonstone Cottage after his death.

He'd haunted the place until Aunt Henleigh died a few years ago.

Hen was certain he had been here merely waiting for her aunt to join him. In truth, on summer nights such as this beautiful one, she felt the romantic strength of their love for each other and could imagine them dancing upon the moonstones that shimmered beneath the water on the clearest, crispest nights. It was said those moonstones glowed brightest when love was in the air.

The Duke of Malvern might jest about such things, but she

knew love was real and could not be bound by time or place. Hearts meant to be together would find one another.

Was this why he had offered to marry her?

Had he felt this way about her?

She shook her head and hurried back inside, hoping tomorrow would bring answers.

It seemed impossible the duke should choose her out of all the young ladies in the realm—and not only choose her, but decide on it within a few minutes of knowing her.

How could love possibly be this strong?

Well, she was *assuming* he loved her.

It was quite possible he did not and had chosen her for other reasons entirely. Not necessarily any bad reasons. Perhaps he felt calmed by her. After all, he was a man in turmoil, unable to shake off the effects of war.

Having the ability to soothe his anguish was a valid reason. How he must ache for his soul to be at peace. Perhaps he wanted her because she reminded him of someone familiar and pleasant.

Well, she simply did not know.

The day had exhausted her in every way, and she fell into a deep sleep before her head even hit the pillow.

Since Hen liked to sleep with her drapes aside, she was awakened early the next morning by the gleam of sunlight across her face. Eager to start the day, she threw off her covers and opened the doors that led onto her balcony. From her vantage point she had a view of her garden, and beyond it to the blue waters of their cove.

She watched the sunrise over the water.

How could London ever compare to the natural beauty of this little part of Cornwall?

The dew was still on the ground, a silvery coating upon the flower petals and grass. Indeed, everything shimmered at this fragile hour, and even the sea sparkled as though touched by faerie magic.

"I'll need a bit of that magic today, Aunt Hen," she said, addressing the soft morning breeze. "Will you help me? I think I botched my chance with the duke."

She sighed, knowing it was foolish to believe the ghost of her aunt and the sea captain might still be lingering in Moonstone Cottage.

Hen washed and dressed for the day, tied her hair back in a simple ribbon at her nape, and then went to look in on her sisters.

Both were still fast asleep and cozily tucked in their beds.

She would not disturb either of them now. Instead, she silently made her way outdoors. Her intention was only to walk to the edge of the garden where it met the cottage's cliff steps so she could look out over the sea. Those steps led down to the beach, but after yesterday's mishap, she was not going to walk there alone for a few days yet.

She changed her mind when she saw a figure standing by the water's edge.

It was not difficult to identify the tall and muscled man.

"Cain," she whispered, liking the sound of his name on her lips.

Despite his request, she was never going to call him that. He was the Duke of Malvern to her.

Why was he here? Perhaps to study the cottage's stairs and rebuild his to match?

He must have sensed her watching him, for he turned suddenly and stared back at her.

She held her breath, uncertain what to do.

Then he smiled and began to make his way toward her.

She had not done up her hair, and now gave it a pat in dismay. Well, this was no social call, nor a suitable hour for visitors. He could not expect her to look perfect. Nor was he properly dressed, clad only in his shirt and breeches.

She heard the soft clomp of his boots as he started up the stairs.

"Good morning, Your Grace." She glanced back toward the house, then started down to meet him partway. "What are you doing here?"

"The name is Cain. I told you, I do not want formality between us when we are alone." He brushed a stray wisp of hair off her cheek, and his knuckles remained lightly pressed against her skin. "You look lovely, Hen. I like you with your hair down."

The wind was a little brisk this morning and blew the stray wisp back onto her cheek. "I only tied it back loosely. It isn't practical, but I did not expect to find anyone out here, or I would have done it up properly."

"I'm glad you didn't." He stood two steps below her and still met her eyes.

She smiled at this big man. "You haven't shaved. I was wondering whether you would."

He emitted a rumbling chuckle. "Do you want me to?"

She shook her head. "Chloe thinks you are a talking bear disguised as a man. But I don't mind the way you look. Flouting convention suits you."

His hair, too long to be fashionable, was drawn back in a tie at his nape.

"I wondered what I would think when meeting you again," he said, his voice deep and resonant. "I wasn't mistaken—you are lovely beyond belief."

Heat shot into her cheeks. "I'm sure I am not."

He took her bandaged hand and held it with care in his palm. "You are, Hen. Your eyes shine the like the stars of heaven. But I did not come here to court you or seduce you."

"Then what are you doing here?" She was more relieved than disappointed, because this man would have her agreeing to anything if she were not careful. No one had ever spoken to her as he did.

Oh, she'd had compliments tossed at her when in her first Season, but she easily saw through them as lies. The duke had a way of making her believe his every word, made her feel the intensity of them, and this was far more dangerous.

How could she possibly be someone special and miraculous

to him?

She slipped her hand out of his, needing to put a little distance between them before she found herself melting in his arms.

No wonder women climbed walls to get at him. The man was irresistible.

She could see the flex of his muscles against the fine lawn of his shirt. His buff-colored breeches hugged his trim torso and firm thighs. He wore brown boots that looked worn but obviously were of the finest leather.

"I could say I wanted to look at your cliff stairs and possibly copy them in the restoration of mine," he said. "But I really had no purpose in coming here other than my heart led me here. I did not expect you to be awake at this hour."

"I went to bed early and woke as the sun came up. I don't know why I came out here either. I was restless, I suppose, and could not stay indoors." She cast him a wry smile. "But I learned my lesson when almost drowning yesterday and had no intention of going anywhere near the beach."

He glanced in the direction of the water. "Then I won't ask you to join me. Your sisters will never forgive us if they lose you again, even if it is only for a few minutes."

"Will I see you later?"

He nodded. "If I am still welcome."

"Of course you are. My sisters and I plan to walk into town later this morning to pick up cakes from Mrs. Halsey's tea shop. She makes the best cherry tarts in all of Cornwall. Have you tried them?"

"No, but sounds tempting."

"We'll serve them for your visit. Do you have any particular favorites?"

He grinned and held out his arms. "Do I look as though I am particular about food?"

She laughed. "You are big, but quite fit. All hard muscle. Nothing soft about you."

He climbed up one step so that his head was a little above

hers and he stood awfully close. "And you are all softness. Ah, you are frowning at me. Shall I go now, Hen?"

"No…that is…not on my account. I wasn't frowning. I was merely thinking."

"About what?"

His lips and the nice way they had felt against hers.

But how could she tell him this?

He was studying her, his eyes taking her in. Was he going to kiss her again?

He grinned. "Do you want me to, Hen?"

Her heart began to race. "Do I want you to what?"

"Kiss you."

How did this man understand what she was thinking?

He chuckled. "Your cheeks are red as fire."

"Was I that obvious?" She could behave priggishly and deny it had entered her mind. But she would only be denying herself the pleasure. "It felt nice the first time."

"I thought so, too." He took her hands in his and tugged her close, his touch purposely gentle so as not to hurt her injured palm. "I know you are still puzzled by whatever this is between us. But I want you to know, you are a wish come true for me."

"Don't say that."

"Why not? It is true."

"How can I be? You are one of England's most eligible bachelors. You can have any woman you want. Why me?"

"To be honest, I don't know. I saw you yesterday and my heart came alive. This is the only way I can explain it. I was sure I would wake up this morning and realize my mistake, dismiss my feelings as momentary madness. But seeing you again now…" He shook his head and emitted a light groan. "I know I made the right decision."

He leaned forward and pressed his mouth to hers, this time prolonging the touch of their lips. Yesterday's kiss had been light as a feather, but this one felt more urgent. Hungrier and unmistakably real. His lips sank deeper onto hers, still gentle but probing and possessive, as though he wanted her surrender.

Not that it was a battle.

But with this kiss, he was staking his claim.

He placed his hands on her hips and drew her up against him. There was no denying the feel of his body against hers or the power of it. He stood one step below hers, and they were now thigh to thigh, and hip to hip.

Her breasts softened against the hard wall of his chest.

"I am going to marry you, Hen." He wrapped her in his arms and deepened the kiss.

She placed her arms around his neck and moaned, the sound resembling something between a sob and a whimper. Mostly, she felt relief that he still wanted her.

These feelings he stirred were new and struck her with the powerful force of a storm wave.

She could not stop her body from tingling, so she held on to him. She'd never touched a man so beautifully formed…muscles upon muscles…taut and divine.

He wanted her.

"Dear heaven," she whispered when he ran his tongue along the seam of her lips to tease them slightly apart.

"Heaven, for certain." He wound his fingers in her hair, slid them through her windblown curls.

Her ribbon loosened and blew away, leaving her hair as free and wild as the beat of her heart.

She could not get enough of this man.

"What you do to me…" he whispered, his voice raw.

"I fear you do the same to me."

He drew his lips off her mouth and began to trail kisses down her throat. "I knew you would taste sweet as nectar. I need to stop kissing you before I take this too far. I don't want to do something we shall both regret."

"What is there to regret?"

"Nothing, I suppose." But he emitted a pained groan and drew away.

She wanted to draw him back. Her head was spinning and her body reeling with these fiery sensations of delight.

"Cain?" She was pleading for him to hold her again, craving the strength of his arms and the warmth of his body.

"I'm right here, Hen." He swallowed her up in another embrace.

She inhaled the arousing scent of sandalwood on his skin. "Is this how our married life will be?"

"Yes, all this and more. Whatever you want it to be. Are you accepting my offer of marriage?"

She gazed up at him. "Are you still offering?"

He nodded. "Yes. My mind is unchanged."

"Thank you." She hugged him and buried her head against his shoulder. "I want to marry you. It isn't because I need you to defeat my cousin. Is it selfish of me to want you for myself? Please tell me we are not insane. I want this to be real. Promise me this is not a mistake."

He laughed. "Does it feel wrong?"

"No. But how can it possibly be right on less than a day's acquaintance? If either of my sisters had come to me in this absurd manner, I would have locked them in their rooms for a month. I am supposed to be the sensible one."

"Love doesn't have to make sense."

She gasped and drew away to stare up at him again. "Is this what we are feeling for each other? Love?"

"Perhaps not yet. But in time, I hope so. Hen, you are fluttering. I have obviously ruffled your very pretty feathers."

"How did we leap from necessity to love? Why are you so calm about this?"

He took her hands in his. "Because I feel at peace when I am with you. I felt this way yesterday and again today. I look at you and know that I am home."

"I am your home? No. We are moving much too fast. There's still too much to discuss."

"We'll have plenty of time for discussion this afternoon.

Write down terms that are important to you. I'll make certain they are included in our betrothal contract."

"We really are doing this? A betrothal contract? It could be all for naught. My weasel cousin may never sign it."

"He will not dare refuse. Not only am I a frightening beast," he said in jest—although how could he be so calm and unaffected?—"but I am also a favorite of the royal family. I have powerful connections, Hen. Your cousin might defy me, but he will never dare defy them."

"I don't want anyone else brought into this dispute, certainly not a member of the royal family. They will take a pound of flesh from you in return for a favor. It is too steep a price for you to pay. Is this not true?"

"No, Hen. They would not make demands on me in return for a favor. But I have no intention of involving anyone else unless it becomes necessary. It is just you and me for now. We can do this on our own. But once we reach London, everyone will be watching us. They will sense immediately if you are scared. So, you need to be brave. Confident. You need to be a lioness."

She laughed. "No, that is Phoebe, not me. But you are a great golden bear, so I shall try my best to be a respectably fierce she-bear."

He kissed her on the nose. "Very well, my bear mate. This is what you must be to protect yourself and your sisters. What terms shall I include for you in the betrothal contract?"

"I don't know. Nothing that will hurt you. As for me, I ask that you do what's right to protect Phoebe and Chloe."

"And you."

"Yes, me too." She trusted him, odd as it seemed. But she had known his father, and he had been a man of honor. More important, his father often spoke with pride of this son he had raised. Mr. Weston always spoke highly of him, too. "Do terms of intimacy go into a contract?"

He arched an eyebrow and cast her a rakish grin. "Care to

elaborate?"

Her cheeks heated. She cleared her throat. "Sleeping arrangements. I did not know if such things were ever mentioned."

"If the circumstances call for it. Hen, I know you are untouched. Unspoiled. I do not expect you to share my bed. If this is what worries you, then rest easy. As my duchess, you'll have your separate quarters adjoining mine."

"Oh, adjoining?"

"Does this not suit you?" He frowned. "Do you wish us to be kept farther apart?"

"No, adjoining is all right. I thought…that is… Are you certain we shall never share a bed?"

"I don't know. Is this how you want it?"

"Is it not the custom?" She did not know what else to say, so she stayed mute. He was the duke. He would know better how these things were supposed to work.

"I am a restless sleeper. It is better we keep to our separate quarters." Pain flickered in his eyes. "I had better return to the Grange. You ought to return to your cottage."

He gave her a quick kiss on the cheek and left her on the stairs.

She watched him as he walked along the sand, hoping he would turn around to look at her. But he never did.

Hen sank onto the step and buried her head in her hands. She had been swept away by his kisses and the ache he stirred in her body.

But he was a man still haunted. Still scarred by war.

Could she trust any of what he was feeling? She did not doubt his word, but it was the word of a man in torment.

Perhaps he was lying to himself. Which meant he was lying to both of them.

Inadvertently, of course.

At heart, she sensed he was an honest man.

It was so odd, the way they behaved around each other. Apart, they could both think logically, but together, neither of them seemed capable of rational thought.

She watched him briskly stride toward the Grange. When he was almost out of sight, she hurried down the steps to retrieve her ribbon that had fallen into the sand. Frugal times called for frugal measures…only, she had just agreed to marry a wealthy and powerful duke.

What were they doing?

She got the sense neither of them really knew.

Was he always going to insist on their maintaining separate quarters? Was it possible to convince him they ought to share a bed?

What if he refused?

Chapter Six

THE SUN SHONE brightly, but the breeze was cool off the water as Henley and her sisters walked to Moonstone Landing to run their errands later that morning. Their cottage and St. Austell Grange were situated on the heights above the village that lay nestled in a pleasant cove below.

Although not large, the village had everything any resident would need—a church, a schoolhouse, a bank, postal office within a general mercantile store. A doctor, blacksmith, fishmonger, several taverns, a tea shop with bakery, and a fine inn. Every Wednesday was market day, when the local farmers would sell their fresh grains and produce in the village square.

Moonstone Landing was also expanding, since the army had plans to enlarge the ancient fort's barracks and improve the local docks. She hoped these additions would increase prosperity for the local residents. Now that the war was over, there would be an influx of soldiers returning who would need employment.

Also not to be overlooked were the well-heeled Londoners who were starting to take notice of their quaint village with its charming streets, flowered squares, and beautiful blue waters. She and her sisters thought it was an ideal place to live out one's life. Were it not for the need to confront her London cousin, she would happily spend all her time here.

"Will you be stopping at the bank?" Phoebe asked as they

walked down the cobblestone main street and greeted villagers in passing.

"Yes, but I doubt there will be anything for us. Cousin Willis is not going to repent his ways without a nudge in the right direction. And by nudge, I mean a hammer fist to the face. Well, not really a fist, but a legal assault."

"I like the idea of a fist better," Chloe remarked.

Phoebe laughed. "Me too."

Hen nodded. "It is nice to dream of such a thing. He is a horrible man and deserves his comeuppance, but I wouldn't want the duke to get into any trouble on our account. Not even a duke can hit an earl without there being repercussions. But if he does hit him, I hope he lets me watch."

Chloe giggled. "You must write to us in detail if he does. Seems to me he could get away with it. Dukes are more powerful than earls, and they don't come more powerful than the Duke of Malvern. Oh, I do wish you had agreed to marry him."

Hen stayed silent.

Phoebe groaned. "Hen? What is that look about?"

Hen felt her cheeks heating again.

"Has something changed since yesterday? I knew you were oddly quiet at breakfast this morning."

She sighed. "I may have done something."

Phoebe took her by the arm. "Something good or something bad? Well? Go on. Don't keep us guessing."

"All right." Hen winced at the thought. "I happened to see the duke on the beach early this morning."

"Our beach?" Chloe asked.

Hen nodded. "I think he must have come by to inspect our stairs and did not expect to see me there at that early hour. But he walked over to greet me. Obviously, he could not ignore me…and one thing led to another…"

Phoebe laughed. "More kisses? You really are setting a terrible example for your sisters, you know."

Hen nodded in agreement. "Yes, a terrible example. Chloe,

do not ever do anything as I have done—certainly never accept an offer of marriage from a man you've known less than a day."

Phoebe gasped. "Accept? Is this what these latest kisses led to? You have agreed to be his wife?"

Hen put a hand to her heart. "Oh, Phoebe! What have I done? Seems I cannot think straight when he is close."

Chloe began hopping about and clapping her hands. "We are saved!"

"Don't say that. We don't know anything about this man, truth be told. And we were not completely helpless," Hen insisted. "I would have figured out a way to restore our trust fund."

"You did," Phoebe said gently. "You took the only logical step and brought the duke into our dispute. We may not know him well, but we have read enough about his exploits to know he is valiant and heroic. Also, we knew his father. And Mr. Weston surely would have said something if he did not think the duke was a good man. But you have also gotten something splendid out of solving our woes."

"What is that?"

"You have gotten a man who loves you."

"Phoebe, he—"

"He must love you, Hen. Do you not believe in love at first sight? Is this not what you felt for him, too? You've just said it yourself—the two of you cannot think straight when you are around each other. It is wonderful."

"It is frightening. Oh, it may be fun to read in stories, but how can I be certain this is real? He does not know me and I do not know him. What if we cannot adjust to each other?"

Phoebe gave her a playful nudge. "Only you would worry about such a thing. Do you think any other woman would give a fig about the duke's feelings? No, they would simply grab him and all they could get out of him. This is why he is so sure of you. As for you, if that man cannot get on with you, then he is a hopeless curmudgeon who will never get on with anyone else. You are the kindest, most sacrificing person I know."

Hen shook her head furiously. "We've hardly had to sacrifice yet. Nor will I ever allow Cousin Willis or anyone else to take advantage of us."

"I know, but hurling fists is not your manner. You ensorcel men with your charm."

She laughed. "Phoebe, stop. I am hardly an enchantress. Can you imagine? It is ridiculous."

"The duke doesn't think so. And look, he and Mr. Weston are riding into town. Oh, they've seen us."

Chloe shot into the quiet street and waved at the two men. "Good morning, Your Grace. Mr. Weston. We've come into town to buy cakes for our afternoon tea. Will you be joining us as well, Mr. Weston?"

Weston glanced at the duke, who nodded. The kindly estate manager doffed his hat. "It appears I am, Lady Chloe."

"Indeed, Mr. Weston. You are most welcome," Hen assured him, noting the duke's consent.

The men must have been on their way to purchase supplies for the repair of the Grange's cliff steps, but had spurred their horses forward upon seeing them instead of turning off toward the mercantile store. Both now dismounted and approached them.

Mr. Weston tipped his hat to them again. "I understand congratulations are in order, Lady Henley."

She regarded him with dismay. "Oh, His Grace has told you?"

The duke chuckled. "Hen, that is the most despondent reply I have ever heard. Do you think you might be a little more cheerful about our betrothal?"

"Hen told us on our walk here. We are thrilled about it." Phoebe stared pointedly at her sister and then gave her a not-so-subtle nudge. "Aren't we, Hen?"

Chloe was all smiles and giggles. "Your Grace, may we let everyone know?"

"Of course," the duke replied. "It is no secret."

She clapped her hands again with glee. "I am certain there will be an extra pie in it for us when we tell Mrs. Halsey. She'll be delighted, especially if she is first to hear the news. That woman loves to gossip. Word will spread throughout the village within five minutes of our telling her. What a coup it will be for her. Yes, we might even find two extra pies tossed in."

"Make sure one is apple." The duke cast Chloe a wink. "It is my favorite. But I hear her cherry pies are equally delightful."

How could he jest about pies when the marriage could turn out to be a disaster?

"Hen," he said with a chuckle of amusement, taking her arm. "I assure you, marriage to me will be a lot less painful than a tooth extraction. Weston, will you escort the young ladies to their shop? I'll follow along in a moment with Lady Henley."

Once the others were out of earshot, the smile faded from his lips. "Do you want to back out? I fear it will be too late to do so in another minute."

"I don't. I am happy about it."

"Then why the frown?"

"I never do things on impulse. I am cautious and deliberate by nature. Phoebe claims I sometimes think things to death. These strong feelings I have for you scare me. Do they not scare you? It has only been a day, and we are taking a plunge into the waters of a lifetime commitment. *A lifetime.* And what do we really know about each other?"

He shook his head. "I know that you are kind. Thoughtful, as you just confirmed. Beautiful to look at and delightful to kiss. I have excellent instincts. If I am not scared, then neither should you be. Are we all right, then?"

"Yes…mostly."

He arched an eyebrow. "Mostly? What still troubles you?"

"You will think me foolish."

He tucked a finger under her chin to raise her gaze to his. "Tell me."

"The sleeping arrangements."

His expression darkened, and he immediately tensed. "What about them? You've made it clear you do not wish to share my bed, and I will not force you to it."

She shook her head in confusion. "You think I do not want to...you know...share? What gave you that impression?"

Now it was his turn to appear confused. "Did you not say so this very morning? Well, you said nothing when I suggested it. But you did not seem pleased by the idea. I was not going to push you. Few men of my rank share a bedchamber with their wives, and I assumed your silence meant this was what you preferred."

She let out a breath. "No, this is not what I want. I thought it was what *you* wanted. I do not mind sharing. I like being in your arms. I think it would be nice to fall asleep while held by you. I just... Everything is so rushed, that's all."

He eased noticeably as she rambled.

She probably made no sense at all, because her thoughts were so scattered. But he seemed to understand the gist. A shared bed. A shared bedchamber.

"Hen, let me make it easy for you. This is all new to us. Once we are married, I'll have you settled in the duchess's chambers. Next door to mine, and we shall be close. But..." He took a deep breath and sighed. "My sleep is troubled. I was not merely saying this out of hand. It is a serious matter. It is possible I will lash out when caught up in one of my nightmares. Let's see how it goes, all right? We can change things if my dreams ever calm down. What matters is that we are always under the same roof."

"Does this mean you have no intention of sending me away?"

He emitted a pained groan. "Send you away? I want to hold on to you with every ounce of my strength. I want to clutch you so tightly, I'm afraid I'll break you in half."

She smiled. "You do?"

Before he had the chance to answer, they heard a shriek from inside the tea shop. In the next moment, Mrs. Halsey's daughter tore out of the shop and started waving down their neighbors.

"Oh dear," Hen said.

"It is done," the duke murmured. "The news is out."

"And it is going to spread through the village like wildfire."

He took her hand and gave it a light squeeze. "Are you all right?"

She nodded. "It was never my intention to call it off... Well, I might have done. But only because it was moving so fast. This is something to learn about me. As I mentioned, I like to mull things over slowly and with due deliberation. Perhaps I think too much, as Phoebe claims. I do like you, Your Grace. This was never an issue."

"Cain."

She groaned. "It feels so odd to call you that."

"Then you may call me something else. An endearment, perhaps? My darling? My love? My dearest beast?" He cast her an affectionate smile that melted her heart. "Or is it too big a leap for you right now, my cautious Hen?"

She shook her head. "You are teasing me, but I am not afraid to test it out...my darling."

"There, that didn't hurt at all, did it?" He laughed. "Sounds nice."

She nodded. "It does. But this is what frightens me. Not frightens me, just...confuses me. I like being in your company. And I liked your kisses, especially the scandalous one you gave me this morning."

"It was tame. You'll know when I kiss you without holding back. But about this morning, I believe I owe you a hair ribbon."

She tucked her arm in his as they started toward Mrs. Halsey's tea shop to pick out their baked goods. "No, I found mine in the sand after you left. I retrieved it."

"I should have known. Cautious and frugal, that's what you are." He arched an eyebrow in wicked amusement when she began to fret her lip. "Ah, you are overly thinking again."

"See, this is precisely my fear. That you will wake up tomorrow and realize—"

"I am going to kiss you in public if you do not cut out this nonsense. I see that you are a worrier, too. Heavens, I think I am about to marry Mr. Weston. This is him to the last detail—cautious, frugal, worrier, deep thinker. Only his body is nothing like yours. Quite unappealing, actually. But yours is hot and glorious. Hen, I am teasing you. What must I do to make you feel more at ease?"

They paused a moment to stand clear of a passing carriage before walking on. "I will calm down. It just takes me longer to absorb things than most other people. You trimmed your beard. Did you do this for me?"

He nodded.

She cast him a sincere smile, quite liking the way he had cleaned up. Oh, he still had the look of a wooly bear, but one who might pass in polite society because he was so handsome. "It looks nice."

"I'll shave it off and have my hair trimmed once we reach London. I will be more effective if I fit in with the fashion of society's elite. The look of a wild man shipwrecked on a deserted island is not going to win anyone over."

"It won me over," she admitted.

His eyes crinkled at the corners and his smile was mirthful. "Good. You're the only one whose opinion matters to me. Perhaps I'll grow it back once we return from London. Which reminds me, we still need to find you a suitable chaperone. And what about your sisters? Will they be all right without you here? Should I engage someone to stay with them while you are gone?"

"I think they will be fine with the Hawkes to attend them. Would you mind if Mr. Weston stopped by from time to time to look in on them as well?"

"In truth, I think he was going to do it anyway."

Hen waited for him to open the door to the tea shop and escort her in. The delicious scent of warming pies, of apple and cherry and apricot, of cinnamon and raisins, enveloped her. But she had not a moment to breathe them all in before Mrs. Halsey emitted a joyful cry and flew around her counter to hug her.

Then the kindly baker remembered herself and bobbed a curtsy to the duke before giving Hen another heartfelt hug. "I knew it! Mr. Halsey, did I not tell you our lovely Lady Hen was perfect for His Grace? And now they've gone and done it!" She was still bobbing curtsies and giving Hen hugs as she rattled on. "Betrothed! We are so happy for you both!"

Hen cast her a gracious smile when she finally managed to free herself from the enthusiastic embrace. "Thank you, Mrs. Halsey."

"We shall have everyone from the village up to celebrate at the Grange upon our return from London," the duke said, placing a possessive arm around Hen's waist. "I'll leave all the arrangements to Lady Henley and her sisters."

He then turned to her. "Weston and I came to town to pick up supplies for the repair of my cliff stairs. We had better be off. I will call upon you later."

She nodded.

He cast her a look that had her quietly melting again.

She wanted to kiss him, but it would be scandalous to kiss him the way she wished to do it…ardently, and with great depth of feeling.

He grinned and looked over at his companion. "Come, Weston. We had better collect our lumber from Mr. Bedwell's mercantile if we're to have any work done today."

Hen watched the duke stride out, surprised by how empty she suddenly felt inside.

Was it possible she was already in love with him?

He had a commanding presence, not to mention impossibly good looks. No one could overlook him when he entered a room.

Phoebe nudged her. "You are staring at that door like a bereft puppy. Come on, Hen. Let's pick out the pies. You will see him in a few hours."

Hen shook her head. "I wasn't staring."

No one believed her.

She sighed. "Mrs. Halsey, what do you recommend for our

afternoon tea?"

Hen and her sisters walked home an hour later laden with packages because they'd bought too much. But in their defense, Mrs. Halsey was a marvel and everything in her shop looked delicious.

Their housekeeper met them at the front door. "Let me take those bundles, my loves. Oh, Lady Hen! Why did you not tell us this morning you were betrothed to that gorgeous man? What joyous news!"

"Do forgive me, Mrs. Hawke." Hen handed over the pies. "I thought the duke wanted us to keep the news a secret. Clearly, I was mistaken. It is now out, and we are both immensely happy."

"I knew it the moment I saw the two of you together. It is a love match, I told Mr. Hawke. Well, I'll make something extra special for tea today."

"Yes, please do. Mr. Weston will be joining us as well."

The sturdy woman nodded. "He's another fine man. Too bad he's never found the right lady for himself. But I suppose he is married to his duties."

Phoebe and Chloe had gone inside while Hen remained behind to speak to Mrs. Hawke, but Phoebe came running back out a moment later. She was waving a letter in her hand. "Hen! I think we've solved the problem of your escort. Our cousin, Prudence Landers, has asked if she may come to visit. We must write back to her at once and ask her to serve as your companion in London. She's a widow and would make the perfect chaperone. Come, let's not waste a moment."

Mrs. Hawke returned to the kitchen with their parcels while she and Phoebe went into the drawing room and sat together at the writing desk.

"I did not want to say anything in front of Mrs. Hawke," Phoebe said quietly, "even though she is the kindest person and I do trust her. But Prudence is clearly experiencing the same issue we are with wicked Cousin Willis. Here, read her letter. She does not come right out and say it, but I am certain this is what has her worried."

Hen read the letter. "It isn't a far ride from here to Plymouth. Perhaps the duke would send his carriage for her. If she came right away, she'd also have a few days to spend with you and Chloe before we went off to London."

Phoebe nodded. "Do you think the duke would look into her trust fund as well?"

"I'm sure he would." Hen took out the quill pen and inkpot. "But I feel awful about dragging him deeper into our affairs. I was hesitant about involving him in our own situation, and now to add Prudence? I suppose it cannot be helped. That weasel has cheated all of us, and it may be to our mutual benefit to approach him as a united front. A judge might overlook one complaint, but if he is cheating his entire family, it has to be obvious he must be removed. I'll speak to the duke about it this afternoon."

"You don't look happy, Hen."

"Cousin Willis is such a vile little clot. I am glad we are about to take him on. But how much do I dare foist on the duke? Will there not come a point where he says enough is enough and requests to be released from our betrothal? I will accept without question. We cannot be officially betrothed without Willis's consent anyway."

"He won't ask to be let out." Phoebe placed a hand over hers. "He will not leave you to fight this on your own."

The time passed quickly, and the clock soon chimed the four o'clock hour.

Hen had changed into one of her favorite gowns, a cream silk with an overlayer of pale green voile. She wore a single strand of pearls at her throat and had added pearl clips to her upswept hair. Her gloves were a delicate cream lace. "How do I look, Phoebe?"

Both sisters had joined her in her bedchamber. "Perfect," Phoebe replied. "The duke will not be able to take his eyes off you."

Her sisters then twirled to show off their own gowns. Phoebe's was a pale blue silk and Chloe's was a pink muslin. "You both look beautiful," Hen said. "Oh, I think I hear riders approaching."

"It must be the duke and Mr. Weston." Chloe squealed and tore out of Hen's bedchamber.

Phoebe and Hen were not far behind.

Hen's heart melted at the sight of the duke.

She watched him dismount his enormous black stallion with a casual grace and hand the reins to Mr. Hawke. Mr. Weston did the same, handing his roan into Mr. Hawke's care.

The pair then marched to the door Chloe had already flung open. "You are right on time. How perfect of you! We have news to share."

Hen groaned. She hadn't wanted to bring up the topic of Prudence immediately. Did the duke not deserve to have his slice of pie in peace before he was assailed?

"What news?" he asked, following after Chloe as she led the way onto the terrace. It was their practice to dine outdoors whenever the weather permitted, and today was a lovely summer's day. A gentle breeze blew off the water and rustled through the lush shade trees.

"We received a letter from a cousin of ours, Mrs. Prudence Landers," Hen began. "She is a Killigrew like us, the daughter of my father's cousin, and a widow for several years. Her husband died early on in the Napoleonic Wars. My father took it upon himself to provide for her. I suppose you know where this is going—our weasel cousin is trustee over her funds as well, and she has not received anything since he took over."

"I see." The duke rubbed the nape of his neck.

Hen sighed. "I've already told my sisters…if you wish to end our betrothal, I will completely understand. You may rely on me to sign whatever documents may be necessary. However, since Prudence seems to be affected by his dishonesty, I would like to ask her to accompany me to London. As a widow, she is the perfect chaperone. Whether you are willing to help us or not, we must go. I think we may do better now that it is not only me and my sisters he's cheated, but others in the family who are willing to come forward."

"I am not breaking off our betrothal," Cain said. "Stop worrying that I will. In truth, having her with us will make it easier for me to bring this dishonest cousin of yours to task. Who else in the family has been damaged by his actions?"

"Two elderly cousins of my father's. They live just outside of London. I am certain we shall have their cooperation."

"They are a bit dotty," Phoebe added, "and live together in a small house with a pleasant young couple as caretakers because they cannot get around by themselves. Father used to visit them every week. We meant to do the same, but Wicked Willis kicked us out, and we are no longer able to look in on them as we'd like."

"We write to them often," Hen continued, picking up where Phoebe left off, "and would like to bring them to Moonstone Landing. But I don't see how we can manage it without enough resources even for ourselves."

The duke nodded as she handed him a slice of pie. "You and I can plan it out once we are in London, Hen. I've also been giving thought to where you are to stay. Now that we are betrothed—"

"Unofficially. Wicked Willis, as Chloe calls him, must give his consent," she reminded him.

"He will. And we are betrothed. There is no 'if' about it. I want you and Mrs. Landers to stay at my Mayfair residence."

"Malvern House?"

"Yes, and I shall take rooms at one of my clubs for the duration. It will be no imposition for me to move out. I keep very little at my home anyway."

"Oh dear."

"You are fretting again." His eyes were alight with amusement. "You seem to worry more for my comfort than I do. Rest assured, I am not shy. I will let you know if I decide I do not like the arrangement."

Hen set down her teacup and turned to him. "But all of it is so unpleasant."

"And none of it is of your doing." He dug into his slice of apple pie. "This pie is delicious. Send my compliments to Mrs. Halsey next time you are in her tea shop."

Hen frowned as she refilled his cup of tea and then her own. "How can you be so calm?"

"Because there is nothing we can do from here. We will confront the problem once we reach London. In the meanwhile, enjoy yourself. The pie is very good. You ought to try some."

She raised her cup to her lips. "I think you must have ice in your blood."

He cast her a steamy look that shot tingles through her body. "I can assure you, Hen. My blood flows hot as volcanic lava when I am around you."

She choked on her tea, setting her cup down with a clatter.

Chloe and Phoebe giggled like peahens. Even staid Mr. Weston cracked a smile.

Hen shook her head and laughed.

Their party broke up two hours later, and the duke took her aside a moment while the others strolled indoors. "I want to let you know that I've already sent word to my Bow Street runner, a very capable man by the name of Homer Barrow. He and his men will do some investigating for me. We'll have helpful reports awaiting us by the time we reach London. Unless your cousin is a complete idiot, which he may very well be, this matter will be dealt with quite efficiently."

"You seem to have everything in hand. I feel as though I've contributed nothing."

"Don't ever say that, Hen. There are many things in which you will take the lead and I will happily sit back and let you go about your business. What your cousin is doing is no small matter. He is emboldened because our English laws ignore the plight of women, treating them as a man's chattel. Until these laws change, you are fighting an uphill battle. In effect, our laws give him the castle on the hill, the defensive moat, and the army. It gives you nothing, not even rotting cabbages to throw at his fortified walls. But now you have me."

She knew he was right. "And what are you?"

He grinned. "Your battering ram. Your flaming arrows. Your thousand-man army prepared to lay siege to his castle."

She reached up and kissed him on the cheek. "You are enjoying this, aren't you?"

He nodded. "Immensely."

He kissed her back, not a light kiss on her cheek but full on her mouth, deep and urgent, evoking sinful waves of pleasure from her. "Oh, goodness."

Cain cast her a smug smile of satisfaction, but turned serious a moment later. "My parents were a love match. Did you know this, Hen? They were a team, unbeatable when standing together. This is what I hope we will become. It isn't a question of who has the strength and power. At times, you will have it. At times, I will. But never against each other."

She loved listening to him, learning the workings of his mind. "I think you must have been a magnificent leader, inspiring your troops as you engaged in battle. I am glad you are on my side and not my enemy. I doubt I would ever win a fight against you. I'd probably embarrass myself and surrender to you before you ever got off a single shot or uttered a single demand."

"I hope our fights are few and far between. I'll likely lose all of them."

She thought he was in jest.

"I'm serious, Hen. Seeing you sad and overset would hurt me more than it ever would hurt you. I'll stop by tomorrow. Write to your cousin."

"I will."

She watched him stride away, then ran up to her bedchamber and stared at the portrait of Brioc Taran Arundel. There were several portraits of the sea captain throughout the house, but this one hanging over her mantel captured him in his most natural expression and was her favorite. For this reason, she had not taken it down to replace it with something more feminine. In truth, she had not touched a thing in his bedchamber.

"Brioc! Aunt Hen! Can you hear me? Did you bring me this man? If so, I am forever in your debt."

There was no response.

The pair had disappeared upon Aunt Hen's death.

Still, she liked to think they were somewhere close by, watching over her and her sisters. She knew the sea captain existed because she and Phoebe had seen his ghost and even spoken to him when they were younger and had visited their aunt.

He was gone now.

The duke had appeared in his place, very much alive, and, for whatever incomprehensible reason, wanted her for his wife.

Well, she was a worthy catch.

But *he* was nothing short of a miracle.

Yet she was too sensible to believe in such things. "Is he too good to be true? Is there something I should know?"

Her hairbrush clattered to the ground.

It had been sitting across the room atop her bureau, and she had not touched it.

Her heart sank. Was this a warning to be cautious?

Did Cain have secrets he was keeping from her?

Chapter Seven

CAIN HAD TAKEN to stopping by Moonstone Cottage in the afternoons to visit Hen and her sisters. He often brought Weston along for the purpose of better acquainting him with Phoebe and Chloe, since Hen would be leaving them behind while Cain and she went off to London.

He hoped his estate manager would look after the girls as though they were his own, for Hen would never rest easy thinking they were being left alone to fend for themselves. Of course, they would also be in the capable care of Mr. Hawke and his wife, who had moved into the caretaker's cottage on the property and would see anyone coming in or out.

Still, they were merely a couple in service and not trained in the art of defense.

One thing he had not discussed with Hen was the possibility of the Earl of Stoke trying something underhanded, perhaps attempting to abduct her sisters while he and Hen were off in London.

He intended to set up precautions.

Not only would Weston look in on them each day, but he would have the local authority, Constable Angel, do the same. He also considered hiring professional guards and perhaps speaking to the major in charge of the local army barracks. It would not hurt to have the army take extra patrols near Moonstone Cottage.

Of course, he dared not mention it to Hen.

First of all, he doubted her cousin planned any such thing. It was highly improbable and would have her needlessly fretting.

Second of all, Hen would insist on taking her sisters with them if she believed they might be in any danger, which would put the girls in closer proximity to their cousin and assuredly place them in greater danger.

"Weston," he said, striding toward the estate manager as he supervised the workmen securing the steps that led from the cliff walk down to the beach, "Lady Henley's cousin, Mrs. Landers, has arrived. Join me today when I ride over."

The man mopped the sweat off his brow and grinned. "All right. Give me time to wash up and make myself presentable. Are you asking for my opinion about this woman who will be guarding Lady Henley's virtue during your stay in Town?"

"No, don't be ridiculous. I'm sure she will be charming if she's anything like these Killigrew sisters. I just want her to know who you are and understand she can trust you."

"All right, but she will have little reason to engage with me, since her time will be spent in London with you."

"Do you not want to meet her?"

Weston sighed. "I'll go. You're right. She ought to know my face."

"All three sisters seem to like her. I understand she is bringing correspondence between her and the earl."

"That man is such a horse's arse. Rest assured, I won't let him get anywhere near those girls."

Cain rubbed his damp nape, for the day was particularly hot and the sun had been beating down on them relentlessly. "Constable Angel is assigning two of his best guards to watch over Phoebe and Chloe. They all know to report to you and obey your instructions. I'll introduce them to you after we call on the ladies."

"I think you are giving the wretched earl too much credit for cunning and deceit."

"Probably, but I dare not underestimate him. If I were he, I would certainly use these girls as pawns in the battle."

Weston frowned. "What would he gain by harming them?"

"Not to harm them, but he could demand they be taken under his wing. After all, he still has guardianship over them. Chloe in particular is vulnerable because she is only twelve and too young to stand up for herself. Phoebe is a little lioness, and I think she can take care of herself. If he dared take her away from Moonstone Cottage, she would bite his head off."

"What are you going on about? Lady Phoebe is a sweet girl."

"She is, but she also has fight in her. Perhaps I'll have a chat with the commanding officer overseeing the new army barracks in town. The more eyes on those girls, the better."

"You are bringing the army into this? I'm not sure I like the idea of having young soldiers around those girls."

"They would not be permitted inside the house, just to patrol it." Cain sighed in the face of Weston's continued disapproval. "No, I suppose you are right. Probably inviting more trouble to have young men swarming nearby. I'll leave it to you and the constable, then. Keep close watch on Hen's sisters."

"You know I will."

Cain patted him on the back. "Another thing's come up, something that will also require my attention while I am in London."

"What is it, Your Grace?"

"I received word about the Marquess of Burness," he said, referring to his best friend, Cormac Stockwell. "Apparently, he was badly injured in the days immediately after Waterloo."

"I'm sorry. I know you and he are as close as brothers. I'll keep him in my prayers. This is why you are so keen to have these extra eyes on Moonstone Cottage. Your friend's situation may keep you in London longer than you had planned."

He nodded. "I hope it will not be necessary. Cormac is tough and determined, but his wounds are severe." Cain felt a tug to his heart. Although they were not brothers by blood, they had been friends since childhood and had grown even closer throughout the war years. These bonds of friendship forged in battle were often stronger than any blood ties.

"How badly is he hurt?"

"I'm not sure yet. But if he is dying, I need to be by his side."

"I see."

"I can do both, Weston. I can be a friend to the marquess and take care of Lady Henley's situation. I've given her my word. She will have my full attention."

Weston eyed him dubiously. "Keep that in mind. War takes its toll on men. You are still struggling with your own demons. I think your friend's wounds will affect you more deeply than you realize. Just don't disappoint Lady Henley. She'll never complain, but you made her a promise and must keep it."

"Enough lecturing, Weston. I know my duty. I'll meet you at the stables in an hour."

Cain strode back to the Grange, his thoughts on Weston's comments. He did not have to choose between Cormac and Hen. He would do all he could for both of them. Abandoning Cormac in his time of need was out of the question. Hen would understand, for would she not sacrifice anything for her sisters? Was this not the very reason she had agreed to their betrothal?

He slowed his pace as he marched across his park toward the grand manor house.

How was he to tell Hen? He had to talk this over with her.

Would she resent his divided attention? Having offered himself up as her savior, was it fair to then devote significant time to his friend? Not that he needed to do more than visit regularly and offer his companionship. Cormac had a younger brother who worshiped him and was shouldering the burden of his care now that Cormac had returned home to recover from his serious injuries.

The hour flew by, and before Cain knew it, he and Weston were striding into Moonstone Cottage. Chloe, as had become her habit, swung open the door to greet them with her typically effervescent cheer. "We cannot wait for you to meet Cousin Prudence! She is eager to meet you, too. Come in! Come in! How are the repairs on the cliff steps going? Mr. Weston, you look as though you've got a bit of sun on your face." She grinned at Cain. "You still look like a wooly bear."

He laughed. "I've promised your sister I will shave my beard once we reach London."

Chloe clapped. "I know you will be the handsomest man in all of England once you do."

He tweaked her nose. "Let's hope your sister thinks so."

They marched through the house and onto the terrace, where the afternoon breeze and the shade trees managed to make their outdoor tea spot comfortable. Hen's eyes brightened the moment she saw him.

This was why he needed her. She lightened his heart with her angel's smile and those sparkling eyes. How could any man not be drawn out of despair when in the company of this girl?

He allowed Hen to make introductions all around.

While his gaze was mostly on his betrothed, he also took the measure of her cousin, Prudence Landers. The sisters thought highly of her, but he was not so quick to accept her. If one cousin could be a weasel, who was to say that trait did not run in the Killigrew family? He did not want anyone taking advantage of Hen and her sisters.

But it did not take him long to assess the widow and come to a favorable conclusion. She was about ten years older than Hen, he estimated, for she had a few gray strands in her dark hair and her eyes looked careworn. Her gown was several years out of fashion, but she wore it with elegance.

"A pleasure to meet you, Your Grace." She cast him a friendly smile. "I thought you might walk in wearing a halo over your head, for this is how my cousins described you." She then turned to Weston. "And you as well, Mr. Weston. It is indeed a pleasure to meet you."

"As it is you," Weston said, and bowed over the woman's

hand.

It did not escape Cain's notice that his estate manager never took his eyes off Prudence Landers for the remainder of their visit.

What was it about these Killigrew women?

Phoebe remarked on it when Weston took Chloe and their cousin for a walk on the beach. "I thought Mr. Weston was a confirmed bachelor, but I see it is only that he has not met the right woman until now. What do you think, Hen? Will he ask Cousin Prudence to marry him today? Or will he wait until you return from London?"

"Phoebe, that is absurd. They've hardly known each other, an—" Hen blushed and abruptly clamped her lips shut.

Phoebe laughed. "What were you going to say, dearest sister? That they've hardly known each other an hour? You are one to talk. What do you think, Your Grace?"

"Perhaps it is something in the Moonstone air that makes bachelors suddenly want to give up their freedom," Cain replied. "Perhaps it is just you ensorceling Killigrews."

Phoebe nodded. "I think he will ask her when you return, because Mr. Weston is as conscientious as Hen. He will not say anything to distract her from her chaperone duties. But once you are home, he will ask her the moment she steps down from the coach, and she will accept him."

Hen rolled her eyes. "You are getting carried away."

"Not at all. I think it is wonderful, this knowing on the spot that you have just met the man of your dreams. Or woman of his dreams, in Mr. Weston's case. I think this knowledge must be buried deep in our souls, do you not think so, Your Grace?"

He gave a moment's thought before agreeing. "I do. Had you asked me a week ago, I would have scoffed at the notion. Whether this knowledge springs from one's soul or is simply madness in the air, I do not know. But it exists."

"To me," Phoebe said, "it is like looking at a puzzle with pieces haphazardly strewn across a table. None of the pieces make sense, until you find the important one, and suddenly all becomes clear and everything falls into place. How did it feel to you, Hen?"

"I am still trying to figure it out," Hen replied.

"Rubbish," Phoebe retorted. "It hit you like a bolt of lightning. Only you are our cautious Hen and insist on thinking things to death. You cannot think about lightning. It strikes too fast. But I hope this happens to me. I cannot imagine what sort of man might be my perfect match. Perhaps a more quiet, professorial type to balance me out, since I tend to be too vocal and opinionated."

Cain laughed. "You would walk all over a man like that. Stomp on him as though he were nothing more than grapes to be trampled in a wine press. And I doubt there would be any lightning bolts between you."

"That isn't fair! I can be sweet when I want to be."

"You are all delightful. I did not mean for you to take offense." He shook his head, still laughing. "But you need a man who will challenge you."

"Oh, Phoebe," Hen said. "Do not think too hard about it. You'll just know when the right one comes along."

The others returned, putting an end to their conversation.

"WHAT DID YOU think of Mrs. Landers?" Cain asked Weston as they rode back to the Grange, their horses at a gentle lope.

"You're not going to believe me when I tell you."

"Not only will I believe you, but I expect I already know what you are going to say. You did not take your eyes off her the entire time we were there."

Weston laughed. "I thought you were mad to propose to Lady Henley, but it seems this madness is catching. I was lost by the time I bowed over her hand at our introduction. I will not say anything to her now, of course. You need her full attention to deal with that weasel cousin and be a proper chaperone to Lady Hen. But…"

Cain frowned. "What is that 'but' about?"

"I just realized, I am no one of consequence. You are marrying Lady Hen. Will you forbid me from marrying Mrs. Landers? Assuming she will have me. You and I would then be related by marriage. It is one thing to be in your employ…"

"But quite another to be in my family?"

Weston nodded.

"You are one of the best men I know, you old warhorse. She could not find a finer husband. I'd sooner have you as a relation than the Earl of Stoke." Cain meant it, too. Titles did not make men noble or worthy. While he would not deny he enjoyed the privileges offered by his rank, he never considered himself above all other men.

He valued honesty, loyalty, and strength of character. Bloodlines were irrelevant.

"High praise, indeed," Weston said with a laugh. "I am honored you prefer me to the Killigrew family weasel."

They rode directly to the Grange, but they had no sooner stabled the horses and walked toward the house when Cain's butler handed him a letter. "Your Grace, the messenger said it was urgent."

"Thank you, Manton." Cain took the letter off the salver and motioned for Weston to accompany him to his study. "It's another one from the Marquess of Burness's brother, Lord Stockwell. I recognize his seal."

Weston followed him in and closed the door. "You are frowning. What does the letter say? The news cannot be good about your friend."

Cain's heart sank. "It is confirmed. They are going to amputate his arm. They have to do it before gangrene sets in."

"I'm so sorry."

"So am I." He forced back tears, knowing how devastating this had to be for Cormac. Had his friend been the bookish sort, he might have taken the loss better. But Cormac was the sort who grabbed life with both fists…only he was about to lose one now. "I have to go to him."

"What about the ladies?"

"I am not forgetting them." He began to pace, his mind now awhirl with newly formed plans. "They can travel together to London the day after tomorrow, as planned. I'll leave them the use of my carriage. Nothing has changed, only I will ride on ahead of them. I'll leave first thing in the morning. The ladies are still to stay at Malvern House. I'll—"

"They cannot travel on their own. It is absurd to consider it. Even if you assign six footmen as outriders for the carriage, it simply isn't the same. They need to be under *your* protection. What sort of message will it send to that weasel earl if they arrive separately from you?"

"Blast it, Weston. I did not ask for your opinion."

"Yes, you did. Why else have me come in here while you read the letter? You wanted me to be the voice of reason."

"I don't need you telling me what to do."

"You cannot abandon them, not even for your friend. His arm is lost whether you reach him tomorrow…which you cannot do even if you kill your horse riding through the night. He'll be at his London townhouse recovering. Whether you reach him in three days' time or five, he will already have lost his arm. And what will Lady Henley think if you ride off now? How will you ever gain her trust if you abandon her now?"

Cain raked a hand through his hair. "She will understand. I am not abandoning her. I will be in London waiting for her."

"Go ahead and convince yourself of it, but do not be surprised if she is doubtful."

Cain slammed his fist on his desk, not out of anger but frustration. Weston was right, as always. However, Cain's heart was in a roil, and he simply could not remain here. "I have to go."

"Then I suggest you ride back to Moonstone Cottage and ask Lady Henley if she would not mind leaving first thing in the morning."

"What if she refuses?" In truth, this was something he had not thought through entirely, this having to take someone else's feelings into consideration.

"Then grit your teeth and stick to your planned departure. It is only a matter of a day or two. As I said, your friend's arm is lost no matter when you leave. Just ask her. She won't deny your request."

"I hope you're right." He strode out of his house and called for his groom to saddle Galahad again.

Within moments, he was flying across his parklands and onto the road toward Moonstone Cottage. Chloe, the family's little watchdog, must have alerted Hen, for it was she who ran out to greet him as he dismounted. "You look terrible, Your Grace. What has happened?"

"Stop calling me that. I am to be your husband. I am Cain." He hadn't meant to sound harsh, especially since she was in the right.

Mr. Hawke had run forward to take his horse, so he and Hen were not alone. But it was hard to keep his temper in check when good men such as Cormac suffered while her weasel of a cousin got away with stealing.

"Sorry, I am out of sorts and taking it out on you."

She tucked her arm in his. "Come inside and tell me what's wrong."

Her touch put him more at ease, but he still was not fit company, and he did not want the other women hovering.

She must have sensed this, for she suddenly tugged him away from the house. "Let's walk along the beach where we can speak privately. The tide is low," she said, casting him an endearing smile, "so no danger of either of us drowning. Tell me what has you so riled."

He told her about Cormac as they walked along the sand.

He spoke not only of his friend's injury but of their longstanding friendship. Hen was a good listener. The tide was starting to rise by the time he had finished pouring out his heart to her.

Well, there was also much he *hadn't* said. He and Cormac had experienced things in battle that he would not burden her with. They had also caroused their way through London's cathouses in their younger days, and those stories were *certainly* not fit for Hen's innocent ears.

The waves now lapped too close to where they stood. He took her hand and led her to sit on the steps where they would be well away from the rising water.

He read her the letter he'd received from Cormac's brother.

She showed nothing but sincerest concern. "We must leave without delay. Prudence has not unpacked yet, so it will be nothing for her to be ready by morning. I'll ask my sisters to help me sort out the gowns I am to take. You needn't worry. We shall both be ready to leave first thing tomorrow."

"Thank you, Hen. I'm sorry to put you through the rush."

"Don't be. He is important to you. Would you prefer to ride ahead? I don't want to slow you down. Prudence and I can follow—"

"No. Weston has already taken me to task for considering this very thing. He is right, as always. I've given you my promise and will see it through. My friend is in loving hands with his brother. My presence will not change his circumstances. He will lose his arm whether or not I am there. But he will need my friendship more than ever. I must make time to see him while I am in town."

"Do you think he would consider staying here with us when he is feeling stronger and can travel? I mean…it feels odd that I will soon be your wife and living with you at the Grange. We can put off our wedding if you wish. I don't want to be in the way."

Cain laughed. "You will never be in the way. And I don't want to put off our wedding. If anything, I want to move it up. I think I'll need you more than ever over these next few weeks. I do want to invite Cormac to the Grange. I think it will be good for his recovery. Hen, thank you for understanding. You don't know how much this means to me."

She placed a hand on his arm. "I still don't understand what you see in me, but I'll stop questioning it and simply accept my good fortune."

The wind blew softly through her curls. He put a hand to them and lightly brushed the loose strands off her cheeks. "Just look in the mirror. How can you not see the beautiful light that you are?"

She cast him an affectionate smile. "More compliments from Chloe's golden bear. You shall put me in a swoon if you keep this up. But if we are to leave tomorrow, then we had better finish this conversation and get to work."

They'd climbed no more than halfway before he held her back. He'd arrived in turmoil, and she had soothed his aching heart.

There was something magical about Hen. This girl was his angel. His salvation.

He wanted to wrap her in his arms and kiss her into forever.

He had two arms to wrap around her.

Two arms.

Cormac would never be able to do this with the woman he loved. Knowing his nature, this loss would make him a bitter wretch, one who would never accept love or believe in love even if it smacked him in the face.

Cain felt guilty about having his own chance at happiness.

Finding Hen. Having all this.

He crushed his lips to hers, desperate to rid himself of these feelings of anger and frustration, needing to absorb her and gain relief for his aching heart.

She stared at him oddly when he ended the kiss, for it had been rough and filled with raw emotion. "I'm sorry, Hen. Did I bruise your lips?"

"No." She cast him a worried look and then turned pensive. "But I need to know exactly what you are sorry about. Your friend? Or being betrothed to me?"

Chapter Eight

CAIN TRIED NOT to show his impatience, for it wasn't Hen's fault his carriage made slower progress than he would have liked because of the rain. The road to London was in good enough condition that a moderate downpour would not have held them up too badly. But there was no moderation to the rain that came down in sheets at times and required them to wait for hours while the flooding receded.

These days of bad weather felt like a harbinger of doom to Cain.

However, the delay was not nearly as bad as it could have been, and they reached London with barely the loss of a day. A heavy mist wrapped them in a blanket of gray as they entered the bustling outskirts of the city.

"You are frowning again," Hen said, shaking him out of his musings. The hour was late and they were all tired. She and her cousin were seated across from him, as they had been the entire journey. Even having a bench to himself did not relieve his feeling of confinement, for the summer's heat made riding in these cramped quarters unbearable.

He had left his big Friesian behind in Moonstone Landing because he knew he would never have time to properly exercise the beast while occupied in Town.

He cast her a wry grin. "My impatience is showing."

"For your friend. You are eager to see the Marquess of Burness." Hen peered out the window. "Look at all the coaches on the road at this late hour. Yet I think it cannot be more than an hour before we reach Malvern House."

He followed her gaze. "No, that is optimistic. Closer to two hours, I should think. It will be midnight by the time we arrive."

"Much too late to visit your friend," Prudence said. "I'm sorry, Your Grace. I know how eager you are to see him."

He shrugged. "I'll call on him and my Bow Street runner tomorrow."

Hen nodded. "Prudence and I will manage for ourselves while you do. Don't worry about us. I'm sure we will be in good hands with your staff. As for tonight, just drop us off and then be on your way to your club."

Prudence nodded. "Yes, do not let us detain you."

These Killigrew ladies were not the demanding sort, something he would appreciate more if not for his distraction over his friend's condition.

But this only made him feel worse. He had made a promise to Hen and did not want her to think she was being pushed back to a secondary concern.

"Is there anything you would like me to do tomorrow?" Hen asked.

He shook his head. "No, just remain at Malvern House. Do not go out. This applies to both of you. I don't want you going anywhere without me. I have no idea what your weasel cousin will do once he hears you are back in town."

"As you wish," Prudence said. "We are so very grateful for your assistance. That man is such a toad…or weasel…vermin, for certain. I am not a malicious person by nature, but I will take great delight in seeing him brought down."

Cain leaned forward. "I have not done anything for you yet. I cannot promise immediate success. All I can do is try."

Hen put her hand on his. "It is more than we ever dreamed possible."

He sank back against the squabs, knowing Hen and her cousin held high hopes. He needed to take down the Earl of Stoke and kick him back into the hole from which he'd emerged. He also needed to see Cormac.

The unfairness of life ate his insides raw.

He had never come to terms with the damage done to good people while the bad, the petty, and the dishonorable got away with so much. Yet who was he to take on the role of avenging angel? He could not fight every battle or every injustice. To attempt it would drain all the fight out of him and leave him a shell of a man.

Not to do anything would dishonor all he held dear… No, he had to choose his battles wisely.

He felt a great weight lift off his shoulders when they reached Malvern House. It was late, close to midnight, just as he had predicted.

The ladies were happy to finally settle in. Cain escorted them inside to make certain their bags were brought up to their bedchambers and a light repast prepared for them.

Hen cast him a tired smile as his housekeeper, Mrs. Crawford, showed them to her quarters. "I have never slept in a more beautiful room. I feel like a queen."

"It is the duchess's suite of rooms," Cain said, dismissing his housekeeper to give her leave to attend Hen's cousin. Only once she had left them did he comment again. "I saw no reason to place you elsewhere, since I hope we will be married before the week is out."

He had expected one of her shimmering smiles, but she did not look pleased.

"What's wrong, Hen?"

"How stupid of me not to consider…my sisters won't be here for our wedding. It did not feel real to me before, but the finality of it is now settling in."

He took her hands in his. "It will not be a grand affair. Indeed, no more than a few witnesses and a quick ceremony performed the moment Stoke signs the betrothal papers. I'll hold a pistol to his head if I must. We'll have a proper celebration once we are back in Moonstone Landing. I dare not delay. It is best to have it done as soon as possible for the safety of your sisters."

"You are right, of course. It is the only sensible course of action."

He kissed her on the forehead. "Will you be all right? Shall I stay a little while longer?"

"No, you needn't. You must be exhausted too. I'll see you tomorrow." She glanced across the hall, where Prudence was now comfortably settled. "You've seen to everything for us. I think I'll turn in as soon as I wash the dirt off my face and hands."

"Then I'll be off." He kissed her once again. "Sweet dreams, Hen."

"To you as well," she said, casting him a tired, but still radiant, smile.

He climbed back in his coach, pausing for a word with his coachman. "Farnum, once you drop me and my bags off at my club, return the coach to Malvern House and get yourself a good night's rest. I may have need of you again soon, but not tomorrow. Sleep the entire day away if you like. Be ready for my summons any time after that."

"Aye, Your Grace," Farnum replied in his thick Cornish accent.

Farnum was another longtime family retainer, a grizzled former soldier and tough as old boots. In their own way, Farnum, Weston, and other retainers long in service to the family provided a bedrock foundation for Cain. It showed him life went on and daily routines were carried out no matter what chaos swirled around them.

Well, England had not been a battleground this time around, so the buildings and family ways had not been disrupted. Still, few families had been spared the ravages of war—so many of their sons had gone off to fight, and too many had not returned.

It took no more than another ten minutes to reach Bedford

Place and the row of exclusive clubs. The steward on night duty at the Malabar Club was most solicitous of him when he arrived, quickly seeing his bags were taken upstairs and his quarters prepared to his liking. "Are you in need of a valet, Your Grace?"

"No, all I need is a good night's sleep. Send a valet up to me in the morning. I'll leave my boots outside the door for him. See they are properly polished."

"Of course, Your Grace."

Cain undressed, dropping all his clothes onto a chair for the valet to attend to in the morning, and then poured himself a glass of wine from the bottle of excellent vintage set out for him. A basket of light fare had also been brought up and placed on the side table beside the wine, its contents including some fruit, cheese, and a few scones.

After washing up, he opened the window to allow in a cooling breeze. However, the air felt warm and too dank against his bare skin to provide much comfort. The club was not far from the Thames, and his room soon filled with the odors of the river and the city.

Well, it was better than breathing in the acrid scents of battle, he supposed.

The steward had also sent up a bottle of the club's finest aged brandy and left it for him atop the bureau. But Cain did not touch the bottle. He would open it tomorrow. For now, the glass of wine was enough.

He drank down the smooth liquid and stretched out atop his bed. His body was too hot to bother with sheets or a coverlet. The moon was visible through his window—not quite a full moon, but silvery and big, as it tended to be in the summer months.

He poured himself another glass of wine, for his demons were stirring and he knew from past experience his sleep would be restless.

But drinking did little good.

He would have to imbibe the entire bottle to get drunk

enough to drown his sorrows, and then he'd wake with a splitting headache, a churning stomach, and that always-present ache in his heart.

He did not bother to finish the second glass of wine. He needed to keep his mind clear for tomorrow. What he also needed was an undisturbed night's sleep.

But it was not to be.

He awoke in the middle of the night in a cold sweat and the sheets coiled about his body like a constricting snake. The moon was no longer up, so no silvery light shone in through his window.

All that surrounded him was a tomblike darkness.

He inhaled, taking several deep breaths. But the air felt acrid, and his nostrils filled with the earthy scents of London, too reminiscent of decaying corpses.

He sat up and tried to calm himself, shake off his dread.

Had anyone heard him cry out?

There were only four bedchambers available at this exclusive club, not often used in the summer months, since most men of means spent their time puttering about their country estates at this time of the year. The members of this club could afford such niceties, and all had country homes.

It was such a tidy way of life. One of ease and privilege.

His hands were shaking and his body soaked by the time he finally regained control of himself.

He listened for footsteps, but heard nothing. No one was stirring along the halls.

"Hellfire." How was he to sleep with Hen if this was what she would be subjected to nightly?

He was not worried about merely disturbing her sleep. What if he accidentally struck her while he was thrashing about?

He could not bear the thought of hurting her.

Well, she would have to sleep in her own quarters. He had already discussed it with her. Was it not common for a married duke and duchess to maintain separate chambers? He would visit her often enough, just never risk falling asleep beside her.

This arrangement would have to do. It wasn't as though he intended to seek anyone else to wrap in his arms.

Hen was the only one for him.

Yes, this would have to be enough.

Besides, Hen had shown she was never one to complain.

He fell back into a fitful sleep, awakened by the club's valet when he slipped into the room to take Cain's clothes and freshen them. "Your Grace," the young man said, his eyes rounding in dismay when saw Cain stir. "I did not mean to disturb you."

"You didn't. I was already awake. Have a bath ordered for me and breakfast brought up."

"At once, Your Grace."

Cain debated whether to shave off his beard today, but decided against it. Homer Barrow would not care what he looked like. Cormac would have a good laugh when he saw him, and was likely in desperate need of a laugh.

Hen was already used to him looking this way and had not been scared off. In truth, she apparently got a quiet thrill from him looking like a big bear.

The notion made him smile.

Within the hour, he was on his way to Homer Barrow's office. The man was a portly fellow, a grandfather type with a bulbous nose and keen eyes. Little got past this very clever Bow Street runner. "Your Grace, I've been expecting you. Do come in. Please, have a seat."

Cain settled in one of the sturdy chairs beside the man's desk. The desk itself was piled with papers, mostly reports, no doubt, for Mr. Barrow had an excellent reputation. Indeed, Cain would call it a nose for digging out information others wished to hide. "I was eager to speak to you. Have you found out anything for me?"

Mr. Barrow smiled. "I happen to have a helpful acquaintance at the Bank of West London. This is where Lady Henley's trust fund is held, as you indicated in your letter to me. The accounts for her sisters are held there as well. It seems the Earl of Stoke is trustee on several other accounts managed on behalf of various female family members. I took the liberty of asking my, er…helpful acquaintance to provide information on those, too."

"Well done, Mr. Barrow. I was going to ask you to do this for me, but I'm pleased you have anticipated my request and already attended to it. I've brought Lady Henley and her cousin, Mrs. Prudence Landers, with me to town. Is Mrs. Landers one of those family members you mentioned?"

"Yes, Your Grace. She is indeed."

"Anyone else?"

Barrow nodded. "Two others who I am told are elderly ladies. My acquaintance found only those accounts managed by him…or should I say, mismanaged? Shall we continue our search?"

"No, not on my behalf. That covers everyone in Lady Henley's family. The scoundrel is cheating them all. The only question is, how badly?"

"As far as we can tell, he takes the interest out each month, but instead of sending it to the ladies, he deposits it in a secret account under an assumed name for himself. This way, nothing shows up in his regular accounts. He uses the secret funds to pay for the vices he and his wife maintain."

"Lady Stoke is in on this?"

"Oh, yes. She is as much a part of it as he is. The woman enjoys gaming but is not very good at it. Not even stealing from the family coffers is enough to cover all her losses."

"And the earl? What are his vices?"

"While his wife attends the more elite gaming clubs, he prefers the copper hells," Barrow continued. "He doesn't gamble much but will go upstairs to enjoy enticements of the female persuasion. They are a low pair, Your Grace. I've had a man assigned in their house as well. They treat their servants poorly. Not an ounce of generosity in them."

"What of the bank manager? How deeply involved is he in abetting the earl?"

"Another slimy scoundrel, but he will turn on the earl as soon as the funds are cut off. There is no friendship between them, only the lure of easy money. The bright spot in this sordid arrangement is that they have not yet taken more than the interest. The principal of each trust remains intact. Perhaps they feared to be too bold because they are still new to this game and did not wish to draw too much attention to themselves at the start."

Cain nodded. "Well, I am about to hit them over the head with a hammer. That ought to gain their notice."

"What will you do, if I may be so bold as to ask?"

"The Marquess of Burness has a brother who is chairman of the bank's board of directors. The marquess happens to be my best friend. I am on my way over to visit them next. Burness's brother will quietly look into the information you have provided and freeze these accounts. Neither the bank manager nor the Earl of Stoke will be permitted to touch them. We'll get all the testimony necessary out of the bank manager in exchange for a lighter punishment. But rest assured, he will go to prison."

"Aye, to betray the trust of his employer and the bank depositors should earn him no less."

"Burness's brother will be livid for certain. That dishonest manager could have ruined the bank. He may have done extraordinary damage already, depending on how many others like Stoke have been able to bribe him. Well, I'll leave it to their board of directors to interrogate him about any other account thefts. As for me, I just need him to testify against Stoke."

"Your Grace, even with this discovery, having the earl removed as trustee could take months in court." Barrow arched an eyebrow. "You do not strike me as a patient man. What are you planning to do?"

"It is quite simple, really. Threat of exposure and public humiliation if he does not immediately resign and turn over all accounts to my supervision. Lady Henley is quite a clever young lady. She has read her father's trust and knows the document gives the current trustee power to appoint his successor. I will call upon her father's solicitor later today to confirm this is correct, although I have no doubt of it. Then it is a simple matter of confronting Stoke with the evidence, having him appoint me to succeed him, and in the next stroke of the pen, have him resign."

"We are at your service should you require witnesses. Often, men such as these are slow to understand their game is at an end."

Cain smiled. "Perhaps I will ask for this acquaintance of yours who is conveniently situated in the bank to come forward. But rest assured, I will leave him out of it unless we have difficulty getting the bank manager to spill all he knows. I understand how carefully you've cultivated your informants and would hate to draw attention to this effective man. His name won't be mentioned unless I have no other recourse."

"Thank you."

Cain stood and reached out to shake Barrow's hand. "You have saved these ladies," he told the Bow Street runner, "and I mean it sincerely."

"Aw, Your Grace." Barrow rose and came around from his desk to escort Cain to the door. "It is my job. However, it is gratifying to know others are helped because of my nose." He tapped on the bulbous protuberance and laughed. "I do what I can to clean up this world. I know it is only in little ways. But I like to think it is something." He handed the reports to Cain.

"It is a very important thing you do. Thank you again, Mr. Barrow. I will let you know the outcome, although I expect one of your informants will deliver the news to you within five minutes of its occurring. Is there anyone in London you do not know?"

Barrow chuckled. "Oh, I am aware of all the scoundrels. Very few escape my notice."

Cain felt as though one weight was now lifted off his shoulders.

He had expected Barrow to be successful, but not this soon.

The rewards of his diligence were a pleasant surprise. Hen and her cousin would be delighted.

Since the hour was still early and the day bright with sunshine, he chose to walk along the Thames embankment toward the Belgravia residence of his friend, the Marquess of Burness. It felt good to stretch his legs after all those days in the coach.

The Burness butler opened the door as soon as he was seen striding through the gate. "Your Grace, do come in. I'll inform Lord Stockwell of your arrival at once."

Cain was led directly into the family's private salon instead of the visitors' parlor and offered refreshments. "Nothing for me, Merrick."

The butler bustled out, closing the door behind him.

It did not take long for Cormac's brother, Lord Stockwell, to rush in. "Cain, thank goodness! I was hoping you'd come. Cormac is in terrible shape. He's upstairs, spends most of his time in a howling temper. My wife wants to take our little girls to our country estate because Cormac's shouting is upsetting them all."

"I'll see what I can do for him, John." Cain set Barrow's report aside on a decorative writing table. "I'll need to speak to you about these papers after I see your brother. It is an important matter concerning your bank. Read through these reports while I am with your brother—they're important."

"Of course. Let me take you upstairs to Cormac first. Come join me in my study when you are done. Thank goodness you are here. I don't think there is another man in the world able to talk sense into him at this moment."

Cain followed Cormac's brother up the grand staircase, his heart already pounding and his muscles in a tense coil. He dreaded what would confront him, this proud, valiant friend now suffering the loss of his arm.

The stench of blood and sweat accosted him as soon as he walked through the door into the large bedchamber fit for a marquess. "Cormac, it's me."

"Bloody hell. Who let you in here?" his friend said in jest.

There was a chair beside his bed, so Cain settled in it. "I won't ask how you are feeling because you'll only bark at me and tell me to go to hell. Is there anything I can do for you?"

Cormac, already propped against a mound of pillows, opened his eyes and stared at Cain. Dark rings had formed under his eyes, which were quite bloodshot. He looked awful and was obviously in intense pain. How much of it was physical, Cain simply did not know. "You could leave me alone and let me die in peace."

"Forget it. I am not going to leave you alone, and you are not going to die. I'll chase you into hell and drag you back if you dare go before your time."

Although he had prepared himself for this visit, his friend's condition still came as a shock. He had never seen a man look more anguished. Cormac's dark hair was matted and damp. His complexion was sallow, save for those dark circles under his eyes, which were almost purple from exhaustion. He looked ill. He looked angry.

"All right, no death," Cormac replied. "I am not going to kill myself, Cain. Not that I didn't briefly consider it when the doctor brought out his saw and began to cut through my bone, but doing myself in would destroy my brother."

"He loves you so dearly."

Cormac nodded. "I know. He is a better brother than I deserve. But he cannot grow an arm back for me, and neither can you, so kindly spare me your platitudes."

"Do you talk to him this way, too? He would give his life for you. So would I."

"I know."

"Your situation could be worse."

"Are you going to lecture me now? Tell me I'm not the only soldier to have lost a limb? I've heard that lecture already."

"Then I won't repeat it."

Cormac waved his good arm to indicate his room. "And don't tell me I'm one of the fortunate ones, that I have the means to take care of myself. First of all, this is all possible because of my brother. He took care of the family fortunes while I was off fighting, and he's taking care of me now."

"John is a very good man and always has been."

"He's the best brother any man could have. Which only makes it worse."

"Why? Because he is your little brother? You always looked out for him when you were younger. He is merely repaying all you did for him when growing up. This is how families ought to be. So, don't be an obstinate arse."

"Damn it, you are still lecturing me."

"And you are still behaving like a four-year-old tyrant. I hear you are in a constant rage, and your shouting scares his wife and their little girls. That is no way to repay their kindness. Are you going to behave, or must I knock sense into you?"

Cormac laughed. "Good to see you, too. No, I am not going to behave. I am still angry as hell."

"Why? Because you were an idiot and got yourself shot *after* the battle at Waterloo had ended?"

"Yes, it was very stupid of me. But that's only part of it, as well you know." Cormac shook his head. "They all walk on eggshells around me. I cannot abide their pity."

"It is love for you they are expressing, and frustration they can do nothing to change your situation. Nor can you. But you are alive and, assuming infection does not set in, should be able to resume most of your activities."

"I am a cripple who cannot even pull up his own trousers without help."

"You'll figure out a way to button your falls. Who's your doctor?"

Cormac grunted. "George Farthingale. He's the best around and understands battle conditions. He treated wounded soldiers in the Peninsular War."

"Good, then he ought to know what he is doing. Have you asked him how a one-armed man pulls up his drawers? Perhaps he can also tell you how a one-armed man undresses a lady.

That's what has you most frustrated, isn't it?"

"I take it back—you can show me some pity. I am not liking your bluntness," Cormac said, cracking a smile. "Women used to flock to me like moths to a flame."

"I am sure you can convince them to undress for you instead of taking on the chore yourself. Speaking of which...well, it isn't really on the topic, but I wanted you to be the first to know. I am getting married."

Cormac struggled to an upright position and gaped at Cain. "Are you jesting? Why are you getting married? Who was clever enough to lure you into a compromising position?"

"I wasn't lured."

"You asked her willingly? I don't believe it. Who are you marrying? The gossip rags reported that you fled London to escape the ladies."

"I did leave, but they were wrong about the reasons. I ran to Moonstone Landing and met someone there. Do you recall my father built a house just outside that Cornwall village on the seacoast?"

Cormac nodded. "St. Austell Grange. You called it an absurd monstrosity."

"It is big, but not really so bad. I may have been out of sorts when I remarked on it. In truth, it has been a haven for me. It is quite splendid, and the views are magnificent. It has cliff walks, hidden coves, and a splendid beach."

Cormac arched an eyebrow. "Don't tell me about the house. I want to know about this girl who caught you."

Cain briefly told him about how he and Henley met.

"Don't tell me—you fell in love with a mermaid."

Cain's grin spread wide. "The point is, she almost drowned because she could not swim. Fortunately, she had the presence of mind to save herself. One thing led to another, and I asked her to marry me."

"Hold on, I think you missed a few steps."

"No, Cor." He raked a hand through his hair. "You won't

believe this, but I took one look at her and knew she was meant for me. She's in London with me now. I hope to bring her around one day soon so you'll have the chance to meet her. She has also suggested I invite you to visit us at the Grange. You are welcome anytime. It will do you a world of good."

"Blessed saints, Cain. So you are really going to settle into wedded bliss?"

"Yes, but I'm still me. Flaws and all. The only difference is that she'll be the only woman sharing my bed from this day forward. Consider visiting us at the Grange. The invitation is an open one. Come whenever you like and stay as long as you like."

"I'll think about it."

"I hope you do," Cain said. "That place changed me. Henley changed me. Lady Hen is what everyone calls her. But she is not one to cluck and fuss, nor do her feathers ruffle easily. I want you to meet her, but you have to clean yourself up. Is it all right if I bring her around tomorrow?"

Cormac's grin faded. "No, I am not fit company."

"Are you running a fever?"

"No."

"Thank goodness. Are you contagious?"

"Of course not."

"Is there a reason you cannot wash up? Shave that scruff you call a beard attempting to grow on your chin?"

"You are one to talk. Look at you. How does your Lady Hen see you beneath all that hair? And if you dare say she sees into your soul, I am going to vomit."

"I intend to shave the beard off tomorrow. So what do you say? May I bring her around to meet you? It is important to me, Cor. No one means more to me than you."

Cormac cast Cain a wistful smile. "Lady Hen will take my place now."

Cain shook his head. "You are a brother to me. She will be my wife. I expect I will grow more deeply in love with her each day. But you and I, we've been through the fires of hell together.

We are bound to each other whether or not we share the same blood. There is ample room in my heart for both of you."

"All right, damn it. I'll meet her. You know I would not do this for anyone else."

"I know. It means a lot to me."

"Don't get mawkish about it. But do me a favor and keep your visit short. I am not back to full strength yet. I'll even shave and wash—how's that for friendship? But all is not well with me, Cain."

He reached out and patted Cormac's shoulder. "Nor am I well, but that is something I will have to work out with Hen once we are married."

"Still suffering those bad dreams?"

Cain nodded. "The horrors of battle haven't left me. In truth, trying to adjust to peacetime seems to have made them worse. I am haunted by these dreams. Dark, frightening visions. I cannot seem to shake them. I want Hen to share my bed, but how can I ask her when it is not safe and I could hurt her?"

"Does she know?"

"Not all of it yet. Oh, she understands I do not sleep well, but she has no idea how intense these dreams are or how dangerous they can be. I'll talk to her about it before we are married because I have to be honest with her."

"What do you think she'll do?"

He shook his head and laughed. "She will look upon it as a challenge. Any other woman would accept sleeping in separate quarters and not care in the least. But Hen won't. She'll push me to take her into my bed. I will only do it once I am certain these nightmares have stopped."

"And if they never do?"

He leaned forward, his expression confident. "They will. Hen will chase them out eventually."

"I hope so, for your sake. You look happy, Cain. Truly happy."

"I am," he said with a nod. "So will you be when you meet

the right woman. Don't fall back into your sulk. I vow, you will know it the moment you set eyes on her…unless you're too drunk to see straight. Don't let frustration get the better of you."

"Ha! You think this is merely frustration? Have you not heard? Lady Seline wants nothing more to do with me. The thought of being held in my arm… Get it? I no longer have two arms to hold her, and it disgusts her."

Cain emitted a soft growl. "That is her failing, not yours. You are better off without her, as you well know. She would only have made you miserable whether you came to her with one functioning arm or two."

"You never liked her."

"She is and always has been completely wrong for you. But you've always had poor taste in women. What draws you to these shallow, scheming beauties anyway?"

"Same reason you were once drawn to them, and not so long ago. They are easy. I know exactly what they want from me, and it has nothing to do with love. I am a coin purse for them and more than capable of providing all the pretty trinkets they desire."

"Expensive trinkets," Cain said.

His friend shrugged. "I can afford it. The point is, they can be bought easily, and they place no demands on my heart. Still, I will admit Lady Seline caught me off guard. I knew she would drop me, but I never expected her to do it so quickly. She was quite heartless about it. This is what comes of shallow relations, I suppose. There's no real caring involved. Just an elegant way of exchanging money for sex. That's what it boils down to, doesn't it? However, I would have stuck with her if the circumstances had been reversed."

"Because you are honorable, even if you are a dolt at times."

Cormac laughed again. "I'll likely continue to be a dolt. I don't need a good woman in my life, especially not now. I would only hurt her badly. So I'll stick to the shallow, scheming vipers for the moment. I like to think I'll know when it is time for me to open my heart. Who knows if the right woman exists for me?"

"She does." Cain slapped his hands on his thighs and rose to leave. "Are we good? I'll bring Hen around to meet you tomorrow. I have business to discuss with your brother right now."

"What sort of business?"

"Hen and I will tell you tomorrow. It concerns her. Has nothing to do with you." He strode to the door. "You had better be washed and clean-shaven when we call."

"So had you. Go away, you arse."

"Stop scaring your nieces."

"Gad, get out of here or I am going to throw something at you."

"It's good to see you, too."

He marched down the hall and strode downstairs, feeling better now that he'd seen his friend. But Cormac had a long way to go before healing.

What could Cain do to help? He and Hen would return to Moonstone Landing once her situation was resolved. Nor did he expect them to return to London much over the coming year, perhaps only when Parliament was in session.

No, he had to get Cormac to Moonstone Landing.

But how was he to convince his friend to join them?

Chapter Nine

CAIN RETURNED DOWNSTAIRS and was led to the study, where Cormac's brother awaited him.

"Ah, how did it go with my stubborn brother?" Lord Stockwell ushered him to one of the wing chairs beside the unlit hearth and settled himself in one of the others. "I heard the two of you laughing. Thank you for that. I wish I could do the same, but we are so different in character. We care for each other, but we certainly don't understand each other. It is so frustrating, especially at times like these. He is hurting so badly, and I don't know what to say to him."

"He has agreed to see me again tomorrow."

"Good—I think he needs you more than he does me."

"No, John. Don't ever think that. He is giving you a hard time because he knows he can get away with it. But never doubt how important you are to him."

"Thank you." John laughed wryly. "I think I needed to hear that. He thinks I am stronger than I truly am and can take all he dishes out. But I'm not. He has always been the strong one in the family, physically and in spirit. Our father was livid when he went off to war. I was the spare and should have been the one sent off, but Cormac would not hear of it. He told our father I was the brains in the family and needed to be left here to run the Burness holdings."

"You've obviously done a good job."

He shrugged. "Cormac could have done it, too. He's just as clever as I am, only he was too busy chasing the ladies to put his mind to business matters. He went around with the worst sort of ladies, too. Unfortunately, he has no intention of changing his ways."

"I know." Cain winced. "We sowed our wild oats together from boyhood and through the war years, but those days are over for me."

"I'm not sorry Lady Seline ended their relation as brutally as she did. I hope he learned a lesson from it."

"Even if he had, he would never admit it to you."

John nodded. "I know—he's too stubborn and prideful."

"He'll come around in his own good time. I am bringing Lady Henley, my betrothed, to meet him tomorrow. He has promised to make himself presentable. See to it that he does."

John cast him a genuine smile. "I will make certain he is scrubbed from head to toe."

"Good. I think he responds better to demands than to pity."

"You know me, Cain. He's my big brother and I've always worshiped him. I cannot help but be soft with him."

"Try to growl at him just a little. Let me know if he needs to be given a solid kick in the arse. I'm happy to oblige."

Cormac's brother laughed. "I won't hesitate to send word if I need your help."

John was a gentle soul, and so was his wife, Charlotte. In truth, the woman was as timid as a mouse, sometimes irritatingly so. She was a fluttery, easily unsettled sort, and Cain knew that had she been the one trapped on his beach with the tide coming in, she likely would have drowned.

Indeed, Lady Stockwell and Hen were both gently bred ladies, but this was where all similarity ended. Hen had a spine to her. Lady Stockwell would have cowered against the rocks and allowed the water to overtake her.

He shook out of the thought and moved on to the urgent

business of the bank. When he was done recounting Hen's situation and the embezzlement his Bow Street runner had discovered going on with the assistance of the bank's manager, John was appalled.

He stared at Cain in dismay. "Dear heaven, I must get in touch with the other directors immediately. I dread what else might be going on under our very noses. We could be ruined over this. Who will ever trust us with their funds if word gets out?"

Cain nodded. "The faster it is addressed, the better. But I think you must not keep it quiet. Get ahead of the news, let your depositors know you are ever vigilant and have safeguards in place that helped you to discover an attempted theft. But I strongly suggest you retain Mr. Barrow to dig in to all your accounts. I think your manager has done no more than petty pilfering up to now, but you had better make sure of it."

"I will get on it at once." John reached over and shook Cain's hand. "If Lady Henley's losses are not restored by that thieving Stoke, rest assured I will restore the funds out of my own pocket."

"No, John. It isn't necessary. I'll take care of Hen and her family. Just make sure those accounts are put out of Stoke's reach until I can get him to step down as trustee."

"Consider it done. And by the way, Lord Justice Arnold happens to be on the bank's board of directors. If there are any pleadings to be filed, as I expect there must be if you wish to remove Lady Henley's cousin as her guardian, I suggest your barrister file them with him. Rest assured, you will get prompt action."

They both rose, Cain once again assuring Cormac's brother he would return tomorrow. "I am staying at the Malabar Club for the sake of propriety while Hen and her cousin are at my house. Send word to me there should you need me. The club's steward will know how to reach me."

"Thank you, I will."

Cain was pleased with all he had accomplished in a morning and looked forward to seeing Hen next. He intended to take her to her father's solicitor to make certain they understood the terms of the trust, and they would have the man prepare the proper documents for Hen's weasel of a cousin to re-sign. Cain's soon-to-be wife was no peahen, and he wanted her to be a part of any discussion concerning her future and that of her sisters.

He walked through the London streets with a purposeful stride and reached Malvern House as the distant church bells chimed the twelve o'clock hour. "Dinsmore, where is Lady Henley? Would you ask her to join me in my study?"

"At once, Your Grace," his butler said. "She and Mrs. Landers are seated outdoors, enjoying the garden on this very pleasant day."

"Even better. I'll go to her." Cain strode to the parlor and through its double doors that opened onto a terrace overlooking the garden. Hen and her cousin were seated in a shady spot on the lawn, a blanket spread under them, and each of them with a book in hand.

Hen scrambled to her feet when she saw him. "Did your Bow Street man have any news for us? Oh, forgive me." She grinned impishly. "How are you…my darling?"

He laughed. "Quite well, now that I am with you."

Her cousin now got to her feet. "I am sure the two of you would rather speak in private. I'll—"

"Stay, Prudence," he said. "This news concerns you as well."

She inhaled lightly. "Very well."

Both ladies now stared at him, obviously eager to learn what had happened.

"My runner uncovered everything," he said. "I never quite appreciated how good the man was at his job until now. He's already discovered a secret account held by the earl and traced the source of its funding to your trust accounts. The months of payments which should have gone to each of you went into this secret pocket of his instead."

Hen was listening with avid interest. "What happens now?"

"I know the chairman of the bank's board of directors and have advised him of what has been going on. He is about to sack the bank manager, but will offer a lighter sentence in exchange for information against the earl. He will also dig through every account the bank holds to make certain there were no other victims."

He glanced from Hen to her cousin. "Your accounts will now be placed under the immediate control of Lord Stockwell. He is the brother of my best friend, the Marquess of Burness, and is also the bank's chairman. From this moment on, no one will be permitted to touch the Killigrew accounts but him."

"Hoorah!" Prudence cheered. "That weasel will have a surprise coming to him."

Cain nodded. "I'm next on my way to see your father's solicitor, Hen. I know he was handling your affairs and you have faith in his abilities. I'd like you to come with me to review the terms of the trust with him. I'll ask to review yours too, Prudence. But if you don't mind, I would like to go alone with Hen. There are other matters we need to discuss privately with her solicitor."

"Of course. I cannot thank you enough for all you are doing," Prudence replied. "I shall be perfectly comfortable awaiting both of you in this magnificent house."

Hen ran upstairs to grab her bonnet, gloves, and reticule, and then hurried back down. She stared up at him, her big eyes filled with wonder as she and Cain stood at the front door waiting for his barouche to be brought around. "Did you have a chance to see your friend? How is he?"

"I'll tell you once we are on our way. Ah, good. Here's the carriage." It was a sleek, polished black conveyance with the Malvern crest embossed on the doors and an open top that was kept drawn back on pleasant days but could be drawn forward to provide some shelter for the riders in cold or rainy weather.

He settled his large frame in the carriage beside her. "You are frowning, Hen."

"Is it wise for you to be seen with me just yet? Won't it tip off my cousin?"

He nodded. "Your account is secure by now. Lord Stockwell immediately summoned his board and has gone down to the bank himself to sack the manager and have him taken into custody for criminal charges. Rest assured, the board members will act swiftly. It is their investment, their entire wealth put at risk by the actions of your cousin and their untrustworthy manager." She listened attentively as he took a moment to explain how banks were structured. "The directors reap the profits, but they also are fully exposed for any losses. If depositors start taking out their funds, they will all be ruined."

"So if it is a matter of their downfall or my cousin's," she said, taking it to the next logical step, "they will see my cousin destroyed."

"Do not feel bad for him, Hen. I can see that soft look in your eyes. Just remember, he gave not a care for you or any of your relations. It is time for news of our arrival to start leaking out. I want him to feel the noose tighten around his neck, as he will feel it when he learns you are ensconced at Malvern House. You look lovely, by the way. Have I mentioned it yet?"

She laughed and shook her head. "And you still look like a big, scruffy bear. Ridiculously handsome, of course. But I thought you were going to shave."

"I will, first thing tomorrow morning. You may not recognize me when I turn up at Malvern House. By the way, Lady Fielding is hosting a dinner party tomorrow evening. I expect there will be an invitation awaiting us when we return from our errands this afternoon. I'll make myself presentable well before that. I may even cut my hair."

"Stop," she teased. "You are making me swoon."

He winked at her, but quickly sobered. "I ought to warn you that your weasel cousin will likely be at Lady Fielding's."

Her eyes widened. "Are we to confront him at her party?"

"No, Hen. All you need to do is behave like a woman in love.

I will be formally announcing our betrothal there."

"But how can we when we need his consent? He'll never give it."

"By this time tomorrow, it will not matter whether he does or not. Control of you and your accounts will be out of his hands. In truth, if he has a brain in his head, he will be running out of London as fast as he can."

"What of his guardianship over my sisters?"

"They will be out of his reach as well," Cain replied. "This is why we must see your father's solicitor. He will take care of the trust details."

"What details?"

"Stoke's designation of me as his successor and then his immediate resignation. That covers the financial assets. We shall then pay a call on my solicitor, who will also be set to work."

"On the matter of the transfer of guardianship? What will that involve?"

"It will require a judge's blessing."

"But that could take months," she said. "Oh, I am not concerned for my sake, since I will turn twenty and one soon, but what of Phoebe and Chloe? I've heard how some of these judges appoint their friends, who might be worse than Stoke. At least he only stole the interest. What if the judge appoints someone other than you?"

He arched an eyebrow. "Seriously, Hen? Do you doubt the extent of my power? I have a very long reach. Not even the most crooked judges will dare defy me. And what is Stoke to bribe them with now that your accounts are out of his reach?"

She groaned. "It is a good thing I like you. Well, actually…it is a good thing you like me. We would have been lost without you."

"I suppose finding you gorgeous helped persuade me to help you." He cast her a wry smile. "But I like to think I would have come around and helped a neighbor. Mr. Barrow, that Bow Street man I retained to investigate your situation, said something that struck me as deceptively profound."

She turned eagerly to listen. "What did he tell you?"

"He is a modest man and gruff in appearance, but that belies his sharp intelligence. He is best in his field, intuitive and experienced. It is not the hefty fees he is paid that spur him on. It is the ability to help those who cannot otherwise help themselves. He calls them little victories. But they are not little to the people he helps. Nor to all whose lives are bettered because someone wicked is gotten out of the way."

She nodded. "I understand perfectly. His accomplishment spreads like a ripple on the water. His information has saved me and my sisters, Prudence, and our elderly maiden aunts. Well, it was not just him. You have had everything to do with our turn of fortune."

"It is not done yet. But we are underway."

"Yes, and I must admit it feels good. But you know what the best part of it is?"

"No. Enlighten me."

She cast him another grin. "Since you have been so efficient in taking down the Killigrew family villain, it may not be necessary for you to shave your beard."

He kissed her on the tip of her nose. "No, I think my wooly bear days are over. But there is more I need to talk to you about. It concerns us and our marriage."

"You are not smiling, so it must be something serious." She inhaled lightly. "Of course, I should have understood. It may not be necessary to marry me. You've been quite efficient in saving us all."

He took hold of her hand. "Only time will tell if I have been successful at wresting control from Stoke. As for our marriage, I have no intention of begging out, even if he capitulates this very day. It is completely wrong of you to think so, and I hope never to give you cause to doubt me on that score. My offer is sincere. My desire to marry you has never wavered. But you may be taking on more than you realize."

"How so?"

"We'll talk about it later. We're here at the Inns of Chancery." Her father's solicitor and his own were merely across the courtyard from each other, having established their bureaus in the various buildings comprising the old judicial inns.

They went to her solicitor first.

"Good day, Mr. Garrick," Hen said, and quickly introduced the two men.

As soon as they were led into his office, Cain recounted all that had been going on.

"I knew I did not like him the moment he sauntered into my office and declared he was taking control of the Killigrew estate and guardianship over the girls," Garrick said. "He did not even ask to review the terms of their trusts before he sacked me and left. I am at your service, Your Grace. I'll do whatever you need to be rid of that scoundrel. I can have the designation drawn up today appointing you as his successor. I'll have his resignation ready today as well."

"There is one more thing I need you to prepare on behalf of Lady Henley, and that is a list of her terms for our betrothal contract," Cain said.

Hen laughed. "That is simple. I have no demands. Whatever you wish to give me is up to you."

"Fine, then I will advise my solicitor to give you everything. Houses, carriages, an obscenely large allowance."

"You are the most irritating duke I have ever met. You cannot give me everything."

"Why not? Much of it is mine to freely bestow, except for the entailed properties, which must go to our eldest son. Provision must also be made for our other children. However, once I am gone, I will not have you dependent on anyone for your comforts."

She cast him the softest smile. "What would I need if I did not have you?"

He was not surprised by her response. He knew she wanted

him and not his wealth. For this reason, he wanted to give her all that was his to give. "Ignore her, Mr. Garrick. First, make certain the betrothal contract clearly states she is to keep control over all assets she brings to the marriage. Hen, you can do whatever you wish with the rest you will inherit from me. Use it for charitable endeavors or whatever else you like. I know you'll apply it wisely. Besides, if our sons are anything like me in my youth, they'll need to be kept under tight control. I was a brash idiot, and I fully expect they will be no different."

"I'm sure you were always wonderful. Your father adored you." She turned to Garrick. "Do your best. Come up with something fair to me, but keep in mind, my needs are modest."

They left him and crossed the courtyard to pay a call on Cain's solicitor, Mr. Chiswell. His bureau was far grander than Garrick's, and he had a small army of clerks at his beck and call. "Your Grace, do come in," he said, immediately ushering them into his rather grand private office.

"I won't keep you long," Cain said, noting others were waiting to see the busy man. This was another advantage of being a duke. Appointments did not matter. He had only to walk in and he would jump to the head of the line. In this instance, he took advantage of the privilege.

He introduced Hen to Chiswell and quickly told him all that had been going on. "Stoke needs to be discharged as guardian, and I must be appointed in his place. The barristers to which you refer your trial matters have clout with the judges. Get them to work on the petitions right away. He needs to be removed from all trusts concerning the Killigrew family. If they can get these documents in front of Lord Justice Arnold, have them do it."

"Of course, Your Grace," Chiswell replied. "Need I point out, it is an obvious conflict of interest, since he is a director of—"

"That is Stoke's problem. Let him try to have Lord Arnold's decision overturned. Who do you think the other justices will side with? A distinguished colleague or a thief?"

Chiswell cleared his throat. "Yes, I see your point. We should have the petitions ready by the end of the week."

Cain arched an eyebrow. "Have them ready by end of today."

The man's jaw dropped. "Please, Your Grace. It isn't possible."

"Make it possible. They need to be in Lord Arnold's hands by tomorrow morning at the latest. Send your clerks out to take affidavits from my Bow Street runner and Lord Stockwell. He and his board of directors are meeting on this matter as we speak. Lady Henley and her cousin, Mrs. Landers, are also willing to attest to his villainous conduct."

"But this cannot be done without his knowledge. No judge will remove him without giving him the opportunity to plead his case."

"He has no case," Cain said. "He and his wife have been stealing from these accounts for months. They will run from London the moment he is served papers. Have him temporarily removed, if that is the best you can do *ex parte*. Just make certain I am temporarily appointed to replace him. I only need guardianship over Lady Henley for a few days, just long enough to give my consent for us to marry. After that, we can go through whatever steps are necessary to permanently put all the Killigrew sisters, as well as their cousin and elderly aunts, under my care."

Chiswell mopped his brow. "It will be done."

Cain nodded. "There is also the matter of a betrothal contract between me and Lady Henley. You will receive a list of terms from her solicitor shortly. As for my terms…there are none. You are to give her whatever she asks."

Chiswell's eyes widened in alarm. "Your Grace, perhaps this is something you and I ought to discuss privately."

"I can assure you, Lady Henley wants nothing from me. But my wishes are that you give her a generous portion upon my demise, and none of it in trust. She is to have full control of her inheritance. My Moonstone Landing assets are to be included in that portion. In addition, her assets are to remain her own and in her control during our marriage."

Hen was frowning at him again. "Can this contract be amended after we are married?"

The solicitor nodded.

"Good, because the duke and I may need to make changes at a later date." She turned to Cain. "You have done so much for me already. And I think you are enjoying tossing your wealth and status around. But I do not have lavish tastes and hope never to develop them. At the moment, I cannot imagine myself retiring anywhere but in Moonstone Landing. Thank you for thinking of this in our contract."

"Of course, Hen."

"But don't overindulge me. You know this is not why I wish to marry you. And I hope you also know that as between us, there need never be anything in writing. Whatever you ask, whatever I can do to help you, is yours."

The duke spared a glance at Chiswell, who was regarding them in the same gaping-mouth manner as Garrick had. One would think Cain and Hen had known each other their entire lives, but it was not yet even two weeks. This trust they had in each other was remarkable, but she made it easy to trust her.

He had never warmed up to anyone this quickly.

However, he was no fool, and understood human nature quite well.

And Hen did not understand how she had gained his trust in so many little ways over their short acquaintance, ways that revealed her character. It was not only the kindness and sacrifice she showed toward her sisters, but toward others as well. It was in the respectful way his workers had spoken of her. That she even acknowledged them revealed her considerate nature. Despite being worried about her own funds, she still saw to the needs of those who had fallen on hard times.

It was in these small gestures that his feelings for her solidified—the bread delivered to a hungry family, or a smile and a moment to chat with a local. Others, like her weasel cousin and his wife, would sneer at those lesser in stature and deem them beneath their notice.

The opposite was true with Hen.

She had shown her kindness again just now in her willingness to share all that was hers with him. Of course, the law would deem her property his upon their marriage, but even if they were not married, if he was in need, she would help him out.

How could he not view her as perfect and want to protect her with all his might?

He had never trusted a woman to this extent before. It made him laugh to think of what an idiot he had been over Lady Alexandra, a woman never to be trusted. He'd known it even as he fawned over her as a foolish youth. That lady, as so many others to this day, had sought him out for his wealth and title, nothing more.

Hen looked at the man he was.

She liked him as he was.

She also liked to stand on her own two feet. The more he did for her, the more uncomfortable he seemed to make her.

She remained pensive as they rode back to Malvern House. The streets were congested and their carriage moved slowly, but Cain was in no hurry for their time together to come to an end. "What are you thinking, Hen?"

"How much you've accomplished in one day. It isn't even four o'clock yet and you've managed to stir up at least a dozen hornet nests. You have bank directors, top solicitors, top barristers, and probably the entire King's Bench hopping to your instructions. And you are doing all this for me. I don't know how to repay you."

"You already have."

She dismissed the comment with a shake of her head.

"There's something more I need to talk to you about." He took her hand in his. "I suppose this is as good a time as any to discuss my situation. I want you to know this before we are married…although knowing you, I don't think you will be deterred. Marriage to me will not be easy."

She regarded him in puzzlement.

"Hen, I am not well. We've briefly touched upon it, but it is time you knew everything. I do not refer to my physical strength. Obviously, I made it through the war physically unscathed, nothing more than a few scars. But my soul was damaged. Quite badly. I am always restless... I'm not sure I know how to explain it. I do not sleep at night."

"I gathered as much the first day I met you. You work yourself to the point of exhaustion in the hope you'll be too tired for dreams."

"They haunt me, Hen. They aren't merely bad dreams. I have no control over when they come on, but when they do, I cannot make it through the night without thrashing about violently. It feels as though I am being tossed in a grave and buried alive. I don't know how to make this feeling stop. It overtakes me sometimes in my waking hours, but usually I can manage it then. But I find myself choking, struggling to catch my breath."

"Cain, I'm so sorry."

"I've situated you in the duchess's chambers, and this is where you must remain after we are married. I'm not sure this is even enough of a safe distance for you. It is possible I walk in my sleep."

"Have you ever done so?" she asked.

"Not that I am aware. But the duchess's bedchamber has been empty until now. I don't know what I'll do once I am back in my quarters and you are in the room beside mine. You had better keep our adjoining door locked."

"Keeping you out?"

"It must be this way," Cain said. "At least for now. I'll still come to you every night because I don't think I can keep my hands off you. But you cannot let me fall asleep in your bed. I have to get away from you, and you must be diligent in keeping that protective barrier between us."

"It feels so wrong."

"I know. I want so badly to wake up after a peaceful night and find you sleeping in my arms. I'd love to see your morning smile and the glow in your eyes when you first open them. But it would destroy me if I found your face bruised because of something I had done. This is how our marriage has to be. I'll still be with you, but only while I am awake."

Tears formed in her eyes.

He caressed her cheek. "It won't be so bad. Most *ton* couples do the same. In truth, most of them see each other as little as possible, whether awake or sleeping."

She cast him a smile of encouragement. "We will work on it."

"Don't expect miracles. All right? This problem isn't going to magically disappear. For all I know, it could get worse. And I vow, I will lock *my* door against *you* if you dare crawl into my bed to test it out while I am sleeping. I will never have a moment's rest if I cannot trust you to be careful. Promise me you will never do this, Hen."

"You have my word," she said in all earnestness. "But can you promise me one thing in return?"

"If it is in my power."

"Can you promise me that we shall always live under the same roof?"

Chapter Ten

CAIN WAS NOT certain he could make that promise to Hen. To reside under the same roof? Of course, he wanted this. But not if it would hurt her.

She was not happy when he refused to make her that promise.

"I do not say it lightly," he tried to explain, but could see he was only riling her. "I will try my best to keep us together."

"As will I, even if I have to sleep in a medieval suit of armor. We have to remain under the same roof, Cain. I do not want our marriage to fall apart."

"Blessed saints, it never will. I will never break my wedding vows."

He returned her to Malvern House, but remained only long enough to check the salver on the table in the entry hall. He needed to be certain there was no urgent message waiting for him. He found an invitation from Lady Fielding for her party.

It pleased him.

Hen caught him smiling. "Word certainly gets around fast. I suppose you will not be joining us for supper tonight or tomorrow, then?"

"Perhaps not tonight. There's still much to do. But I am invited with a guest to Lady Fielding's party. Of course, that guest will be you."

"Oh, I am not certain I have a suitable gown to wear. I did not think…how foolish of me. But Phoebe might have packed one for me."

"If she hasn't, then go to your modiste right away. Have her put all your purchases on my account. Promise me you will do this, Hen."

She bristled. "Let's just not make promises to each other, all right? I will take care of my gown for Lady Fielding's affair. I am not yet your wife and don't like to be thought of as your… I don't know. It does not feel right."

He could see she was still aching over his refusal to promise her a cozy marriage. But he was not going to lie to her. Nor would he ever allow himself to become a danger to her.

She stiffened as he leaned over to kiss her on the cheek.

He sighed and kissed her anyway. "I'll see you tonight if I finish with this ugly business earlier than expected. If not, I'll come by first thing tomorrow."

He wanted to stop by the bank to see if Lord Stockwell needed his help. It would be closing to the public shortly, not that any doors would ever close to him. Dukes were not *the public*.

The guards were locking up just as he arrived. "Your Grace," the porter said, immediately allowing him entrance. "Lord Stockwell and several of the board's members are in his office. He told me to bring you straight up should you come by."

The man quickly secured the doors behind them and escorted him up the marble stairs to the private offices.

Cain noticed four directors in addition to Cormac's brother standing around a seated man who had a frightened look on his face and could only be the bank manager. Also in the room were two clerks seated behind writing desks set up in the corner, no doubt to prepare the necessary affidavits to be taken to Cain's solicitor.

Lord Stockwell made quick introductions as he strode in.

Cain was familiar with most of these men.

"How far have you gotten with this cur?" He posed the question to all the directors present.

"We were just getting started," Lord Easterly, one of the older gentlemen, replied. "But he does not appear to want to cooperate."

"Is that so?" Cain kicked the chair out from under the manager, causing the stunned man to tumble to the floor. He then grabbed the manager by his lapels and dragged him upright. "Let me be clear about this, for you will get far worse treatment in prison if you do not cooperate fully with us. You are to tell these lords what you have stolen from their depositors, what Lord Stoke has stolen from his family, and whoever else assisted you in these thefts. If you omit any detail, I shall personally see you hanged, drawn, and quartered. Are we clear?"

The man nodded, his face now ashen and the sly gleam in his eyes extinguished.

Cain knew he had shocked the directors as well, for these were gentlemen and probably regarded him as mad.

Well, let them all think he was a little mad. He did not mind playing the role of devil in this situation. After all, he still looked the part.

As the directors were about to resume questioning the manager, the young guard who had led Cain upstairs suddenly hurried back in. "My lords," he said, addressing all of them but settling his gaze on Cain, "Lord Stoke is at the door asking to be let in."

They all looked to Cain.

He smiled. "I will deal with him."

The manager gasped.

"Cain, dear lord." Lord Easterly hurried out after him. "You're not going to…"

Cain arched an eyebrow. "No, I am not going to kill him. As to anything else, I give you no promises."

He walked out with the guard, knowing he'd left these men worried about what he meant to do. In fact, he intended to do absolutely nothing.

"Have you let him in?" he asked the young man.

"No, Your Grace. He is standing on the steps. I haven't unlocked the doors. We have a strict protocol at the bank not to open them after we close."

"Good. Just leave him standing there. Do not respond to his knocks or his shouts. He'll get the message soon enough. No one is to get inside unless Lord Stockwell authorizes it. Do you understand?"

"Yes, I am clear on that, Your Grace. I have taken the liberty of alerting the night guards on Lord Stockwell's behalf. They came on duty when the bank doors closed, and they are all here now." The guard straightened proudly. "I will be staying, too. Until matters settle, it is wise to keep watch over everyone."

The man was young and affable in nature, but Cain was concerned he was not up to the task of supervising others, especially those senior guards who had worked here before this young man was even born.

If others were involved in the manager's misdeeds, was it not likely these took place after hours and guards were involved? These conspirators would be scrambling to cover their tracks.

Cain kicked himself for not thinking to bring in his Bow Street runners. But this reminded him—Barrow had told him about a source at the bank.

There were a few clerks and tellers still finishing up downstairs. Was one of them his source?

The young man cleared his throat, his manner suddenly serious as he kept his voice low. "Your Grace, rest easy. I am not a fool. Mr. Barrow came by not an hour ago and told me what to look out for. Do not let my easy smile and jovial manner deceive you. I am on alert. And do you see that guard over there? His name is Mick. He is Mr. Barrow's best man. Between us we are making note of everyone employed here as they make their way out."

Cain was going to give Barrow a hefty bonus for this.

He patted the young man on the shoulder. "I ought to have

known. It eases my mind greatly. There are clerks and tellers still here. Is there a back way out for them? And is it also being guarded?"

The man nodded.

"Good, show it to me. I'll take my leave as well." Cain went next to his solicitor's office to check on his progress.

"The barrister has the pleadings drawn up and is merely awaiting the affidavits," Chiswell said. "But he tells me Lord Justice Arnold will not take this matter because it would give the appearance of impropriety."

"Lord protect us from honest judges," Cain muttered. "Does he not understand how important it is to his own interest in the bank?"

"He fully understands, and this is why he will recuse himself. He has arranged for one of his colleagues to hear the matter tomorrow morning."

"And then what?"

"And then nothing, Your Grace. The presiding judge will make his decision on the facts presented. Hopefully, he will rule quickly. But do not expect a miracle. The judicial system is a process, and you are also asking for the Earl of Stoke, a peer of the realm, to be removed of his authority over his own family. Not only removed, but removed without notice to him. Even commoners have the right to defend themselves from such allegations. As a peer, he has all this and more. He will exert his privilege and avoid any punishment."

"We'll see about that."

"Your Grace!" Chiswell said. "It is obvious this man is a bounder and a villain, but there is only so much the law can do. You cannot mete out your own justice. It will destroy your life as well as his. What would Lady Henley say? Do you think she wants you to violate the law on her behalf? Proceeding against one of her own relations, no less?"

"Calm down, Chiswell. I am not going to murder him, so you can stop wringing your hands. Just keep the pressure on him.

That is all I need you to do."

Cain walked out, needing air.

But the air was damp and carried the scent of rotted fish off the Thames. The skies were now overcast and threatening rain.

Having set everything in motion, he knew he ought to simply allow Chiswell, Lord Stockwell, and Mr. Barrow to attend to the business he'd set out for them. They were all honest, competent men.

He decided to return to Malvern House and share a quiet supper with Hen and her cousin. However, his demons were working themselves up inside him. He needed to walk off his anger and frustration first.

He hadn't walked far before a carriage drew up alongside him and slowed to match his pace. A beautiful young woman popped her head out the window. "Cain, darling. I thought that was you. I had no idea you were back in town. Why did you not send word to me?"

"Should I have, Alexandra? I doubt your husband would have approved."

She shrugged. "Fenwick's off at his country estate mucking about the stables with his horses. The man hasn't touched me in months. All he thinks about are the Newmarket races. I vow, he cares more for his horses than he does me. What are you doing this evening? Have supper with me tonight."

"No, I'm busy."

The rain began to fall, merely intermittent droplets at first, but quickly turning into a more persistent patter. "Do not be a fool," Lady Alexandra said. "Hop in before you are drenched. I'll drop you off at Malvern House. It is on my way. Why are you so reluctant? It is only a carriage ride. Although you know how much fun you and I can have in a carriage." She cast him a seductive smile. "All you have to do is ask nicely."

The rumble of thunder sounded in the distance and the rain began to pound down on him with force.

"All right. Just the ride, Alexandra." He had to return to Malvern House and patch things up with Hen. He did not like leaving things as they were between them. But how could he have promised to keep them under the same roof? He wanted it, of course. Was that also not made clear to her?

She had to understand his concern.

He could also bring her up to date on all that had transpired since he'd left her side. Having set all in motion necessary for Stoke's demise, all they had to do was wait for his downfall to occur. Hen would appreciate his keeping her abreast of all that was going on. It was obvious she did not like to be kept out of things.

Alexandra squeezed close to him, regaining his attention. "Will you not talk to me? You seem miles away. That is very rude of you."

"Forgive me, but I have a lot on my mind."

She cast him a practiced pout. "You are a beast. Can you not think of me while I am beside you? There was a time when you could not keep your hands off me. Or your mouth."

"That time has long since passed."

She was now almost atop Cain, rubbing her perfumed body against him. "It doesn't have to be. Touch me again. Here. Now."

She tried to sit astride him, but he stopped her. "Do not embarrass yourself, Alexandra. I mean it. Our time has passed."

She began to sulk. "But I am so bored. Why have you suddenly turned so prudish? Is this not the ideal situation for you? A woman to pleasure you who is understanding of your needs and asks for no commitment?"

He ignored the question.

She frowned at him, now giving him the silent treatment as she pretended to gaze out the carriage window. There was not much to see other than the swirling mist and still-pelting rain. The streets were mostly empty now, as everyone had run for cover to wait out the passing downpour.

It would pass quickly, as most of these sudden deluges did.

True to form, it was not long before the rain stopped and the sun burst out between the gaps in the clouds. "Well, it has been a joy to see you again, Alexandra," he said, not bothering to hide his sarcasm. "I shall walk the rest of the way."

"Don't be ridiculous. I'll drop you off at home."

Probably not the best idea, but he was not going to argue with her. The woman had a jealous nature and was already in a peeve because he did not wish to serve as her stud bull. To make a thing of dropping him off would only rile her further.

In any event, Hen was unlikely to be standing by the window and watching carriages roll by. His thoughts remained on Hen and what he was going to say to her.

"I heard the oddest thing from a friend of mine as I was riding in the park a short while ago," Alexandra said, breaking the silence and shifting closer to him once again.

Her hand drifted casually onto his thigh.

He drew it off. "Stop it, Alexandra."

"Are you not interested in what I heard?"

"No."

Lord, she was pouting again.

"Then it must be true. Are you betrothed to a little sparrow? Or is it a wren? Some sort of bird. Ah, I have it—a little hen. Lady Henley Killigrew." Alexandra laughed. "That's it. Lady Hen. How droll. How did she trap you?"

"She did not trap me. I asked her and she accepted."

"Of course—who would pass up an offer from a duke? She must be more clever than she seems. What tricks of seduction did she use to pleasure you so mindlessly as to elicit a proposal of marriage from you? Perhaps there is something I can learn from her. Is she demanding anything from you?"

"Nothing at all."

"Do not be absurd. Why else were you walking out of your solicitor's bureau looking so morose?"

"Alexandra, it is none of your business."

"Why will you not admit she trapped you?" She leaned against him, rubbing her breasts against his chest. "You do not owe her your loyalty. I can pleasure you. You used to like the taste of me."

"That was in the past."

"It doesn't have to be. It is a pity, really. You and I ought to have been the ones to marry. Fenwick turned out to be a bit of a limp rag. He doesn't please me, and I no longer please him. Ah, well. It really should have been you for me. But you went off to war, and I wasn't going to wait around for you. Nor did you bother to ask. I had to look out for myself."

He nudged her gently away. "You would not have waited for me even if I had begged. We both know it. Have your driver stop here. I'll walk the rest of the way to Malvern House."

"Not on your life. Are you afraid to be seen with me? Worried your little hen will not believe you when you tell her nothing happened between us? My scent is all over you."

Bollocks.

"I am not worried about her. She trusts me." He certainly hoped so, for Alexandra was going to make this innocent ride look as bad as possible.

He should have walked and taken the drenching.

"Oh dear," Alexandra said as her carriage drew up in front of his house. "Is that your little Hen peering out the parlor window? Shall I kiss you and see what she does?"

He refused to follow her gaze. If Hen happened to be looking… No, why would she be looking out onto the street when she had to be occupied with finding a suitable gown to wear for Lady Fielding's party?

He popped open the door, not needing her footman to do the honors. "Goodbye, Alexandra. Thank you for the ride."

She blew him a kiss. "I'm happy to have you ride me anytime."

He stifled a groan and marched into the house.

"I've decided to stay for supper," he told his butler. "Where is Lady Henley?"

"Right here," Hen said, walking out of the visitor's parlor

with a look on her face that revealed she had indeed seen him stepping out of Alexandra's carriage.

He was not going to apologize or try to explain when he'd done nothing wrong. "Come into the garden with me and I'll tell you what has happened so far."

She arched an eyebrow. "Seems quite a bit has been happening."

He ignored the comment, and also ignored the fact he reeked of Alexandra's expensive perfume. He recounted the progress made at the bank. "Lord Stockwell and several other directors are now interrogating the bank manager. Mr. Barrow has several of his runners inside the bank as we speak. They'll keep an eye out for any activity that appears suspicious. My solicitor has retained his top barrister to bring suit to remove Stoke as your guardian. However, he has made it clear to me that this may take a little more time than expected."

She nodded. "I knew this. You were the one who thought you could throw your weight around and skirt the judicial process. What you have accomplished in a day is amazing. But I never expected a miracle. Not even you can undo the laws of England."

She turned away to stare at the renowned Malvern House flower beds, which had been supervised by his mother when she was alive and were now maintained by his competent garden staff. He did not want to be fighting with Hen amid these vibrant red, gold, and pink blossoms.

He did not want to fight with Hen anywhere.

"Nor do you owe me a wedding, Cain," she said, the heartbreak clearly evident in her voice. "That woman who dropped you off is quite beautiful."

"Yes, she is. But men are trinkets to her, and I have never been nor shall I ever be anyone's trinket. It was raining. I was about to get drenched. I made the supreme mistake of accepting her offer of a ride home."

"Was it a mistake?"

He groaned. "As I said, a supreme one. Nothing happened, Hen. She is married, by the way. Even if she were not, I would have no interest in her."

"She blew you a kiss."

He gave a short, mirthless laugh. "Done purposely to rile you. Lady Alexandra is not a nice person, I can assure you. She takes pleasure in fomenting discord. Obviously, it worked. Turn around and look at me."

She sighed and did as he asked, her expression still wary.

"I promise you, nothing happened between me and Alexandra. It was a chance encounter and a lift home."

She nodded. "If you say so, then I believe you."

He cast her a wry smile. "That sounded pathetic, Hen."

She shook her head and this time returned his smile, but it was a weak one and still obviously filled with doubt. "I do believe you."

He placed his hands on her shoulders and stared down at her. "Then why are you overset? Is it because of our earlier discussion? I want us to share a bed. Lord help me, I crave it. More than you can ever imagine."

"So do I," she said softly.

He kissed her lightly on the cheek. "Your delicious body is what drew me to you first, but your heart is what led me to propose to you. It is the sweetest thing imaginable. This is what enthralls me most about you, this lack of guile and cynicism. Your nature is to be honest and kind. My father taught me early on that while being a duke has its privileges, it also comes with responsibilities. Marrying a woman like Alexandra would only add to my burden. She would plague me with her need for attention and incessant demands. But marrying you will be a delight. You'll make me proud every day."

Her genuine smile returned. "I wasn't jealous of her so much as uncertain. It's just that everything has been happening so quickly. You know me—I need to process things slowly. It strikes me how opposite we are in this. You move with the speed of lightning, and I move like a snail."

"We are a good fit. You slow me down, and I force you out of your comfortable shell."

"Yes, I suppose so. It is a good thing. I need to be challenged because I think I can be too complacent at times."

"You will never have that with me. I move like a rampaging bull. But no matter how idiotic or irritating my behavior, I will never be unfaithful to you. My idiocy does not extend to that. I will never seek another woman for my pleasure, and that is a sacred promise to you."

She groaned. "Now I feel like an utter shrew."

"Don't. I knew Alexandra would try something, but I climbed in anyway. All I wanted to do was get out of the rain. She wasted no time in jumping all over me. Next time, I'll walk."

"And get drenched? I know you will hold to your vows just as I will hold to mine. Perhaps I was a little jealous, but not because I did not trust you. I was jealous of how familiar she was with you, and how she knew you well enough to understand exactly how to rile you. Not that I would ever seek to rile you. But we are so new to each other. I look forward to the day when I understand you that well."

"It will happen in time," he said. "You should have heard some of the ridiculous breakfast conversations my parents used to have with each other, my mother telling my father not to eat the strawberry jam because he would break out in hives. He'd deny it even as the red splotches began to pop on his face. *They're not hives,* he would insist. She'd call him stubborn. He'd call her meddlesome. They loved each other to pieces."

Hen laughed. "Yes, I hope we are just like that." She grew pensive once more as their laughter died down.

"What are you thinking about now, Hen?"

"Speaking of your parents just made me think further about your family. How thoughtless of me never to ask. But somehow you struck me as this mythical being come down from Olympus to join our ranks. Do you have brothers and sisters? Your father never mentioned anyone but you."

He nodded. "I have a half-sister who is much older than me. We share the same mother. Jennifer is married and lives in Aberdeen with her Scottish husband. He's a good man, and they are happy together. They have no children. This is one of the things I am most sorry about for myself, that my parents did not have the joy of knowing I was to marry you. My mother had already passed when my father started building St. Austell Grange. I'm glad he had the chance to meet you. I know from his letters how much he enjoyed your company and that of your sisters."

"Cain, do you have any of his letters?"

"I saved all of them. I ought to read through them again, especially the ones where he mentions meeting the nieces visiting Moonstone Cottage. I don't think he ever referred to any of you by name, but it could just be that I wasn't paying attention to those passages. I'll have to look again."

"Where do you keep them?"

"Here at Malvern House."

Her eyes brightened. "How lovely. Do you think we might… If it is not too personal for you?"

"You wish to read them?"

She nodded.

"All right. Let me get them, but we cannot make a night of it. I want to return to the bank one last time before I retire for the evening. Tomorrow will be a busy day for us. I'll come by to fetch you around ten o'clock in the morning. We're to stop at Chiswell's office first, then on to Cormac's home to pay him a visit. I want you to meet him."

"I'm sure he is curious to meet me, as well. Did seeing him this morning relieve any of your worry?"

He sighed. "No, he's in a bad way."

"I'm so sorry. I'll do my best to make him feel welcome if he decides to join us in Moonstone Landing."

"Thank you, Hen." He kissed her lightly on the lips, intending something short and sweet. But there was something in the feel of her mouth against his that he always found arousing. Perhaps it was the honey taste of her.

Or the crush of her soft body against his brutish own as he drew her up against him.

He took it no further, reluctant to give his staff too much of a show.

"That was nice, Cain." She had that starlight look in her eyes again, this look his soul seemed to take nourishment from and crave.

"Perhaps it is not wise for me to stay. You are too tempting, and I am not at my best just now."

"No, don't you want to see the letters? Please, Cain. Spare a moment to read them with me."

"Yes, all right. But then I must go."

"I won't keep you long, but neither should you be attempting to close this thing up in a day. Be careful. It may not be safe for you to be out after nightfall. From what you've told me, my cousin must now be aware he is being brought to task. He has to be desperate and feeling trapped."

"I can take care of myself, Hen."

"I know. Just be careful, that is all I ask. You left him standing outside the bank, pounding on the door. He will soon learn that the bank manager is under arrest and all accounts are now under review."

"That ought to make for a fun confrontation between us at Lady Fielding's party."

Hen shook her head. "That would be awful for so many reasons, not the least of which is ruining the dear woman's party. If my weasel cousin has any sense, he'll run away from London this very night."

"I hope he doesn't."

She placed a hand on his arm. "Promise me that you will bring him to task verbally and that is all. One solid blow with that big fist of yours could kill him."

He arched an eyebrow. "That would take care of your problem, would it not?"

"Do not dare joke about this. I will not have you strike him. But enough about my horrid cousin. Let's read your father's letters."

"Curious to see what he wrote about you?"

She tipped her chin up pertly. "Of course, and I'm sure he told you how lovely and wonderful I was and how you ought to marry me as soon as you get home."

She spoke in jest, but Cain was suddenly not so sure what his father had said about her. It was not a stretch to believe this was exactly what he wrote. It certainly would explain Cain's asking Hen to marry him within minutes of their first meeting.

"Give me a moment to wash the stench of Alexandra's perfume off me, then I'll retrieve those letters. We'll read them in my study. Meet me there."

"All right."

"Gad, I reek. Don't I?"

"I think Lady Alexandra was trying to mark you with her scent just as a lion marks his territory."

"Heaven forbid. I had better scrub myself raw."

He escorted her back into the house, then took the stairs two at a time to reach his bedchamber.

He marched down the hall, his curiosity now piqued.

He had always been close with his father. Even when they did not agree on matters. There was not a day, not a moment, in his entire life when he did not love the man.

Had his father put this marriage idea in his head?

Chapter Eleven

HEN WAS IN tears as she read the letters Cain's father had written to him. The old man oozed love for his son. *My dearest son* was how he started all his letters. While this correspondence mostly revealed his father's thoughts and fears along with his wonderful character, it also showed glimpses of Cain's character and the close relation these two men had always enjoyed with each other.

These St. Austell men were bred to be honorable and never break vows. She understood now why Cain would not promise to have them live under the same roof. He was truly scared of what his dreams might bring and would rather see her safely out of his reach, even if it meant their living apart.

A warmth spread through her as she sat beside Cain and read the letters aloud to him. Too bad she hadn't gone through them before seeing him with Lady Alexandra and watching her blow him brazen kisses. She would have understood what was going through his mind and known this woman meant nothing to him.

Cain was stretched out on the sofa in his study, his hands casually propped behind his head and his eyes closed as she continued reading.

"I miss you, my son. Stay well and I shall continue to pray for Napoleon's hasty demise and your safe return. Your..."

Cain now opened one eye a crack. "Hen, you cannot cry over

every letter."

"I cannot help it. They're so filled with love. It must have been unbearably hard for your father to endure having you gone all those years."

"I know it was, but he'd raised me to do the right thing, and that was to fight for my country. Leaving him and my mother behind, not being there when she passed, that was awful for me as well. My mother lost four babes between Jennifer and me. Each loss was a heartbreak for them. By the time I came along, they were afraid to breathe around me for fear I would fall ill and die. But I was built like an ox and rarely got sick."

"Then you went off to fight Napoleon," she replied. "Their only son marching into the heart of danger and rarely returning home in all those years. A week, a month, an entire season would not have been enough time for them to be with you." She emitted a ragged sigh. "I don't know how I would have managed to let go of someone I loved that much."

"It was not their choice to make. They knew they could not hold me. I was never one to sit on my pampered arse and enjoy the spoils of London while others were risking their lives for England."

"Still, it had to break their hearts." She had read three letters from his father and now opened a fourth. *"My dearest son,"* it started, just as all the others had. *"The loss of your mother has been quite hard for me. I have dealt with it by immersing myself in building St. Austell Grange. It started as a project for myself, but now I believe I was meant to build it for you. There is a quiet charm about the town of Moonstone Landing. The views of the sea from the Grange are breathtaking. I am convinced this place will calm your soul."*

She glanced up at him. "I don't think it has, but perhaps it will in time."

He nodded. "This is why I ran there when I left London. I look forward to returning as soon as this nasty business with your cousin is over. But go on, Hen. Finish the letter."

"I met my neighbor's nieces today. The eldest is a little angel with

golden brown hair and big green eyes that shimmer like starlight."

Cain laughed. "And there you are. He called you an angel. He was right. You are my angel, Hen."

"We'll see if you still think so after we are married." She smiled and read on. *"She's young for you yet, but she will be of age by the time you come home. I pray that you will make it home."*

He sat up when he heard her suddenly gasp and begin to sniffle. "Hen?"

She took out her handkerchief to dab at her tears. "Oh, Cain. He knew."

"Let me see the rest of it." He began to read the letter aloud to her. *"My son, do not think I am mad. But sometimes, one is struck with something so obviously right. I think my neighbor's niece will bring her starlight into your life. I know the ravages of war and how it can darken one's soul. You need to meet this girl who sparkles with silver light. Her name is Henley, and she is a little mother hen not only to her sisters, but to me as well. I suppose I am getting old and now creak a bit as I walk. These old knees of mine are not what they used to be. Come home soon, my son. I need to see you before I reach my end of life, and I fear that time is not so very far off."*

He paused, needing a moment to compose himself.

Then he gave a raw, bitter laugh and ran a hand through his hair. "Listen how he ends it." He cleared his throat. *"If I do not see you before I move on to reunite with your mother, promise me you will not forget what I have written about little Hen. Starlight is a rare thing to find. I love you, my son."*

She settled beside him on the sofa, her heart beating so rapidly she could hardly catch her breath.

Cain's eyes were watery as he drew her onto his lap. "He was right. Have I not told you that your eyes shine like starlight? My father believed it as well. There's an end to all doubt about having you as my wife. It had to be you, didn't it?"

She put her arms around his neck, inhaling the heat and sandalwood scent of him as she pressed her lips to the arch of his neck and burrowed against him. His shoulders were broad and all of him was divinely muscled. "Thank goodness there wasn't another green-eyed Hen residing in Moonstone Landing," she teased.

He chuckled. "There could have been a hundred and I would have picked you out. The night skies may be filled with the bright light of stars, but it is a rare thing to find in a person. You radiate with it."

He placed a finger under her chin and tipped her head up to kiss her. His kiss was soft, but she felt the raw feeling behind it. "I need you, Hen. I want you so badly."

His hands roamed up and down her body as though compelled to memorize the shape of her and feel each curve beneath his palms. She leaned into him when he cupped her breast and again when he began to lightly knead it, for she now understood they were meant to be united as one.

She gasped as heat coursed through her when he removed the fichu covering the swell of her breasts and dipped his head to kiss her there.

"You are so beautiful." The words came with a wrenching ache as he loosened the bodice of her gown and nudged the fabric aside to take the tip of one fleshy mound between his lips. The little explosions she'd felt before were nothing to the fiery burst she experienced as his tongue licked over the peak of her breast.

Every pulse in her body began to throb, and her blood was now a fiery river.

She feared there would be nothing left of her because he consumed her so completely. This great beast of a man could devour her whole, and she would let him because she was in love with him.

She had always been in love with him.

Even before they had ever met.

She loved him because of the way his father had spoken of him, his voice filling with happiness and pride for his son. She loved him because of how gentle he'd been when treating the cuts on her hand that first day. She loved him because he resembled a big, intimidating bear and not a preening peacock.

She wanted to tell him, and was about to when the clock in his study chimed the six o'clock hour. In the next moment, there was a knock at the closed door.

She froze in panic.

"Hen, it's all right. No one will enter without my permission." He groaned and gave her a soft, lingering kiss to the swell of her breast, then helped her quickly put herself together. Obviously, he was adept at this sort of thing. No doubt he had been caught in the middle of undressing women in inappropriate places and at inappropriate times before.

He'd lowered the bodice of her gown and now raised it back up, secured the fichu atop it for modesty, and quickly tied the lacings. But there was nothing he could do about her face, which remained fiery.

Her hands were shaking, too.

Nor could she catch her breath.

Cain was grinning in a tenderly affectionate way. "Time for us to go in for supper. Too bad. I was quite enjoying my feast of you. Oh, Hen. You look completely undone."

"I cannot help it. I've never…you know…"

"I do indeed, and so will everyone realize exactly what we were doing if you walk out looking as you do."

"Oh, dear. Is my gown not on straight?"

"Your gown is fine." He took her hands in his when she continued to fuss with her clothing. "It is your face that gives you away. Perhaps mine will, too. You tasted so good, like the sweetest cream. I shouldn't have done that to you, but you are temptation itself. Take a deep breath, love."

Her eyes rounded in surprise.

It took him a moment to realize what he'd just called her. She saw the recognition on his face an instant later. "Is this not what we hope our marriage to be? I should have held back, but how could I after we read my father's letters? We were fated to be together."

She slipped her hands out of his and put them to her hot

cheeks. "No, don't say that."

"Why not?" He regarded her and frowned in obvious confusion.

"What I mean is…your father said the loveliest things about me. But I don't want you to be using terms of endearment because it was your father's wish. I want it to be your wish, no one else's."

He kissed her on the forehead. "No one tells me what to do, not even my beloved father. Is it not obvious from the letters? I do a thing because I want to do it."

"Perhaps, but the reason you want to do it is because it will make someone else happy."

"Hen, you are overly thinking things again. This is my fault. I went too far with you, and you were not ready for it. But you really are an irresistible temptation. Come on, let's go before I lock the door and have at you again."

"Wait. I'm not ready."

He sighed. "For dinner or my kisses? Perhaps you are ready for neither. Merely a jest, Hen. You look about to turn purple. Prudence must be waiting for us in the dining room. I'm not going to touch you again. You are far too distracting, and I must leave right after supper."

He escorted her out, holding her arm in his even though she desperately wanted to duck behind him to keep hidden from prying eyes. "Gad, remind me never to partner at cards with you. We'll lose every hand," he teased.

"I am an excellent cards player," she insisted as he hurried her down the hall. "It is not at all the same thing. What we did was…um…"

He cast her a wicked smile. "Yes, it was."

She held him back as they were about to enter the dining room. "How do you manage it?"

He quirked an eyebrow. "Manage what?"

"My body is in spasms and you look as calm as bathwater. How do you do it?"

"Ah, you mean hide my feelings? It is something trained in dukes from an early age. I can assure you, I am burning up inside."

"You are? That is splendid," she whispered as they entered the dining room. Prudence and several of the Malvern House footmen were already there.

Cain's chuckle was quiet but hearty.

They said nothing more as they walked in and took their seats at the table. Hen remained pensive throughout the meal, finding it hard to keep her thoughts on the conversation at hand. It was mostly casual chatter, but she paid closer attention when it turned to more serious matters. Prudence opened up about her situation after she'd learned of her husband's death in battle.

Cain had been listening attentively and now spoke. "It is one of the things I hope to accomplish in the House of Lords. Something must be done not only for the returning soldiers but for the families of those who do not return. This is something the Marquess of Burness and I are quite passionate about. We have the support of other lords who fought in battle and understand the situation, but we are a minority."

"Is there a way in which we can help?" Hen asked.

"Perhaps, but I'm not certain just how. Women do not have a voice yet, so how are politicians ever to hear them? It is especially difficult to get through to the members of the House of Lords. They like things just as they are and have an aversion to any change. These stodgy lords are an impediment to progress, an immovable impediment. Only death or extremely drastic measures ever get a peer tossed out. I don't think a peer has ever been stripped of his title, short of treason. Several have threatened to petition stripping their wayward heirs out of inheriting their title a time or two, but few ever carry through on the threat."

"And this is the problem," Prudence muttered, nodding in agreement. "It is very hard to move a man off his position when he knows he has nothing to gain by a change and everything to lose."

They pursued lighter conversation during the rest of their meal, but did not linger at the table once it was over.

Cain made a quick departure.

Hen and Prudence retired to what had been his mother's salon to have their tea. "All right, Hen," Prudence said once they had been served and were alone, "what happened in the study? I ought to have insisted on being in there with you, but those letters are such a personal matter. I did not feel I had the right to impose. Nor will I ask about their content. But something happened between the two of you. It is my fault entirely. I should not have trusted him to be a gentleman."

"Don't say that. He has always been a gentleman." Hen cleared her throat. "That is, he meant to be. For the most part, he was. We shared a kiss that got a little out of hand, quite minor in the scheme of things. I am still…untouched in every important way, if this is what you are worried about."

Prudence's relief was obvious. "I know he is to marry you, but things remain unsettled. We can never be sure what our weasel cousin might do. I don't want you to be left in a more vulnerable position than you already are."

"Understood."

"Being under that horrible man's thumb has been very difficult for all of us. Did you know he was planning to toss me out of my own home? Well, it isn't actually mine. I never owned it, nor could I ever have, since it is a part of the Stoke entailment. Your father offered to buy me a small place elsewhere, but I was foolish and did not take him up on the offer. My husband had died and I was not thinking clearly for myself."

Hen cast her a sympathetic nod. "How could you do so when you had just lost the man you loved?"

"I will not lie to you. Mr. Landers and I were not a love match, but it was a very good and happy marriage. We liked each other very much, and it was to our mutual disappointment not to be blessed with children. However, when he died, I was relieved not to have given him any. They would have been too much of a burden for me. I cannot even take care of myself, so how would I have managed with small ones?"

"What about his relatives? We have been casting all the blame on Weasel Willis, but did the Landers family not feel any responsibility toward you?"

"No, as it turns out," Prudence replied. "Mr. Landers had risen well above his family's station in life, and we were helping them out as much as we could. But there was not much to spare on an army captain's wages. Even after his death, I loaned them funds to help out. This is all they thought of me, apparently. I was a wealthy woman in their eyes, and they happily took all I was willing to give. Perhaps they would have looked upon me more kindly had I been able to give Mr. Landers children. When the funds dried up, so did their affection."

"I am truly sorry, Prudence."

She shook her head. "No, don't be. I was living in my own little world. In a cloud of fanciful dreams. My parents objected to Mr. Landers and wanted someone better for me. But I did not like the men they brought around. Mr. Landers was handsome and kind. He treated me well and made me laugh."

"That is important, I should think."

She nodded. "We eloped. It was quite the family scandal, but you and your sisters were too young to be told of it at the time. I never thought of myself as a stupid woman, but it turns out I was when it came to finances. I just assumed funds would always be there. Oh, never a huge amount. But enough for me to live out my life in modest comfort."

"My father set up all of our accounts to ensure this for us. Willis is the one who broke faith."

"I am going to sound waspish now, but Hen…you cannot assume someone will provide for you. Make certain the duke protects you financially from the start. Attend to this matter now, while you are young and beautiful and he desires you. This is the moment you hold the most power. Make certain he gives you sufficient sums outright so that you are never at the mercy of someone like Willis."

Hen smiled through clenched teeth. "I am not marrying him for his money. I understand your concerns, Prudence. But I don't need to say anything to him. He will protect me as he sees fit. No doubt he will be overly generous. What I hope to have is his love. It is not a question of power or a grab of his wealth."

"Oh, now you are angry with me. You must think I am a horrible person. But starvation is not pleasant. I hope the duke can save us from what Willis is trying to do. But I plan to marry whether I have that income back or not. Mr. Weston seems to be a man of good character. I noticed how he was looking at me."

Hen nodded. "He is a good man."

"If he asks me to marry him, I will accept. He seems to be very kind, and I will make him a good wife. Some women are strong on their own, but I am not one of them. I like the idea of a man providing for me. I have not done well by myself. Not only because of the lack of funds. I like having a companion and protector. I am simply not the sort who can scratch and claw her way through adversity."

"None of us knows what we are capable of doing until our backs are to the wall."

"I would rather not find out," Prudence said. "I am not averse to work, but I like to be looked after. Perhaps you have more strength than I ever had, Hen. You were prepared to fight our cousin with or without the duke's assistance. I think you would have done whatever was necessary to save yourself and your sisters."

"I would have. It eats at me that Cain is doing all the work. I do little but watch him close the noose around Willis's neck. I hate that I am not doing more, that I cannot do more. But my feelings for Cain have nothing to do with his coming to our rescue. Whether he succeeds or not in removing Willis as our guardian and restoring our funds…I love him."

Prudence cast her a warm smile. "Have you told him?"

"No, not yet. But I think he must realize it, since I seem to have no ability to hide my feelings. He reads them very easily."

"Do not assume he knows it. This is one thing Mr. Landers and I never said to each other, and I am sorry we did not. I think over time we grew to care for each other deeply." Prudence shook her head. "Neither of us was raised to believe love was important. Perhaps this is what we had all along and did not appreciate this special feeling. Yes, I expect it was love. After all, I eloped with him. And he never looked at another woman. There was only me. When he kissed me…it was nice." She shrugged and then shook her head. "If I do get a second chance, I will be more aware. I think it is the nicest thing one person can say to another. *I love you*. It is a powerful sentiment indeed."

"Yes, I agree."

Hen had thought it was too soon to reveal her feelings to Cain, but this was nonsense. They were already about to make the greatest leap possible. In truth, they would have been married by now had her weasel cousin's consent not been required.

Yes, she would tell Cain of her feelings tomorrow.

Perhaps once he knew this, his nightmares would go away.

Love conquered all, did it not?

Chapter Twelve

CAIN HAD THOUGHT perhaps it was possible to get through the night without those violent dreams invading his sleep, but they came on as strong as ever once again. He awoke soaked to the skin, the bedcovers twisted around him, ever the familiar snake cutting off his circulation.

Since he was still alone in that private wing compromising the club's guest quarters, he knew no one had heard him. He sat up with a groan and slowly flexed his muscles as he peeled off the layers and uncoiled the sheet.

He'd gotten so caught up in the damn thing, it felt like bindings.

"Hen," he said in a whisper, "how can I do this to you?"

The sun was barely up, he noted once his body calmed.

He crossed the room to peer out the window. The streets were quiet still, the only movement that of a vendor pulling his wagon to a nearby market square. He remained by the open window and allowed the morning air to cool his still-damp body.

More carts and wagons appeared on the street, their wheels groaning and clattering on the cobblestones as they hauled their wares to market.

He knew the club's stewards would be stirring soon.

It was not long before one of them came up to take the clothes he wore yesterday and freshen them. "Your Grace, you are awake."

"I couldn't sleep, Collin. Have a bath sent up and my breakfast."

"At once, Your Grace."

Cain took his time soaking in the tub and scrubbing himself down with the sandalwood soap provided. Although he had washed the scent of Alexandra off his skin last night, her perfume had remained on his clothes and now permeated the room.

Perhaps this was why his dreams had been particularly unpleasant. He ought to have tossed every last garment into the fireplace and burned them, he was that irritated with her.

No, he ought to be irritated with himself for being so stupid as to climb into her carriage when he knew what was likely to happen.

Thank goodness Hen believed him when he assured her there was nothing between him and Alexandra. He would not have blamed her if she had remained doubtful.

Despite the feelings he and Hen had for each other, it could not be overlooked that they still hardly knew each other. She had no reason to trust him. Their conversation could have gone quite badly, and it would have been completely his fault. He knew what Alexandra was. Deceitful, petty, jealous.

And he did not believe Alexandra was through with him yet. Rubbing herself all over his body and then blowing him that parting kiss was merely a start to her game.

He rose from the tub, dried himself off, and called for one of the club valets to shave his beard and trim his hair.

"Have a look, Your Grace," the man said, his smile wide as he finished the task.

Cain stared at himself in the mirror, hardly recognizing the face staring back at him. His hair was now cropped and appeared more golden in the light. His dark eyes still appeared tormented, but perhaps a little less so now that Hen was in his life. He hoped so, for he did not want another dream as bad as last night's.

Having seen enough, he turned from the mirror and dressed

in preparation for the day. It took him a little longer than usual because he had a role to play. If he was to stand before one of the lord justices this morning, he needed to look the part of a powerful duke who was never to be crossed.

He was also eager to know what Hen would think of his new look.

He strode out of his club and walked to Malvern House. The air was warming but not yet unbearably dank. Nor were the streets too congested. It was a pleasant walk, and it did not take him long before he marched up the steps of Malvern House.

His faithful butler opened the door. "Your Grace…"

Cain laughed as Dinsmore's mouth fell open. "Yes, the duke is civilized once again. Is Lady Henley awake yet?"

"Indeed, she is waiting for you in your mother's salon."

He marched directly to her, his heart melting the moment he caught sight of her. "Hen, you look beautiful."

An understatement, for she was radiant.

The sun shone through the window and bathed her in a circle of light. Her hair was a gleaming honey-brown and her eyes held a starlit sparkle. Her gown was a dark amber, soft and elegant as it hugged her curves and undulated with her movements as she approached him.

"Thank you, Cain," she said, sounding a little breathless. "I hardly recognized you."

But her smile was big and broad, so he hoped she was pleased with what she saw. "What do you think? Do I pass muster?"

He surely did not deserve this beautiful girl.

Her eyes widened as she began to inspect him, her gaze slowly traveling up and down his body, and finally coming to rest on his trimmed hair and clean-shaven face.

"Well, Hen?"

She laughed and threw herself into his arms for a quick but ardent embrace before stepping back to study him again. "You are handsome beyond words. I knew it. You even have dimples when you smile. I cannot get enough of you."

"Better than the old bear?"

"No, I love that old bear. That bearded, wooly look suited you to perfection. But this is just as good. My heart is lost to you either way."

He took her hands in his. "Truly?"

She nodded. "I fell asleep thinking about your father's letters. I adored the way he was so open in his affection for you. This is how a family ought to be. Mine was, and this is how I am now with my sisters. This is how I hope you and I shall always be with each other."

"We will, Hen."

She took a deep breath. "I have something to tell you. Something I am resolved to tell you. At first, I thought it was too soon. I'm still quite afraid, but I must reveal it now because it is important for you to know."

"What is this thing that has you so unsettled?" He frowned, suddenly worried something had happened between last night and this morning. "Tell me. I am ready to listen."

She took another deep breath. "I suppose it is no secret, since I am incapable of hiding any of my feelings. They show on my face like a beacon upon a dark shore."

"Hen, has someone hurt you?"

"No." She shook her head. "Well, here goes…Cain…"

"Yes."

"I want you to know that my heart is yours whether or not you succeed in removing Weasel Willis. My affection for you is not conditioned on anything. It just is."

He wasn't certain why she felt it was important to tell him this now, but he was relieved her distress was caused by nothing more serious.

He knew what she felt for him. He'd always known. First of all, her every expression revealed what was in her heart. Also, a sweet girl like her would never allow just any man to slip the gown off her shoulders and put his mouth on her breasts.

That was her declaration of love to him.

He'd known it yesterday and treasured her for it.

"What I am trying to say, rather ineptly…is that I am in love with you," she continued. "Not just in love, but deeply in love. You have made me happier than I ever thought possible. Thank you for giving me this feeling."

He wanted to let her know he felt the same, but his butler came in at just that moment to report that the Malvern carriage had been brought around.

"Hold that thought, Hen," Cain said. "We will pick up this discussion later."

She cast him a forced smile and tried to pretend she was not disappointed he did not say it back to her.

How could he in front of his staff?

And now Prudence had marched downstairs to see them off. "I hope all goes well. Did Hen tell you she has the loveliest gown selected for Lady Fielding's party? But she neglected to bring a suitable wrap for herself if the evening grows chilly. I'll have to stop by her modiste, but I'll take two of your footmen along with me for protection. And…Your Grace, may I put the purchase on your account?"

Hen was about to protest, but he cut her short. "Yes, she must have the very best. Prudence, add whatever you need for yourself."

"Thank you, I will." Prudence darted off before Hen could countermand his instructions.

"You are frowning again," he said, wanting to kiss her temptingly pursed lips. "It is my pleasure to provide for you and your family. Especially for you."

"It isn't right. You and I are not married yet. I don't want you to think I am after you for your wealth."

"A shawl, Hen? Seriously? You are the only woman in London who even cares. I would give you the world if I could. If it were in my power, I would give you everything your heart desires."

She placed a hand on his arm. "You have, Cain."

He silently kicked himself for being such an idiot when it came to women. Until now, of course. He and Cormac had treated them as playthings, both of them attracted to the "easy" ones. These were the elegant *ton* ladies who were quick to bed, bought cheap, and often were married, so there was no question of promises made and no chance of being forced to the altar.

Alexandra was that sort of woman.

Even before she was married, she was easily bought and quick to bed.

But she would have been an expensive, demanding wife. She would have had his eyes bulging at the size of the bills run up at his expense.

He helped Hen into the carriage and climbed in after her. "Ready to face the day, Hen?"

"Eager for it. I felt useless just waiting around yesterday. You handled everything while Prudence and I sat in your garden and read our books."

"You will always stand out, make your own mark, because you are not empty-headed and will never be a mere appendage to me. You called me impatient, wanting to flout the laws, but in your own way, I think you are just as impatient. You won't accept that there is nothing you as a woman can do about your cousin's misdeeds. The law does not even recognize you as a separate being."

"It is ridiculous and unfair."

"But it is presently the law. So let me take the lead in this and don't toss daggers at me because I am doing so. I am on your side."

"I know. Haven't I told you how grateful I am?" she asked.

"Yes. But you, my lovely Hen, are also a little resentful."

"Never of you, just of the way men seem to control everything. My irrelevance in the eyes of the law just galls me."

"Once you are my duchess, you can set about changing that." He said nothing more as they rode in silence. The laws were not going to change overnight, and he did not want to bring up the matter of her love declaration.

She had given him her heart.

He was giving her a man with uncontrolled nightmares who might physically harm her if she got too close.

Perhaps it was a mistake to hold back his admission of love, for he did love her deeply. But he was starting to understand Hen. If he told her that he loved her, she would do everything in her power to keep him safe. *Him.* As if he needed her to look out for his well-being.

In truth, she was probably already determined to put him first.

But she was the one who needed protecting, especially from him, and nothing was going to interfere in his purpose to keep her safe, not even her.

As they rode to Chiswell's bureau, he began to point out sights of interest. They were in the open carriage making their way through the now-busier London streets, and he made a point of stopping to greet *ton* acquaintances they happened to encounter.

Others, ordinary men and women on their way to work or running errands, also recognized his family crest and shouted greetings. A few came up to their carriage with a word of appreciation for his saving one relative or another. This caught him by surprise, for he truly had not considered his impact on these strangers.

Hen squeezed his hand. "You are everyone's hero."

"Blessings to ye. Ye saved m'brother, Yer Grace," someone called out.

"Ye saved m'husband," a woman said, sounding quite weepy. Several people around her cheered.

"I did my duty, just as any other soldier." Cain acknowledged the greetings with a smile or a nod or a wave of his hand.

More people came up to him when his carriage drew up in front of the Inns of Chancery, and he descended with Hen. He was about to put his arm around her and rush her through, but she did not appear to be at all intimidated by the crowd forming around them. Instead, she made a point to greet each person and ask them how they were doing.

She introduced herself as Lady Henley, his betrothed. "But my family calls me Hen. So does His Grace. He thinks I squawk at him too much."

"And what do ye call 'im, m'lady?" one gentleman called out.

She cast a knowing grin at the ladies in the huddle. "Nothing I dare say in public. The man is gorgeous, as anyone with eyes can plainly see. I think I must call him 'my darling,' and he is indeed that. A kinder gentleman you will never meet."

He led her inside before the crowd around them grew too large. "You charmed them as you have charmed me."

"Nonsense. I made a few jests. You saved their families."

Chiswell quickly ushered them into his office. Hen did not appear at all ruffled by the exchange they'd had on the street. As for Cain, he'd seen the faces as she spoke to each man and woman, and did not doubt she had won them over.

As Chiswell stepped out a moment to call in his clerks, Hen turned to Cain. "Why did the crowds start forming around you today? No one approached us yesterday."

"Perhaps because I no longer look like a snarling bear."

She laughed as she settled in one of the chairs in front of Chiswell's desk. "Yes, that must be the reason."

He sank into the one beside her. "In fact, it is probably true. This is also the reason I waited to shave until this morning. The bank manager almost fainted when he saw me yesterday. This is what I meant to do, put fear into him. I hope it worked. By the way, you handled yourself beautifully out there."

"I enjoyed meeting all your admirers. They were so grateful to you for all you'd done. How could I possibly turn up my nose at them?"

He thought of Alexandra again, taking a moment to compare the two women. Alexandra would have called them a rabble and shown nothing but disdain when they approached. Hen behaved like a true duchess. "This will likely be reported in the papers. Certainly the gossip rags. Everyone will now refer to you as Lady Hen."

She laughed. "I do not mind. But how will you feel to be referred to as my rooster?"

Likely he would be called her big cock, because it was the aim of these gossip rags to be crude and titillate their readers.

They spoke no more about it as Chiswell and his clerks returned. "Lord Stockwell delivered the bank manager's signed confession, along with affidavits from himself and several of the board's directors," Chiswell said.

"Do you not require my affidavit?" Hen asked.

"No, Lady Henley. Lord Stockwell's affidavit is sufficient and will carry more clout." He cast her a sheepish look. "It is the way of things, my lady. However, I have prepared an affidavit for His Grace to sign."

Cain quickly read through it, making certain to hold it so that Hen could read along with him. "You are grinding your teeth."

"I cannot help it. He stole from *my* account, and yet I am completely shoved aside."

"Getting worked up about it will not accomplish anything. The lord justice who will hear the matter is not going to be swayed by anything short of this."

He then signed his affidavit.

They were left alone once more in Chiswell's chambers as he and his clerks scampered off to deliver these documents to the barrister.

Hen's jaw remained tightly clenched, but after a moment she sighed. "Ignore my pouting. I am grateful to you and everyone you have brought in to help. Extremely grateful."

"But you feel you do not exist, because despite this problem being all about you and the women in your family who were preyed upon by that weasel cousin, you are not asked to provide anything. I understand your frustration, Hen. Just know that you are quite real to me, and I will never ignore you."

"I do know this, but you are not the problem." She cast him an impish smile. "Every other man is."

He shook his head. "It is a constant amazement to me that men are allowed to handle anything, considering how badly we seem to muck up every blessed thing we touch. Well, you will have quite a bit of power once you are my duchess. People will listen. Ah, Chiswell returns."

The barrister carried an armful of documents. "I have also prepared a betrothal contract in accordance with the terms provided by Lady Henley's solicitor, Mr. Garrick. He has also sent over copies of the designation and resignation documents. Would you care to read through them, Your Grace?"

"Yes, Lady Henley and I would like to do so." Cain took them one by one and held each up for them to read together. "What do you think, Hen?" he asked when they were done.

"They all look fine to me. As for the betrothal contract, the terms are more than fair. Now all we need is for the Earl of Stoke to sign it. Ugh, I cannot bear to call him that. He is such a horrible man, nothing at all like my father, who was the kindest, most decent man to ever live. It turns my stomach to watch his legacy so quickly destroyed."

Cain gave her hand a light squeeze. "It is all fine, Chiswell. Send one copy off for Garrick to hold. We will be visiting the Marquess of Burness next. Send word to me there if something develops at court within the next hour. Otherwise, we shall be at Malvern House."

Outside, Cain assisted Hen into his carriage, and they rode off.

"Do you think there is the chance of a ruling today?" Hen asked.

He shook his head. "No. Our solicitors have said it is quite unlikely. We've done all we can for now."

She was nibbling her lip again, a sign she had come up with another reason to fret.

He sighed. "What is it, Hen?"

"After we visit your friend, do you think it is possible for us to pay a call on Stoke? After all, he may be willing to compromise now that he knows he is found out."

"I am not bringing you to him. I do not want you under his roof. He is still your guardian and can hold you there against your wishes."

"He wouldn't dare if you are with me," she said.

"We cannot be certain of it. He is not a clever man, as you well know. And Hen, I will maim him if he attempts to keep you captive in his home. You said you did not want violence. I can assure you, there will be exactly that if I put you within his grasp and he dares lay a hand on you. I don't want to be forced to hurt him, but I will."

"Point made. Forget I suggested it."

"Besides, there is no reason for us to go to him. He will take it as a sign of weakness when our position is not weak at all. If anything, he is the one who needs to come groveling to me."

Her cheeks reddened. "I'm sorry. You are right. I can see it was a stupid idea."

"It is not stupid. I hope to force a compromise, and we will confront him. But on my battleground and at the time of my choosing. It will likely be tonight at Lady Fielding's party, where there are witnesses to control his behavior…and mine. He is new to the *ton* and obviously eager to be accepted. But as news of my desire to marry you becomes known, what do you think will happen if he dares deny me?"

"Other than your breaking his fingers?" she said with a wry smile.

"All of his dirty dealings will come to light. He will be shunned. Society will know him as a coward and a thief. He will not be extended any credit, nor will he or his wife be permitted into any elegant salons. I know it does not seem like much to you, but it means everything to that grasping pair. You were happy to be banished to Moonstone Landing. This little weasel craves society's acceptance. His wife perhaps desires it even more than he does. It is a cudgel to hold over their heads."

"I don't know that it will work. He loses too much in giving me up."

"He has lost you anyway, Hen. You are only a few months shy of your twenty-first birthday. Not that I intend to wait that long to marry you. I've told you, I will take you to Scotland if it is necessary. Once we are married, he will lose the rest of it, for I will be the dragon breathing down his neck if he dares take a step out of line. If he attempts to take your sisters from us, I will burn him to ashes. The best he can do is negotiate something for himself."

The carriage drew up in front of the Burness townhouse. "Ah, we have arrived," Cain said.

"Is your friend another one like you?"

Cain grinned. "I think Cormac is worse. Dear Lord, I hope he's made himself presentable."

They were expected and immediately escorted into the family's private parlor. Lady Stockwell, a fluttering bird of a woman, scurried in to greet them. "How delightful to see you again, Malvern. I shall have tea brought in for us. Although I expect you would prefer a heartier libation."

"No, Lady Stockwell. Tea is fine for me." He introduced Hen to her and silently prayed Cormac would arrive soon, because Lady Stockwell's titters were already getting on his nerves.

Hen was as gracious as ever and seemed to sense his impatience. "Your husband, Lord Stockwell, is chairman of the Bank of West London, is he not? I cannot tell you how helpful he has been to me and my family. You must be so proud of him."

"Dear me, I am," Lady Stockwell said. "He is a very good man, always so kind to me and our daughters."

Hen nodded. "How is the Marquess of Burness feeling today? I hope he is well enough for visitors."

Lady Stockwell's hand fluttered to her throat, and she tittered again. "I do not know how he is doing today, or any other day. Burness shuts his door and does not see fit to allow any of us in.

Well, he does allow Lord Stockwell in. But my dear husband and you, Malvern, are the only ones he ever permits close."

Hen cast the woman a sympathetic look. "Men are often terrible patients. They refuse to admit they require assistance and then whine like babies or howl like banshees when it is not immediately forthcoming."

"Yes, and then they resent your help," Lady Stockwell said with an exasperated laugh.

Cain had always regarded her as a timid bird of a woman who felt more at ease maintaining a polite distance. She was not a bad person, just excruciatingly dull and simpering…at least, he and Cormac had always thought so.

Cormac's brother adored her. The reason why still eluded him.

He supposed she was different around him, more her natural self and not intimidated, as she seemed to be around him and Cormac. Still, her fluttering made him itchy.

Cormac had to be going out of his mind. Yet he had to be as much to blame for ranting and raving and bemoaning his fate when none of it was Lady Stockwell's fault, and she was only trying to help. Cormac was disruptive even when on his best behavior. He must have turned into a bellowing tyrant, unmanageably enraged by the loss of his arm.

Cain's visit yesterday may have calmed his friend down somewhat, but only time and acceptance of his situation would ever bring Cormac peace.

Where was he?

Cain would strangle his friend if he was made to wait any longer. Dukes were not in the habit of being kept in abeyance. He turned to Hen for help, for making conversation with Lady Stockwell was one of the most difficult chores imaginable. Given the choice of an hour chatting with her or a tooth extraction, that tooth was getting pulled.

Hen immediately took up the gauntlet, complimenting Lady Stockwell on her gown, which immediately led to talk of the best

London modistes and other conversational topics he found excruciatingly dull.

Hen had a manner that put everyone at ease.

Even Lady Stockwell stopped her incessant fluttering and seemed to relax, laughing pleasantly a time or two, a great improvement over her usual, birdlike twitters.

As the minutes passed, Cain grew restless and was about to excuse himself to march upstairs and haul Cormac down when the man himself strode in.

Cain was relieved to find his friend clean-shaven and decently dressed. But he knew Cormac had purposely kept him waiting for nearly half an hour in the company of Lady Stockwell just to rile him.

It was a small price to pay for insisting Cormac make himself presentable to meet Hen.

He and Cormac could be coarse at times, but he would not tolerate his friend being rude to his betrothed. He tossed Cormac a warning glance.

"I am not going to eat her alive, Cain," Cormac said with a surprisingly genuine smile. "Besides, you would not have brought Lady Hen around if you thought she could not handle me."

Hen could not have overlooked Cormac's missing arm, but if she was repulsed by it, she hid her feelings well. However, Cain knew Hen did not hide her feelings at all. Everything showed on her expressive face, and right now she was smiling at Cormac with sincere pleasure.

Cormac bowed over her hand while they were properly introduced. "I can see why Cain did not stand a chance with you. I'm sure his heart was lost the moment he set eyes on you, Lady Hen."

His sister-in-law pinched her lips. "She is Lady Henley."

Hen's cheeks turned pink, but she kept her tone light. "It is quite all right, Lady Stockwell. I do not mind at all. This is how I am known among my friends, and I do hope we shall all become good friends. As for my meeting the duke, I'm sure I was the first to lose my heart. The feeling was quite mutual, I assure you."

Cormac sank into a chair beside them and picked up the teapot to pour himself a cup.

Cain was relieved his friend did not go for the brandy instead. But in the next moment, he wanted to throttle Lady Stockwell when she gasped and tried to grab the teapot out of Cormac's hand.

When Cormac resisted, because he was more of a stubborn dolt than Cain was, the woman became overset and began to flutter around him. "But it is my place to pour. You are not trained to do it."

"It is my home," Cormac shot back. "No one sets rules for me here."

"Lady Stockwell," Hen said sweetly, "do come sit beside me. I must have your recipe for this delicious treacle cake. As for the men, why should we not let them fend for themselves? They will never learn to appreciate what we do for them if they do not occasionally make the effort to do what we do. And I am certain a man as clever as Lord Burness knows to remove the lid from the pot before he tips it over to pour the tea into his cup."

"That I do," he said with a smirk at Cain, "but I do appreciate the reminder."

While Hen patiently listened to Lady Stockwell chatter about her cake, Cain leaned forward and whispered to his friend, "You are such a stupid arse."

Cormac chuckled. "I know. That lid would have crashed right onto my cup and shattered it. I thought women held the pot in one hand and held the lid down with the other just to look charming. I had no idea it had a practical reason. Deliver my thanks to Hen later."

"I will." Cain's own gratitude to Hen was not merely because of a teapot. That Cormac had come out of his room, suitably dressed, and was ready to pour a cup for himself was a huge gesture on his part, an attempt to show them all he was learning to manage without his arm.

Hen once again interceded with a comment meant to distract Lady Stockwell when the woman began to flutter again. "I understand you have two daughters. Would you mind bringing them down? I would love to meet them."

"Why, yes. If you wish. They are a bit excitable, but do forgive them. They are still young. However, they are such little dears. Excuse me. I'll fetch them."

She scampered out of the parlor.

Cormac groaned. "That woman will be the death of me. I cannot understand what John sees in her, but there must be something I am missing. Thank you for getting her out of here, Hen. You did that seamlessly. Cain's a lucky man. You wouldn't happen to have a sister, would you?"

Hen laughed. "I have two. They are quite happy at Moonstone Landing, and I dare not put them in front of you. Especially not Phoebe."

"Cain is my best friend. You are to be his wife. I would never insult either of you by—"

"Oh, you mistake my meaning," Hen said, her eyes aglitter with mirth. "It is you I worry about. Phoebe can handle herself. She will manage you quite readily."

He laughed. "I doubt anyone can. But good for Phoebe for having the confidence to stand her ground even at her young age. Any progress with your problem?" he asked. "Cain told me all about what the new Earl of Stoke has been doing to your family. John filled me in as well. He wasted no time in getting that manager to confess his misdeeds. I must say, I am impressed by how quickly he rallied the other directors to pay attention. I did not think my gentle brother had it in him to take charge like that."

Hen nodded. "Other than Cain, I think his actions have been the most helpful so far. Without him, my horrible cousin would still be dipping his hands in our funds unchecked."

"Uncle Cormac! Uncle Cormac! You are finally out of your lazy bed!" Two little girls bounded toward him and began to quack like ducks.

He let out a whoop of delight, set aside his teacup, and lifted the two of them onto his lap. "My little ducklings!"

His joy at seeing his nieces completely transformed him.

"Let me introduce you to my friend, Cain, and his lovely Lady Hen. I'm sure she would be pleased if you quacked her a greeting."

They immediately did so, to their mother's horror. Gad, Cormac took too much pleasure in goading the woman.

Hen clucked a greeting back to the girls.

They burst into giggles, certain it was the funniest thing they had ever heard.

Lady Stockwell sighed and bustled out of the room on some made-up errand.

"What sort of name is Hen?" the elder girl asked, scooting off Cormac's lap to draw closer to Hen. The other one followed after her big sister. They were so little and light that they amounted to the weight of a feather.

Cain rose and motioned for Cormac to join him by the window while Hen entertained the girls.

"She's a gem, Cain," Cormac said. "Seriously. Grab hold of her tight and do not ever let her go."

"I know." Cain glanced at her. "But what about you? Thank you for pulling yourself together today."

Cormac nodded. "It was time I got my arse out of that bed…my lazy bed, as the girls called it. No doubt this is what they heard their mother call me…a lazy lay-abed."

"Do not be too hard on Lady Stockwell. She seems painfully shy rather than the ignorant dimwit we see. Hen put her at ease, as she seems to be able to do with all of us effortlessly, and the woman was actually bearable. Then you marched in and she turned back into that prattling peahen. You have a way of rattling everyone."

"That is not likely to improve," Cormac said. "I hate everyone right now, save for you and my brother. I suppose I'll have to get back in society eventually, but it's all changed for me now. I cannot bear the way the ladies will look at me."

"How can you know what they will do? They aren't all going to be like Lady Seline."

"Too many of them will be."

"This was true long before you ever lost your arm. The elegant ballrooms were always filled with young women hoping to grasp what they could. You only need to find the pearl among the grains of sand. She is out there, I promise you."

Cormac shook his head. "I am not like you, Cain. I don't see how one woman can ever satisfy my every need. All the worse if she truly loves me and wants a real marriage between us. If I vowed to be faithful, I would never break my word. But that would leave us both unhappy, would it not?"

Cain folded his arms across his chest and leaned against the wall. "I might have agreed with you as little as a few weeks ago. But this is not the way love works."

"Oh, you are the expert now?"

"Hardly, but I can tell you how my feelings have changed since meeting Hen. Love isn't about your happiness. It is about finding the one who means more to you than anything else in the world. The true joy comes in making her happy. The amazing thing about it is that when it is right, it all comes effortlessly."

"Well, I'll keep this in mind. I am not as optimistic as you are about my success. My fault, of course. I was always more of an arse than you ever were. Perhaps I will become a recluse."

"You? Doubtful," Cain said. "You are a natural leader and people will always flock to you. You just have to stop encouraging friendships with the worst sort."

"They are diversions, never friends. The men are easy to beat at cards and the women are just easy. Seline's sexual pleasures were fairly cheap to buy. Not anymore, though. You should have seen the disgust on her face when I told her I was losing my arm. I suppose I can find a few who will service me without disgust showing on their faces. Some will do anything for the right price."

Cain tried not to lose patience with his friend. "You need to join me at Moonstone Landing. Remaining here is not healthy for you."

"Ah, but it is so much easier to destroy myself right here." Cormac shook his head. "I will right myself in time. Do not fret for me, Cain." He glanced over at Hen and his nieces. The girls were chattering up a storm with her. "I will be all right because of those little girls. My ducklings. I think they are the only thing keeping me sane."

"All the more reason why you should join us at—"

"I am sure as hell not going to live under the same roof as you and Hen when you are newly married. Having me around will be worse than having a mother-in-law breathing down your neck. But I might just buy a lovely stretch of land on the water and build a house near yours. What do you think of that?"

Cain smiled. "I think it is the first smart thing out of your mouth all day. I'll keep an eye out for just the right property. You'll like Moonstone Landing. It will be good for your soul."

He and Hen ended their visit soon after and returned to Malvern House.

To his surprise, they had company.

"Your Grace, I've put the Earl of Stoke in the visitor's parlor to await you," his butler said. "I informed Mrs. Landers about his arrival, but she refuses to come down. I did not know whether to turn him away, as she would give me no instruction."

"You did well to allow him to wait. I shall see him. Have tea brought in for us in the visitor's parlor. He does not set foot anywhere else in this house."

"Understood, Your Grace."

"I'll join you," Hen said, tipping her chin up and daring Cain to contradict her.

He wasn't going to send her away. As far as he was concerned, Hen had an extraordinary ability to handle herself with grace under the worst situations. He would need her voice of reason to keep him from smashing his fist into Stoke's face.

"Fine."

Her eyes rounded in obvious surprise. "Fine?"

He cast her a wry smile. "Yes, Hen. I want you with me."

"Well then…" She handed her hat, gloves, and reticule to one of the footmen. "I wonder what he's come here to do. Surrender? Or threaten?"

Chapter Thirteen

CAIN HAD NOT met this new Earl of Stoke and was curious as to the man's purpose in coming to Malvern House. He did not think it was to surrender, unless something had happened in court that he had not yet heard about. Chiswell would have immediately sent him word.

He took a moment to question his butler before entering the visitor's parlor. "No, Your Grace. No messages for you. But I shall alert you at once if any come for you."

"Yes. Please do." Cain took Hen's hand and placed it on his arm. "Are you sure you want to see your cousin?"

"I am not a coward," she said, "especially when I have a big, growling bear at my side. Yes, I must see him."

"All right." He led her into the visitor's parlor. "Stoke, to what do we owe the pleasure?"

The man's hands were curled into fists, and he clearly appeared enraged. Hen and her sisters had referred to him as a weasel, and he looked like one. An angry weasel, for his eyes were dark and beady, his hair thin and slicked back, and his nose came to a pointed snout. He was a thin man with little style, and he dressed like a popinjay.

Cain wanted to chew this little man up alive.

Hen was also angry that he could feel the tension in the touch of her hand upon his arm. She was aching to take a poke at her cousin. He would not allow it, for the man might hit her back. Then Cain would be forced to kill him.

He made certain to keep himself positioned between Hen and her contemptible cousin. She was built of soft curves and lacked the physical brawn to defend herself if Stoke was demented enough to strike her.

"You know why I'm here," Stoke said. "Do not play coy, Malvern. You have no right to interfere with my family."

"I beg to differ. They will be my family soon, and you have been stealing from them."

"Is this what she's told you? And you believed her lies?"

"Careful what you say, Stoke. She is my betrothed, and I will call you out if you dare utter a word against her."

Stoke glared at Hen. "Seduced him, did you? Has he gotten you with child? Too bad for you, I will never give my consent to marry him. Your child will be born a bastard, and—"

Cain growled. "You idiot, do you think I would not take her to Scotland and marry her there? But it is unnecessary, for we know the terms of her trust. For that matter, I am aware of the terms established by her father for each of his daughters. You lose control when they marry or if they sooner turn the age of twenty and one. Lady Henley reaches that in a couple of months. There is nothing you can say or do to stop her from claiming her funds."

The weasel seemed shocked.

Cain could see the panic in Stoke's eyes—and then quick recalculation as his gaze once more settled on Hen. "But I control your sisters, and there is nothing you can do to take them out of my guardianship."

She took a step toward her cousin. "You shall never get within a mile of them. Dare to try, and I shall shoot you."

Cain held her back, not wanting her within the scoundrel's reach. A trapped creature was not to be trusted. "Bring those girls into this and you shall not walk out of here alive," he said. "I shall dismember you piece by piece. Am I clear? You little gnat, I'll squash you if you dare lay a hand on Hen or her sisters. Nor will you ever get your hands on anyone's trust funds again. It is over, you fool. The best you can do is beg for their mercy, for I shall show you none. You are done. Exposed as a thief. You and your wife shall be pariahs among the *ton*. It is only a matter of days before all is taken from you."

"All?" Stoke suddenly appeared confused. "How can you take my title from me? My entailed properties?"

Cain shrugged. "I cannot, but the Crown has the power to do so. There is unrest enough in the country, resentment seething for the privileged few who are living fat while the ordinary man struggles. What do you think the prince regent will do when he hears you have been stealing from children, a war widow, and elderly women? And he will hear of it. I dine with him regularly."

"I don't believe you."

Cain shrugged. "That is your mistake. The grant of your title is at the pleasure of the Crown. I can assure you, every member of the royal family will be incensed once they hear of your behavior. I do not need to wage a campaign against you within the House of Lords. The royal family will cut you down themselves."

Sweat began to bead on the man's brow.

Cain had taken the measure of Stoke and knew he was not clever. In truth, he was a fairly ignorant man who did not calculate the consequences of his actions. Nor was he familiar with his legal rights and powers. He had not even known that Hen's funds were to be turned over to her when she reached the age of twenty and one whether or not she married.

Had he bothered to read a single document? Or did he not care because he planned to steal it all anyway and thought he was untouchable?

"We can attend to this quietly or I can hang you out to dry," Cain said. "What is it to be, Stoke? You have ten seconds to decide. The count starts now. Ten. Nine."

"Wait! What are your terms?"

"Sign all control over to me. By that I mean for all the women in the family. Hen, her sisters, Mrs. Landers, and the maiden aunts. You are also to consent to Hen's and my betrothal, which I shall announce tonight at Lady Fielding's party whether you comply or not. You and your wife are to restore the funds you stole. You and your wife are also to leave London. Slink back to the hole from whence you sprang. I will not have you sullying our family connection with your unacceptable behavior. I am doing you a favor by demanding you both leave. Your wife is reckless at the gaming tables and will bankrupt you within the month if you do not bring her under control."

The weasel fidgeted and began to reach into his jacket pocket.

"Eight. Seven. Six." Cain prepared to lunge for Stoke if he withdrew a pistol, but the man merely drew out a handkerchief and began to wipe his brow.

"If I agree to this, you will leave me alone?"

"Yes. Five. Four. Three. Two."

"All right! I will go home now and tell my wife."

Cain clamped a hand on Stoke's shoulder when he attempted to leave. "No. You come with me first. There are documents for you to sign."

"But my wife—"

"Do not take me for a fool, Stoke. You do not get to go home until these are signed. Then you can flee wherever you like…on your own funds. By the way, I've had Bow Street runners following your every move since before we arrived in town. I know everything about you and Lady Stoke. You cannot sneeze without my hearing about it."

He called for his carriage to be brought around and had his footmen escort Stoke to it. "Hen," he said, taking her aside a moment. "I cannot take you with me. I dare not have you in the same carriage as that man. He is desperate, and I have no idea what he might do in this situation. Let me be the enraged bull and have this ugly affair finished."

She nodded. "Yes, do what you must."

But he saw the disappointment in her eyes, for she had been

set aside once again as he brought the hammer down on her cousin. She was grateful for it, he knew. But she was also feeling insignificant and useless.

He did not know how to explain her importance to him and how much he needed her. He knew she had strength. It wasn't physical strength. He did not need her to smash a fist into a man's face. "I'll return in time to take you to Lady Fielding's party."

He kissed her, a chaste peck on her cheek, and left.

As he reached his carriage, he thought about going back inside and telling Hen he loved her.

No, he dared not spare the time.

He shook his head and climbed in.

Her cousin was restless, and every minute's delay gave that man extra time to think. Cain could not risk having him regain his courage and refusing to sign the papers.

Cain had brought two of his best footmen along with him to maintain a show of force. Besides, they would also prove useful if Stoke tried to run away. But the man seemed docile enough despite his obvious anger at being thwarted.

When they arrived at the Inns of Chancery, he sent one of the footmen off to fetch Hen's solicitor, Garrick, and bring him to Chiswell's bureau. He brought the other along for no reason other than a continued display of intimidating muscle.

Cain strode into Chiswell's office.

And held his breath until all signatures were set on the documents.

He knew he'd done the right thing in bringing Stoke straight over here, for his wife clearly ruled him with an iron fist and would have stopped him from capitulating.

In truth, the weasel seemed relieved to have all control taken out of his hands.

Hen and her family were now safe.

It did Cain's heart good to know he was free to marry her. But this meant Hen would also be about to face her greatest challenge…him.

Would his night terrors destroy their chance at happiness?

Chapter Fourteen

HEN SPENT THE remainder of the afternoon writing to her sisters and then settling in the Malvern library to read. But she could not decide on what to read, so she began to pace across the large room that held a thousand books, all neatly aligned upon the polished mahogany shelves. "Why isn't he back yet? Should he not be back by now?"

Prudence smiled as she joined her. "You know it is still far too early. I've brought along my embroidery to occupy my time while we await the duke. You are going to wear a hole in his elegant carpet if you do not settle down. Have you ever seen a more magnificent home? And it will soon be yours to live in with that handsome man. Honestly, Hen. Why are you frowning? He's won a brilliant victory for us."

"I know."

"You ought to be more appreciative of his efforts. I certainly am. We could not have accomplished any of this ourselves. We are not as big or intimidating as he is. Weasel Willis is a coward who only responds to the threat of a thrashing. He always was a whimpering, scheming brat even as a child."

"You knew him better than we did. I don't think we had met him more than once or twice. Of course, he always put on a false face to us."

"He had every reason to appear charming, especially toward

your family," Prudence said. "Your father would never have put him in charge of so much as his kennels if he knew the true nature of the man. Hen, do stop pacing. Do you think Malvern will like these handkerchiefs I am embroidering for him? I wanted to do something to show my gratitude."

Hen sighed. "Yes, he will enjoy them."

"Why don't you sit beside me and embroider something nice for him? He will appreciate these thoughtful gestures from his duchess. What he will not appreciate is your sour expression," Prudence said with a teasing grin.

Hen laughed. "You are right, of course. But no sewing for me. Chloe is the wizard when it comes to that. I am all thumbs. I'll read." She grabbed a book off a nearby shelf. The leather was soft beneath her hands, and its binding slightly cracked. "Oh dear."

"What did you pick out?"

"It is a poisoner's handbook. Well, I suppose it suits my current temperament. I truly wanted to do Stoke in for all those months of torment he gave us. He is such a horrible man." She settled in one of the tufted chairs and put her mind to reading. But she merely skimmed through the pages, some of which were illustrated with drawings of plants, and some with drawings of jewelry designed to hide deadly powders.

She had not heard of this before, but apparently it was a popular thing among the Italians to include a compartment in a locket, amulet, or ring in which to hide their poisons. She told Prudence about it. "And look at this ring."

Her cousin set aside her needle and thread and joined her to study the drawing. "It is quite a distinctive design."

"I remember seeing one just like it in a jeweler's shop here in London. This was shortly before my father died and Weasel Willis kicked us out," Hen said.

"The rings themselves look quite beautiful," Prudence mused. "I'm sure most jewelers must carry them. The Italians are known for their artistry. I wonder if they were made here or in

Italy and imported. Goodness, do you think the ones you saw in the London shop had a secret compartment that could be put to such use?"

Hen shrugged. "I never thought to ask."

"I'm sure they would never be used for such purpose now, even if they were designed into these rings. What a medieval notion. But they could be used to hold a lock of a loved one's hair or a miniature portrait."

As the hours passed, Hen closed the book and went upstairs to prepare for Lady Fielding's party. She wanted to look particularly nice for Cain's sake, whether he chose to announce their betrothal or not.

However, she knew this was what he intended to do.

Warmth spread through her, for it was a very good feeling to be wanted, and especially by such a fine man as Cain. He had come through for her, saving her and her family. She only hoped she would be as successful for him.

Prudence had not been invited to attend this soiree, but being left out did nothing to dampen her excitement. She flitted around Hen like a butterfly in a bed of flowers, and chattered incessantly while Hen bathed. "One would think I was going to marry the duke," Prudence said. "My heart is bursting with joy for you. This suddenly feels quite real. He's done it, Hen. Rescued us from those fiends, and now he's going to marry you. How can you be so calm?"

Hen laughed. "I am not in the least. My heart is in a wild flutter, and I feel as though I am walking in a beautiful dream."

Once her hair had dried, the lady's maid assigned to attend Hen began to style her hair. "Molly," she said when the young woman finished, "you've done an excellent job."

"Thank you, m'lady."

The girl was obviously talented and had worked effortlessly to braid and twist her curls to create this soft but intricate chignon.

Prudence nodded. "Yes, a job well done."

"Shall I help you with your gown now, m'lady?" Molly asked.

"Yes, please." As the fabric slid over her curves, Hen felt like a princess in gossamer silk. She was glad Phoebe had had the presence of mind to pack a suitably elegant gown for her along with her other clothes. This was one of her finest, meant to be worn as she entered her second Season, a pearl silk with a small train of aquamarine tulle that floated and swirled whenever she walked.

Her father had died as the season was about to open, so she had never worn it because the family had gone into mourning.

Prudence suddenly gasped. "Oh, Hen. We've overlooked the most important thing. You have no necklace to wear."

"Oh, but I do. A lovely pearl necklace—"

"On the night of your betrothal announcement? No, you must have something exquisite. Nothing as ordinary as pearls for you. How foolish of us not to think of this earlier."

Molly softly cleared her throat. "I'm sure His Grace intends to provide one of his family pieces for you."

Hen laughed. "You are more clever than both of us, Molly. Of course this is what he intends."

Prudence's smile returned. "Yes, the duke knows his duty. You are right—he will never overlook this detail. Do you think he has the exact piece in mind for you? Shall we go downstairs and wait for him?"

They were just descending the stairs when they heard a carriage draw up.

Dinsmore hurried to the door. "Your Grace."

"Good evening, Dinsmore."

Hen drew in her breath as Cain strode in, for he looked splendid in his formal attire. The black of his jacket enhanced the broadness of his shoulders and the fine taper of his body. It also brought out the burnished gold of his hair.

He looked up and saw her. "Hen, you look incredible."

She hurried down to him with a joyous laugh. "So do you. Completely and utterly magnificent."

He grinned. "Sorry I'm late. I had to stop by my club to prepare for the evening."

"Did everything go as you hoped at Mr. Chiswell's office? I began to worry," she said, tucking her arm in his as they walked into the family's private parlor along with Prudence, who was just as eager to hear his news.

"Yes, surprisingly smooth. The man capitulated, as most cowards do when confronted with the inevitable. He must have seen the constables haul the bank manager off to prison, and panic set in that he'd be next. He signed with hardly a whimper. The ink had yet to dry on the parchment before Chiswell sent the documents to the barrister to file. Your Mr. Garrick was present and had your cousin sign the ones he had prepared, which included my designation as his successor and his resignation. Lord Stockwell and his board of directors were also informed. All relevant affidavits are now before the lord justice."

Hen was delighted.

"Our betrothal contract is also signed and locked in Mr. Chiswell's safe. Mr. Garrick has a copy. You can look it over with him at any time. But we'll make any adjustments to it after we are married. I just wanted Stoke's signature on it now."

"Yes, that was most urgent."

"Afterward, I took Stoke to the parish house at St. Martin's Church to sign for the marriage license." He patted his breast pocket and cast her a smile that reached his eyes.

His dimples were also on full display.

She had never seen him so unguardedly content. He looked exceedingly handsome. His entire demeanor lightened as his smile turned endearingly boyish.

"Are you doing anything tomorrow, Hen?" he asked.

Prudence leaped out of her seat and squealed. "Not a thing! Her day is completely open. She'll be ready. What time will you come by to take us to the church?"

Hen laughed. "It cannot be early enough for me. I will not sleep a wink tonight. As it is, we'll get home quite late from Lady

Fielding's party. I am an early riser anyway, so I doubt I'll manage more than an hour or two of sleep."

"Do announce your betrothal early in the evening," Prudence suggested.

Cain nodded. "It is all arranged with Lady Fielding. You needn't worry about Hen. Our hostess is delighted that the formal announcement is to be made at her party. She will gush over us and gloat to her friends all night. They'll find her insufferable, which will make her triumph all the sweeter."

"You seem to be a master at manipulating the *ton*," Hen said. "I don't mean it badly. You know their rules and exactly how to play within them."

His expression softened. "Tactics have always been my strength. But I cannot control everything. For this reason, I dare not wait to marry you. Although Stoke has signed off on all of it, he may yet decide to change his mind. Especially when that shrew of a wife lays into him. He hasn't the power to overturn these documents, but he can still create enough of a tempest to cause delay."

She nodded. "I would not put it past him to do such a thing. I almost feel sorry for him now, having to face that woman and tell her what he did."

Prudence huffed. "He deserves none of your pity. The man is spineless. Unlike your husband-to-be, who is heroic in every way."

Cain cleared his throat. "It will be a simple ceremony. I've asked Cormac and Lord and Lady Stockwell to join us. Prudence, you'll attend, of course. The Fieldings, if they are not too exhausted after their party. Lord and Lady Ashbrook as well, if he is fit enough to step out. I know he and your father were best friends, and it would mean a lot to you to have him present. Then we shall return here for our wedding breakfast."

Hen nodded. "Sounds perfect. That is very thoughtful of you."

It was more than kind of him to think of Lord and Lady Ashbrook. But her heart still hurt knowing her sisters would not be present. She squelched her disappointment, knowing to delay would risk having their victory slip away. This posed the greatest danger to Phoebe and Chloe. Marrying tomorrow was the best thing she could do for them.

Still, it hurt.

They had been through everything together.

Well, she would sit down with them once they returned to Moonstone Landing, and the three of them would plan a special celebration.

Cain caressed her cheek to regain her attention. "My lovely Hen."

"I am fine, I promise. What happens next—I mean, now that our cousin has resigned his trusteeship?"

"Next step is to transfer all the accounts and place them under my authority. That is the simple part. Cormac's brother, Lord Stockwell, already has it underway. The official transfer of guardianship over your sisters to me can only be done by judicial order. The sooner we are wed, the quicker it will happen. Otherwise, it could take months to finalize."

"You need say nothing more to convince me," Hen replied. "I am all for our exchanging vows as soon as possible. Not so much for fear of what our cousin will do, but, as you pointed out a moment ago, for what his wife might goad him to do. I would not put it past her to work up a scheme herself if she cannot persuade him to do her bidding."

Prudence nodded. "It takes a certain coldness to toss out one's own family."

"And deprive them of food and shelter, steal their money, all so she can indulge her gambling vice," Hen added.

"I cannot wait for you to slam the door in their faces, Your Grace. Especially hers. Well, you two run along and enjoy Lady Fielding's party. I have my embroidery to occupy me. I think I shall sew a commemorative pillow, one depicting two weasels sitting on a powder keg with a lit fuse about to blow them up."

Hen laughed. "Prudence! That is awful! Terribly satisfying, but still awful."

"Remind me not to run afoul of you," Cain said. But after a moment, as their laughter subsided, he ran his knuckles along Hen's throat. "We ought to be going, but first come upstairs with me and select a Malvern necklace for yourself."

"Something outrageously expensive," Prudence insisted. "Hen, do not choose something plain and spoil His Grace's pleasure. He intends to show you off. Come along. We'll pick out something dazzling together, something bright and blinding. I will never be a duchess, but I can certainly enjoy your becoming one."

They followed Cain upstairs, and he had them wait in her bedchamber while he brought in a large box. "Only the Duchess of Malvern may wear these pieces. You will be that by tomorrow, Hen."

She understood the importance of presenting herself as his soon-to-be duchess. With Prudence's help, she selected a small tiara, which Molly helped to properly secure to her curls. She also selected a delicate necklace of diamonds with an aquamarine stone in the center to perfectly match the train of her gown. "I think these will do."

Prudence nodded. "Yes, nothing more is necessary. We mustn't have you looking as though you raided a jeweler's shop."

Cain said nothing, but looked quite pleased. His dark eyes glinted with amusement.

After returning the other heirlooms to his chamber, he escorted Hen downstairs and helped her into his waiting carriage. He settled in the seat across from hers, stretched his long legs, and eased his back against the squabs.

"My big bear is smiling," Hen teased. "You look quite satisfied with yourself."

He laughed. "Why shouldn't I be? I am escorting the prettiest girl to the party. You look breathtaking, Hen."

She blushed. "Molly did a good job of fixing me up."

A soft smile played on his lips. "It's all you. You are a little burst of starlight. I never tire of looking at you."

His eyes crinkled slightly at the corners and his gaze simply burned right through her. She liked this lightness in him, for she did not think he was a happy man by nature. Frowning bear was a more apt description, but not tonight.

He looked so handsome when he smiled.

That she had the power to make him happy was not something she would ever take lightly. In truth, it still amazed her.

"I have been trained for this," she said as their carriage wound its way through the London streets. "I was raised as an earl's daughter and taught how to run an elegant household. I spent a year out in Society, and yet I still have butterflies in my stomach. It is just a party, not even a ball. One would think it was my very first Society affair. You look so calm. Are you really?"

"Yes."

She laughed. "Does nothing scare you?"

His smile slipped, and he leaned forward. "Only my dreams. They still prey on my mind."

"Oh, Cain, forgive me. I never meant to make a jest of it. I know you are afraid of hurting me while in the throes of one of those bad dreams. But we'll work it out. We are together in this fight, and together we shall conquer everything."

He took her hands in his.

She thought it was a good opportunity to remind him that she loved him. He did not appear inclined to say it back to her, and she was not going to press him. He would tell her whenever he was ready. A man such as Cain would not admit his affection easily.

To confide in her as he had about his dreams was proof enough of the trust and affection he held for her. She knew he valued her. He had even called her "love" a time or two, and it was no small thing. He was not the glib sort to casually spout endearments.

He was still leaning forward and holding on to her hands

when the carriage drew up in front of Lady Fielding's residence. The elegant townhouse was aglow, candles blazing in every chandelier in the house, the dazzling lights reflecting off the polished crystal.

Liveried footmen were in attendance, present everywhere one turned. Some stood out front as the carriages drew up. One of them, hardly more than a boy, dressed in the Fielding livery that seemed a little too big for him still, and wearing a powdered wig, assisted her down.

Others were in the garden, silent guardsmen positioned beside the massive torches that lined the borders. More footmen bustled about indoors, carrying silver trays laden with glasses of champagne.

This was to be a late evening, for supper would not be served before midnight. Of course, there was still plenty of food and drink to go around.

"Follow me, Hen." Cain grabbed two glasses of champagne and took her for a quick turn about the garden as the sun was setting.

The air had not yet cooled, but soon would now that it was turning dark.

When they found themselves alone for a moment and hidden behind a tree, Hen rose on tiptoes and kissed him on the lips. "I love you."

"Hen—"

"No, you do not need to respond to me. Lady Fielding's footman is coming toward us. She probably wants us to join her now on the receiving line. It was not well done of us to slip past her without so much as a greeting."

"I would have taken you back in a moment."

"Well, we are being summoned now. Let us enjoy the evening. I don't need you to say anything to me. I know how you feel about me."

Music filled the air as they entered the elegant townhouse.

Lady Fielding motioned them over. "Come, my dears. Stand

beside me."

They took their places and dutifully greeted her guests as they passed on the queue. Hen noted the party was small compared to most *ton* affairs, only about eighty guests present for a night of supper and dancing.

This was how exclusive these grand dinner parties were. To be included was a mark of honor.

Lady Fielding turned to her with a bright smile. "Has Malvern mentioned that you are to open the dance along with me and my son, the current Lord Fielding? Immediately afterward, Malvern will announce your betrothal."

Hen was quickly learning that Cain left nothing to chance. "Sounds perfect."

He approached even this soiree with military precision, his battle plan in place before a single note of the orchestra was struck or the first glass of champagne passed around.

"Stay close to me tonight, Hen," he whispered as the last of the guests entered the ballroom.

"Why? Are we still in danger? Have you seen Stoke? Neither he nor his wife were in the queue who streamed past us. But I know they were invited."

He laughed softly. "No, not that sort of danger. But I am going to be accosted by every young woman of marriageable age and their eager mothers. I need you to protect me from them until our betrothal is announced."

She rolled her eyes. "Honestly, you are having too much fun at this. Admit it, you adore the attention heaped on you."

"No, you have no idea how aggressive some of these women can be."

She glanced around and quickly saw that he was garnering everyone's notice. They were quickly surrounded by other guests. Some of them were familiar to Hen from her first Season, and she engaged them in easy conversation.

But her smile slipped when the woman who had dropped Cain off at Malvern House the other day approached them.

Lady Alexandra.

The elegant society creature did not look pleased to see her standing beside Cain, and made a point of treating her as invisible when she greeted him. "Darling, you must dance with me tonight."

Hen thought of her as a cat because of the way she purred and the feline way she tried to rub against him as they spoke.

There was no warmth in this woman's eyes, just envy. Was she capable of loving anyone but herself?

Cain did his best to back away, but there was little room to move in order to avoid her unless he wished to topple the large potted ferns immediately behind them. "No, Alexandra. I'll only be dancing with Hen tonight."

Though the lady wore gloves, Hen saw her claws come out.

"Then perhaps I shall tempt you in other ways," she said with that annoying purr to her voice. "I remember how possessive you once were over me. You could not keep your hands off me. And you would never allow any other man to approach."

"I don't recall it that way, but if you say so. It is a good thing you escaped me long enough to marry." Cain frowned when she did not move on.

"Introduce me, darling. It is impossibly rude of you to hide me from your latest distraction."

"Give it a rest, will you? As you well know, this is Lady Henley Killigrew. Hen, love, Lady Fenwick is an old friend."

"Lovely to meet you, Lady Fenwick," Hen said. "I've heard so much about you. Indeed, quite an earful about you from the duke. By the way, thank you for bringing him home to me the other day."

"I hope you didn't mind his riding alone with me in my carriage," Alexandra replied. "After all, he and I have a history. We were quite the item at one time."

"Yes, but that is old news. Very old. I gave it not a second thought."

Cain glanced at her once Lady Fenwick moved on. "Why,

Hen, was that a bit of wicked sarcasm on your part? I did not know you had it in you."

"That was awful of me. I think this is why I did not mind leaving the London social whirl for Moonstone Landing. People here can be disparaging, always ready to step on others to climb to the top. And look how easily it brought out the worst in me. How much better off we would all be if these manipulative schemers put their efforts into something useful?"

"True, but it will never happen," Cain replied. "Alexandra is a frustrated, angry woman. Her husband is a decent sort and could have given her a good marriage had she allowed it. But she is petty, always wanting what is not hers, and never content with all she has in front of her. She'll never understand that she's brought the misery on herself." He took Hen's hand and led her onto the dance floor behind Lady Fielding and her son.

"She thinks she still has a claim on you."

He arched an eyebrow. "Even as an idiot boy, I understood what she was. Trouble. She never had a serious claim on me and never will. Enough about her, Hen. Our hostess is about to open the dance."

Tingles shot through her the moment Cain put his arm around her waist and took hold of her hand to begin the waltz. These affairs were not usually opened with a waltz, but she was not complaining. There was nothing nicer than being in his arms. He had a way of conveying his feelings with a mere touch, his hold protective and at the same time exciting.

There was the promise of love in his touch.

And yet she could still sense his torment. It was like a ghost circling him, perhaps silenced at times, but always close and threatening.

Well, her strength was in knowing how to put people at ease, and she would do all in her power to help Cain escape its menacing grasp.

The room was large and had been cleared of all furniture to allow for dancing before a late supper was served. The walls were a cheerful yellow trimmed in white, and the ornate ceiling had cherubs painted on it—those plump, childlike angels played their instruments in an Italian countryside.

Cain led her through the steps of the waltz with surprising ease, his movements fluid and graceful. "You are very good at this," she said, not bothering to hide her surprise.

"Did you not know? Bears can dance."

She laughed and missed a step in her distraction, but he so quickly and flawlessly guided her back that she doubted anyone noticed her mistake.

As soon as the dance ended, Lady Fielding gave the nod for her footmen to resume serving champagne. She welcomed her guests and then gave the room over to Cain, who wasted no time in announcing their betrothal.

They were immediately surrounded by a crush of well-wishers.

Hen noticed a few in the background who did not look pleased, several disappointed debutantes, and Lady Alexandra, who had her back arched like that of a hissing cat.

She shrugged off the woman's animosity. The night was a beautiful dream, and she was not going to let anyone ruin it for her.

Odd, how quickly life changed.

A few weeks ago, she was worried about having to mortgage Moonstone Cottage. She and her sisters were scrimping on everything. Now, here she stood in an elegant ballroom, about to become Cain's duchess.

It felt quite nice to be officially betrothed to him.

He grinned as he received everyone's good wishes, that smile sincere and warming her insides as she watched him enchant everyone.

She was also smiling and quite enjoying herself—until she spotted her cousin and his wife.

"Cain," she whispered, her heart shooting into her throat because their presence rattled her. She had not believed they would attend. In truth, she hoped they would pack up their belongings and run from London before news of their misdeeds broke.

"I see them." He put a hand to the small of her back to reassure her.

Lady Alexandra's irritating behavior no longer seemed important, not that Hen was ever concerned about Cain's feelings for his old paramour. He obviously had none. But Stoke and his wife were a danger and would remain so until she and Cain married.

He drew her closer. "Don't leave my side, Hen."

"I have no intention of it. What shall I do if they approach?" Since Cain had taken care of dealing with her cousin since their arrival in London, she sought to take her guidance from him. She did not want to make a mistake and undo all his good work.

"Be cordial, nothing more. I'll whisk you off for a dance if they do not take the hint and move on. He is fortunate I do not toss him over the balcony into Lady Fielding's thorny roses."

To Hen's dismay, the pair approached them a moment later.

She felt Cain's grip tighten around her waist to draw her closer still. "Stoke," he said, his manner aloof, "I expected you to be on your way back to Staffordshire. Did you not have urgent business which required your abrupt departure?"

Lady Stoke tipped her head up in defiance. "Nothing so urgent we could not attend Lady Fielding's soiree and share a drink in celebration of your betrothal to Stoke's ward."

"It is not necessary," Cain assured her. "Lady Fielding has already made the announcement and everyone has toasted us."

The woman was not to be dissuaded. "But people will talk if we do not drink to your and Lady Henley's good health."

"No. Make your apologies to our hostess and leave before I have you both thrown out."

"You wouldn't dare." Her lips twisted in a cruel smile as she gazed at Hen. "Will you deny your own family a toast on your impending nuptials?"

"Indeed, I will." Why was she making such a fuss over a drink? And now the horrid woman was staring avidly at the Malvern necklace around Hen's throat. Hen noted the twitch of her hands. Itchy fingers. Fortunately, the necklace was double clasped and quite secure.

But Hen saw the calculation in her eyes and knew she was figuring out how much she might get if she slipped it off Hen's neck and stole it. How desperate she must be to look at everything as a means to feed her voracious appetite for gambling.

Cain kept a protective hold on Hen as he once again addressed her odious relatives. "Do not test me, Lady Stoke. You are new to this game, but I was born to it and will outmatch you at every turn. I do you a kindness by not exposing your husband's venal behavior toward the family he was supposed to protect."

Lady Stoke sputtered, but held back her outrage, since it would destroy the image of cordiality she and her husband were trying desperately to maintain.

"Stoke," Cain continued, his voice lethally calm, "the late earl left you an estate in excellent condition. Do not allow your wife's grasping nature and your laziness to undo it all. Apply yourself and you will live quite comfortably. Now, go."

The pair moved on with feigned joviality.

Cain turned to Hen as she let out a breath of relief. "Are you all right, Hen?"

She nodded. "Was it not the oddest exchange? What was she hoping to accomplish? But you handled the situation perfectly."

"So did you."

"You are only being kind. I burrowed against you like a coward."

"You still have reason to be wary of those two. Another day and you will be out of their reach. Once you are my duchess, your weasel cousin and his shrew of a wife will fade into the background and become irrelevant to you. Care for another dance? I believe this is the last waltz before supper."

"Yes, I would love any excuse to be in your arms." She wanted to hug him fiercely, loved how ably he rose to every challenge. In her eyes he seemed infallible, but she knew he was not. He hid his torment so well, but this did not mean it wasn't there, simmering beneath the surface.

Stoke and his wife were just taking their leave by the time the waltz ended. Footmen were scurrying about, and the aroma of succulent meats wafted in the air. Hen expected the dinner bell would soon ring, and couples would be asked to the dining room for the evening's featured repast.

A footman approached Cain with a brandy in hand. "Compliments of a friend, Your Grace."

"What friend?" Hen asked, uncertain why a tingle suddenly shot up her spine.

"Forgive me, Lady Henley. I did not catch the name."

"Oh my goodness." She held Cain back as he was about to drink. "Don't put it to your lips. How could I have been so stupid?"

He frowned, more confused than angry when she remained insistent. "What's wrong, Hen?"

"I happened to be reading a poisoner's handbook earlier today."

He burst out laughing. "Should I be worried?"

"Cain, the Italians designed rings with special compartments to carry poison powders. It struck me as odd…Lady Stoke was so insistent on sharing a drink with us. Did that not seem strange to you?"

"A little. But irritating, for certain."

"Then she was staring at my necklace, so I stared back and took note of her jewelry. She had on one of those Italian rings, an exact replica of the one I saw illustrated in the book."

"Hen, is that not a stretch to—"

"She is desperate." She put a hand to the necklace at her throat. "I was sure she meant to grab this Malvern heirloom. Did you not notice the way she salivated over it? I am sure she is up to something because she needs to feed her gambling habit, and now we have cut her off. Or should I say, you have cut her off. But with you out of the way, she may believe her husband can reclaim control of all he has just signed away."

He glanced at the drink in his hand and then back at her. "You really think they mean to harm me?"

She nodded. "I think she does, because she cannot get at our trust funds while you protect me. I'm not sure about my cousin, though. I don't think he has the spine for this sort of thing. For his sake, I hope he is ready to limp back to Staffordshire and give up on all his grand plans. But there is an easy way to find out. Take the drink to him and offer it with your apologies for being curt earlier. Let's see if he hesitates to take it. More important, let's see if Lady Stoke knocks it out of his hand."

Cain cast her a wry grin. "You do realize if this is poisoned, then you will have saved my life. See, I told you I needed you. Stay here, Hen."

"Not a chance. I'm coming with you."

"All right, but stay close and let me do the talking."

She nodded.

He ordered another brandy from a passing footman. When it arrived, he led Hen over to the pair, who were still standing beside their hostess and appeared to be boring her to tears as they lingered over their departure.

Well, if she was right about Lady Stoke tampering with Cain's drink, they were likely stalling to see what would happen next.

Those rotten fiends.

"Lord Stoke, a moment," Cain said, extending the hand that held the brandy earlier delivered to him. "You asked to share a congratulatory drink with me before taking your leave. Here, take this one and we shall toast to family bonds."

Stoke eyed him warily, but was about to drink from the offered glass when his wife knocked it out of his hands. Some of the drink spilled onto his jacket. "Oh, my dear!" she said.

"Do forgive me. We must leave right away and attend to the

stain before it sets."

Cain's eyes bored into her, his glower seeming to immobilize both of them for an instant. "No, Stoke. Hold a moment."

Hen's cousin appeared genuinely confused. "Well, all right. What is this nonsense about?"

His wife paled and grabbed his arm to tug him away. "We must go."

A footman appeared to clean up the shattered glass.

"Stoke, we really must go," his wife insisted.

"But, my dear… Oh, Lady Fielding, I do apologize. I think my wife is not feeling well."

"She'll feel worse in a moment," Cain growled. "Hand over your ring, Lady Stoke."

She shrieked and knocked Hen over as she sprinted out of the room.

Lord Stoke chased after his wife.

Lady Fielding shook her head in confusion. "What in heaven's name just happened?"

"Hen, are you hurt?" Cain did not bother to go after the pair. Instead, he knelt beside her and carefully lifted her in his arms.

"Just winded," she managed to say as she regained her breath. "A little bruised, I think. But nothing broken."

"Lady Fielding, I need to take her somewhere quiet."

"The poor dear! Yes, follow me." Lady Fielding led Cain to the library, nudging her curious guests out of the way to forge a path out of the room.

"I didn't hit my head," Hen muttered, sensing his concern. "I'll be all right in a moment. But I got it."

"Got what?" Frowning, he entered the library and gently set her down on the leather divan. "Blast it, why did you try to stop her? She's twice your size."

"Look." She smiled up at him and held out Lady Stoke's ring. "I grabbed it off her hand when she tried to push me over."

"Tried? She did push you over. You are a little thing, Hen. No match for her size and brawn." He emitted a groaning laugh. "I don't know whether to hug you or throttle you. She might have hurt you."

"Any bruises will fade in a day or two. Let's get the powder in that ring analyzed."

Lady Fielding gasped. "Powder? Ring? What was the horrid woman trying to do?"

Her son now joined them and must have heard a few moments of their exchange. "Shall I call in the constables?"

Cain shook his head. "No, James. It may all be nothing. You see, Hen was reading a book on poisons earlier today, and I think—hell, at least I hope—her imagination got the better of her. Someone sent over a brandy for me, and when your footman could not recall who—"

"Oh, Lord. That was me. I sent over the drink and asked him to keep it anonymous. I can assure you, the Stokes were never near that glass."

Heat shot into Hen's cheeks. "They weren't?"

"Well, I don't think so. I…wasn't watching him the entire time. But surely…"

Hen glanced at Lady Stoke's ring in dismay. "But she has a secret compartment in it. And look, here are the remains of a powder. Oh, heavens."

Cain and Lord Fielding examined the powder.

Lord Fielding cast Hen a mirthless smile. "Seems she is an opium eater."

"In addition to her gambling problems," Cain muttered. "At worst, had she tampered with my drink, the opium might have made me giddy for the night. There isn't enough in here to do a man my size any permanent damage. She probably used it herself before coming to the party."

"What a sad thing," Lady Fielding said with a shake of her head.

Hen sat up, now utterly confused. "But she behaved as though she were guilty. Why knock the drink out of her husband's hands if she hadn't planned this bit of mischief and thought we'd caught her at it?"

Cain had been on his haunches beside her and now moved to sit next to her on the divan. "Because she thought we were going to poison *him*."

"What?" Hen's breath caught in her throat, and she stared at him, wide-eyed. "How could she ever believe such a preposterous thing? You are the most noble man who has ever existed. As for me, I could not harm a fly…even one who needed a good swatting."

Cain's lips twitched at the corners in the flicker of a smile. "There is a French expression, *honi soit qui mal y pense*— shame on anyone who thinks evil of it. She may have been dreaming up plots of revenge to poison you or me. She knew about these Italian rings, since she used the secret compartment in hers for her own powders. She was thinking evil thoughts about us and then assumed we were doing the same when I handed the brandy to her husband."

Lord Fielding laughed. "She believed you were trying to poison her husband?"

Hen was beside herself in dismay. "But we never would!"

"Of course *you* would never do such a dishonorable thing," Lady Fielding intoned. "But she is a low creature and imagined you were capable of it because she was not above attempting it herself."

"Oh dear. Then there was nothing wrong with the drink. What have I done?" Hen buried her face in her hands.

Cain took her hands in his and drew them away from her face. "Hen, look at me. Your suspicions were understandable. And they may yet be proved true, although I don't know if we can retrieve the glass now. It has probably been taken away to be washed."

"So we'll never know for certain," Lord Fielding remarked.

Cain nodded. "The pair did not think twice before getting their sticky hands on your inheritance. Lady Stoke had to know it would all catch up to her someday. She just hadn't expected it to be this soon. Given another day to plan, she might very well have acquired a lethal poison and done me in. I'm sure she did pour some of her opium into the brandy Lord Fielding's footman was delivering to me, hoping it might be enough to fell me. It would have taken no more than an accidental bump into him, a moment's distraction to accomplish the task."

"You are only saying this to make me feel better." She shook her head and laughed along with the others when she realized how ridiculous her words sounded. "You know what I mean."

"I do, love. Thank you for worrying about me and likely saving me from a night of painful cramps…or worse."

Lord Fielding still held the ring. "Shall I turn it over to the magistrate?"

Cain glanced at it. "I'll hold on to it for now, then Hen and I can decide what to do about the Stokes. What do you think, Hen? Shall we send the magistrate after them?"

"Without the glass, how will we ever prove their dastardly intent?" she said.

"As for Lady Stoke's ring, is there a point to holding on to it?" Lady Fielding asked. "She would be depraved enough to accuse Lady Henley of stealing it."

Her son agreed. "I'll have it delivered to her tomorrow, along with a note informing her we are cutting off all association with her and her husband and will advise our friends to do the same."

"Yes, this is exactly what we must do. I heartily agree." Lady Fielding took her son's arm. "Our guests must be wondering what is going on. Come, let's feed them. That ought to distract everyone. Shall I make excuses for you, my dears? I will understand if you wish to leave early."

Hen's cheeks were ablaze with embarrassment as she looked up at Lady Fielding. "Would you rather we left? I cannot apologize enough for this horrid incident. That woman has had me so on edge ever since my father died. And reading that book on poisons, then seeing her ring… Well, we shall never know for certain whether she had touched that drink. Still, I had better put a tether on my imagination."

Lady Fielding cast her an affectionate smile. "Nonsense, my dear. You had every reason to be wary of her. Their perfidy is exposed now, but gossip was already rampant about that pair. A disgrace to your father's title and his decency."

"Everyone in London will be begging my mother for invitations to next year's dinner party," Lord Fielding added with a grin. "Do come join us. Cook has outdone herself. You are a slight thing and probably eat like a bird. But Cain must be famished and ready to eat the furniture."

Hen laughed. "You are far too kind to me. I am happy to stay if Cain wishes it."

Cain took her hands in his. "Are you certain?"

She nodded.

He smiled in obvious relief. "Good. This bear is starved and needs to be fed."

Chapter Fifteen

CAIN BREATHED A sigh when Cormac arrived at the church with Lord and Lady Stockwell shortly before noon the following day. They had been through the worst of times together, and he wanted his friend to now partake in Cain's best day. He was glad their friendship was solid enough to draw him out of the cocoon of misery in which he had wrapped himself since losing his arm.

The Fieldings, mother and son, had also been invited to their wedding, for they had been more than gracious to him and Hen. Despite the lateness of their dinner party, the pair arrived all smiles and looking none the worse for wear.

Lord and Lady Ashbrook sent their regrets, for he was too frail to leave his sickbed. Cain was disappointed for Hen's sake, for the Ashbrooks were a close link to her parents, and she would feel their absence.

"Where's Hen?" Cormac asked, giving him a playful nudge to stir him out of his thoughts. "Has she come to her senses and run off?"

Cain shook his head and laughed. "No, you arse. I just saw her at Malvern House, but I came on ahead to greet our guests. Her solicitor, Mr. Garrick, is escorting her in my carriage. She wanted him to stand in place of her father. He's a good man. They should arrive at any moment."

He had no sooner spoken the words than his carriage drew up. Hen's ebullient cousin, Prudence, stepped out first. Garrick came down next.

Cain drew in a breath as Hen descended, her gown a honey-colored silk that brought out the tawny hues of her hair and delicate green of her eyes. "She's beautiful, isn't she?"

Cormac nodded. "Am I permitted to tease her about last night? Gossip is rampant this morning about Hen tackling Lady Stoke and wrestling her to the ground."

"Blessed saints, is that what they're saying?" Cain laughed again. "Actually, Lady Stoke barreled over her when Hen tried to stop her from running off. Hen went flying. Fortunately, she's only slightly bruised. You ought to have accepted Lady Fielding's invitation and seen Hen in action for yourself."

"Next time."

Which was Cormac's way of saying he wasn't ready to join the social whirl anytime soon.

Cain resolved to talk to his friend about it, but not today. This pain Cormac was going through was no light thing, and could not be addressed within a matter of minutes. It was no splinter that could be drawn out of one's palm and easily cleansed. He knew and understood.

Their bond had always been strong, but had gained in strength over these past few years because each understood what the other was going through. Their demons might not be exactly the same, but they were capable of destroying them each in their own way.

However, now he'd found Hen.

The girl with starlight in her eyes.

Cain forgot everyone and everything as his beautiful bride stood beside the carriage and thanked the footman who handed her the small bouquet of flowers she was to hold when marching to the altar.

This was her strength, this ability to put a smile on someone's face with a kind word or nod of appreciation.

He strode forward to escort her into the church. "I cannot take my eyes off you."

She cast him a glowing smile. "You are quite magnificent yourself. Ready to get leg-shackled, Your Grace?"

"Eager for it. Ah, here's the minister. I had better take my place." He kissed her lightly on the cheek. "Meet you at the altar."

The ceremony proceeded smoothly.

Cain felt proud as he listened to Hen repeat her vows. She spoke them with such sincerity and so much love in her heart.

He hoped to convey the same with his vows, for he wanted their marriage to succeed.

It had to. It would destroy him if he made Hen unhappy.

Before Cain knew it, the minister declared them husband and wife.

He kissed Hen and then whispered, "I love you."

She looked at him as though she'd heard wrong, but he knew he had been clear. This was the right time to tell her, as they stood at the sacred altar and pledged themselves to each other.

Hen was a miracle delivered to him when he needed it most.

Their friends cheered and surrounded them to express their good wishes. Prudence giggled and addressed her as *Your Grace*.

Hen was effusive in her happiness.

Cormac patted him on the back. "I've never seen anyone happier."

Cain nodded. "Yes, she's radiant."

"I meant you," Cormac said with a chuckle. "You haven't smiled so unguardedly since we were children."

"I'm relieved she is now out of danger from Lord and Lady Stoke."

Cormac nodded. "That is no small thing. They will not dare put their hands on the Duchess of Malvern. If only our problems could be so easily resolved. Perhaps yours will be. Hen could very well be the magical cure you need."

"I hope so, but I doubt my night terrors are going away anytime soon. They've grown worse since the war ended. It makes no sense." Cain tried to keep the frustration out of his voice, but probably failed. "I know Napoleon has been defeated and will not escape exile this time. But my soul does not seem to realize it yet."

"You understand the war is over, but you haven't come to terms with your surviving it pretty much unscathed when so many of your friends did not," Cormac said, his manner no longer lighthearted. "Just as I have not come to terms with losing a limb. I seem to have lost my heart along with it. These events haunt us. Destroy us. Leave us raging because we can do nothing about them. You married well, and you know I do not say such a thing lightly. In time, your Hen will calm your anger down. I know she will, for I see the way you look at each other."

Cain nodded. "I hope you find the same someday."

"Perhaps someday." His friend grinned and glanced upward to the heavens. "My perfect woman will have a tougher task with me than Hen is likely to have with you."

A few moments later, Cain escorted his new bride to their waiting carriage.

His bride.

Hen was now his.

It felt good to have her to himself as they made their way back to Malvern House for the wedding breakfast. Garrick rode with Cormac and his family, while Prudence rode with the Fieldings.

Hen snuggled up to him. "You look awfully morose for a happy bridegroom."

He raked a hand through his hair. "I am happy."

"You were as we exchanged our vows. But you have since moved on and are planning ahead. Tonight worries you."

He muttered a lame denial.

"I don't think this is something you can approach with battle tactics and advanced strategy, Cain. This pain comes from somewhere deep within your soul."

"I've lived with it for a while now. But you haven't, love.

Hurting you is all I worry about."

"You won't ever hurt me. I think your need to protect me is also buried deep inside your soul, and it will win out."

"Perhaps, but what if it does not?" This was what worried him most, especially since he knew Hen would push his limits.

"Time will tell, but I am fairly confident of the answer. Love conquers all. It does, Cain. I believe this with all my heart. Did you mean it when you said you loved me?" She cast him a gentle smile. "I wanted to leap into your arms and smother you with kisses. But the minister seemed eager to get on with the ceremony. So was I. Not to be your duchess, but eager to be your wife. I love you too."

"I know, Hen. I see it in the way you look at me, the way you light up and glow when I approach. Dealing with me will take every ounce of that love."

"We'll start with little steps," she said. "I understand we need separate bedchambers for now. Nor must we answer to anyone but each other. We'll have the house to ourselves for the next few nights, since Prudence will be staying with Lord and Lady Stockwell. Whatever happens will remain between us. Nor does anything need to happen. We need not have our wedding night…I mean…nothing needs to happen until—"

"Hen, I am not holding off." He cast her a wry grin. "Don't pat my hand as though I am a little boy. I'm not worried about what I do while I am awake. Blessed saints, I'm going to devour you. You'll like that part, I assure you. I have no intention of holding back." He kissed her softly on the lips. "However, you are going to lock your door and keep me out before you fall asleep. I want your promise on it."

She nodded with obvious reluctance. "We've already had this discussion. Yes, you have my promise."

The rest of the day passed smoothly, and Cain found himself surprisingly at ease by the time the guests left and he was finally alone with Hen. It was not very late, only eight o'clock in the evening. But they'd eaten all day and had gotten little sleep the night before, so they were both ready to turn in.

Hen's maid was waiting for her in her duchess's quarters.

His valet awaited him in his ducal chamber.

Cain dismissed them both, then opened the door between his bedchamber and Hen's. "I'll claim the privilege of undressing you tonight."

Hen gave a laughing snort. "You haven't seen the clasps and laces on this gown. It might take you a while."

He shrugged out of his jacket and waistcoat, then took her in his arms. "It won't. I shall approach your delectable body as I do a battlefield," he teased, easily undoing the laces and distracting her with soft kisses along the curve of her neck. "Surveying all the obstructions and deciding where to charge first."

She cast him an impudent smile. "Shall I do the same with yours?"

"Have at me while I have at you?" He arched an eyebrow and gave her a wicked smile. "Go ahead, give it a try. I'll do my best to distract you."

She began to fumble with his shirt.

He distracted her by licking her throat as he removed the Malvern necklace. Next came the tiara. He removed it and gave her a feather-soft kiss on the lips.

Then a deeper kiss.

Her eyes were now closed and her breaths came quicker.

He easily undid the rest of her gown and soon had it off her. She now wore nothing but her corset and shift.

"You are falling behind, Hen. You have yet to undo a single button of mine."

She opened her eyes, her expression wondrous as she laughed softly. "Your tactics are completely unfair. You trailed your tongue along my neck, and now I cannot concentrate."

He planted a steamy kiss at the base of her throat. "Shall I stop, love?"

She closed her eyes again and licked her lips. "No, that's heavenly. Oh…my…"

He tossed her corset aside, but did not immediately remove her shift. Instead, he unbuttoned his shirt and slipped it off.

Her eyes were open again, and he liked how avidly she watched the play of his muscles along his bare arms and chest. In return, he noted the rise and fall of her exquisite bosom as she anticipated what was to come next.

He took her back in his arms, liking the warmth of her skin against his and her light blush.

Soft light filtered into her chamber, casting her in the gentle aura of twilight.

A golden light.

He removed the pins from her hair and watched the intricately styled twist come free and her curls tumble loosely over her shoulders and down her back. "You look so pretty, Hen."

He buried his fingers in her hair and drew her close for a deep, lingering kiss.

The last of their clothes were shed by the time he carried her to bed and began to tease her with his kisses, explore her with his caresses. He had been aching to see what lay beneath the layers of clothing, suspecting he would find skin as soft as cream and silky to the touch.

She stole his breath away.

Truly, she was perfection.

He stared at her lovely breasts and their dusky rose peaks, then cupped one and took its peak into his mouth.

She gasped as he began to suckle her. "Cain," she whispered, clutching his head and emitting several breathy moans.

"Close your eyes, love. Feel each sensation." He was atop her as she lay on her back on the bed, but he was careful not to put all of his weight on her slight frame.

He was feeling each sensation as well, for in all his experience, he hadn't imagined anyone could be this beautiful, this soft and warm and captivating.

She tasted as sweet as honeysuckle.

Her hair was drawn off to one side so that it tumbled over

one shoulder and the tawny curls partially hid one breast. He moved those tresses aside with a caressing brush of his hand and then lowered his lips to this creamy mound and flicked his tongue across its hardened peak. "I cannot get enough of you, love."

She was ready for him by the time he moved his hand lower to stroke the intimate spot between her thighs. Ready and responsive, clutching his shoulders and moaning as her passion built, eager to take him in when he entered her.

His senses were roaring, for she was deliciously hot and delighting in his every touch. But he moved slowly, holding back the rutting boar inside of him because he dared not lose control when it was her first time.

He did not rush their coupling, but took his cues as to her readiness from the lick of her lips, the soft pucker of her mouth when she moaned, the desire on her expressive face.

An odd feeling came over him as he watched her respond, as he fully embedded himself inside her and claimed her as his own. He'd expected the fiery build as their bodies joined, the pulsing heat and throbbing pleasure. But he had not appreciated the intensity of this marital bond now forged between him and Hen.

The act of love was physical and pleasurable, but with his every thrust also came a promise to protect her, to love her, to always cherish her.

These were promises he meant to keep.

She was easy to love, for she had a beautiful heart and an outrageously glorious body. Her smile was sunshine.

Her purrs and breathy moans were a delight, her passion so exquisitely honest and unrestrained that he could not get enough of watching her. When she tipped over the edge and found her pleasure, so did he.

His seed spilled into her, but the act meant so much more than a moment's gratification. With it, he was pledging his love. He would love her always, for this was the only way he could ever be with Hen.

"Cain," she said, wrapping her arms around him as they lay

together afterward, their hearts still pounding and their bodies damp with the scent of their sex. "I had no idea this is what people meant when they spoke of a wedding night."

He chuckled. "This is why parents guard their daughters like hawks."

"It felt splendid. How was it for you?"

"Better than splendid, love. Powerful. Perfection." He kissed her lightly on the lips. "These feelings were a first for me, too."

"I'm glad."

He shifted her so that she lay atop him, for he wanted to see her face and soak in her smile. Her heart was still racing; he could feel its rapid beat against the wall of his chest. He could also feel the fullness of her breasts as she rested atop him, and felt aroused once more. "I cannot get enough of you, Hen."

Her tawny curls cascaded over her shoulders and onto his arms. He brushed her hair back and then drew her forward for a deep, lingering kiss.

"Does this mean you won't leave me yet?"

"Do you want me to go?" He frowned, knowing he ought to return to his bedchamber, but he wasn't nearly ready yet. In truth, he would never be ready to leave her side.

However, this was her first time, and she was not used to this intimacy.

"No, I would love for you to stay. Is there any harm in your holding me for a little while longer?"

"No harm, love." He stroked her hair, loving its rich, lustrous feel. "In truth, I wasn't anywhere near done yet."

She inhaled lightly. "There's more?"

"Yes, but not if you are too sore. There are other ways to pleasure you."

"There are?" She was like a little sponge, seeking to soak up all the information she could. "Will you tell me?"

"It is better if I show you," he said with a soft, bearlike growl before rolling her back under him and gently parting her legs. "Any objections?"

Chapter Sixteen

MOTHER IN HEAVEN.

Hen had no idea a man could put his mouth *there*.

She had never realized such pleasure could exist, and had not a single objection.

Nor had she ever imagined such a powerful bond could develop after experiencing these intimacies. Cain now knew all of her, for there was not an inch he hadn't explored, touched with gentle hands, or tasted with soft lips.

She responded passionately, for he seemed to know just what to do and how to touch her in ways that made her shatter.

"Hen, love…I had better go," he said after bringing her to pleasure a second time with the touch of his mouth.

He was now holding her in his arms; their bodies were wrapped around each other like clinging vines as she recovered her composure.

He had called her beautiful several times, but he was the one with the truly magnificent body. His was a masculine beauty, big and rugged. He had a few scars, but none too serious, or so he insisted when she ran her hand lightly along each disfiguring mark. The one at his back was particularly long and puckered pink. The one above his ribs was mostly hidden in the light spray of gold hair along the span of his chest.

She inhaled his scent, that heady mix of sandalwood and

maleness she found impossible to resist. She was not ready to have their night end but dared not protest and add to his already increasing tension. "All right. This was nice, Cain."

He cast her a wry smile. "Hell of a nice way to fall into bed. I'll see you in the morning, love. Make sure you lock that door between us."

"I will." She rose with him, trying her best to hold back her tears because she did not want him to see her crying. First of all, this had been a joyful day and an even more joyful night. She was not unhappy about any of it except having to part from him now.

The sadness was for him, not for herself.

She loved having him beside her. But he was the one who truly needed her, a need that sprang from a deep, dark place, from an emptiness within his soul. She'd felt his desperation as he claimed her and inhaled the scent of her, memorized each curve of her body.

Well, he was her bear.

Big, golden, and beautiful.

She kissed him and wished him sweet dreams, then hid her heartache as she barred her door to him and climbed back into bed. After a moment, she realized he had left his clothes behind in her room.

Perhaps this was his way of assuring her of his return.

She stared at the thick oak door between them.

He wasn't coming back tonight.

Sighing, she slid back under the sheets and fell asleep holding tightly to the pillow carrying his sandalwood scent.

Sometime in the night, she heard him cry out.

She wanted to go to him, but he had been adamant that she was not to go near him or ever open that door between them.

Having given her sacred promise to him, she simply held tight to her pillow and tried her best to stem her tears.

His cries died down soon after.

She awoke just after sunrise, not quite as refreshed as she would have liked.

It was still early in the morning, and she did not think her maid would come in to attend her for another hour or two. Wondering whether Cain might also be awake, she donned her robe, then gathered his clothes and knocked lightly at the connecting door between their chambers. "Cain, are you up?"

She heard nothing, so she knocked softly again. "I guess not."

She had just resolved to return to bed when she heard his muffled voice. "You can unlock the door, Hen."

She quickly turned the odious lock and swung open this unwanted barrier between them. Well, he wanted it, mistakenly believing it was for her protection. Perhaps he was right, but she felt to the depths of her soul he would never hurt her.

"Good morning," she said.

He cast her an affectionate smile that had her insides melting. "Good morning, Duchess. You're awake early."

She nodded, her heart doing little somersaults as she looked at him. "I enjoyed last night."

He laughed lightly as he took his clothes from her arms to set them on a nearby chair. He had just washed up and shaved, for his hair was damp and she caught the refreshing scent of lather on his skin. He wore nothing but a towel wrapped around his hips and looked simply divine. "So did I. Care to continue where we left off?"

Her eyes rounded in surprise.

His smile turned naughty as he led her to his bed. "Come, my beauty. I see you need corrupting. Yes, Hen. We can do this in daytime, too."

"But what about your valet?"

"He knows not to come up unless I ring for him. Same for your maid. I left strict instructions we were not to be disturbed." He lifted her in his arms and carried her to his bed.

She thought he would now remove his towel and her robe, but he merely lay down beside her and took her into the circle of his arms. She was fascinated by the sculpted strength of his arms and the breadth of his shoulders, the way his muscles bunched and corded with an easy, flowing grace.

He kissed her on the forehead. "I suppose you heard my demons last night."

"Yes." She swirled her fingers in the dusting of hair across his chest.

"The attack wasn't as bad as usual."

She emitted a shattered breath. "It sounded awful."

"Last night was mild in comparison, but do not make too much of it. I had hoped these bad dreams would go away for once and allow me to sleep soundly. We were tired, and last night's activities left us both well satisfied."

She caressed his cheek. "Were you truly satisfied?"

He groaned. "Hell yes. All I can think of is you and your luscious body."

"You are going to turn me into a wanton. But I suppose it is a good thing for a wife to crave her husband's touch. So you say these um…marital activities can also take place in daytime. Such as now?"

"Yes, love. Shall I show you?"

"Please do." She held her breath as he shifted their positions so that she was once more under him and he atop her, with his elbows propped on either side of her to absorb the bulk of his weight.

Her hair was unbound and now splayed across his pillow, but he seemed to like this untamed look. His eyes turned dark and smoldering, and he began to kiss her, one deeply erotic kiss that involved lips and tongues and conquest, followed by lighter kisses down her body.

She thought he would now slip the robe off her, but he merely touched her through the thin overlayer of fabric, something she found surprisingly arousing. Perhaps it was the slight lacy friction against her breasts to blame.

Whatever the reason, her senses were now exploding.

He peeled the garment off her shoulders with smug confidence and smiled as her breasts were now revealed. At the same time, he slid the hem upward so that she was exposed to her waist. He teased her as he did so, sliding his hand up the inside of her thigh, finding her core with his thumb.

She was gasping and eager for relief by the time he entered her, wild for him and lurching her hips forward to take him fully inside her. She cried out softly when he caught the tip of one breast between his lips and teased it.

"Cain…oh, my…oh!" She clutched the sheets, and then clutched him as she tumbled, shattered. Starlight burst all around her.

She cried his name.

His own release followed soon after, no less explosive although perhaps less noisy. He collapsed onto his back, breathing heavily and laughing. "Hen," he said, emitting a sexy growl as he took her back in his arms, "that was spectacular. I would have married you within a minute of my meeting you had I known just how incredible this was going to be."

She laughed along with him. "You must have had a hint, since you hardly knew me an hour before you proposed."

He kissed her on the forehead. "Yes, my heart knew."

They lay quietly in each other's arms for a while, then Hen began to fidget with her robe. It was still hiked up around her waist while the bosom of it was still off her shoulders and her breasts were spilling out.

"Don't, love." Cain put a hand over hers. "I like the way you look."

He was naked beside her, having tossed his towel to the foot of the bed sometime during his kisses that left her breathless and mindless.

She blushed. "I think we would shock Molly and your valet if they walked in on us now."

He grinned. "Oh, Hen. This is still fairly tame. Just wait. There's so much more."

Her face turned fiery, for if he considered this tame, then she dared not imagine what else was in store for her. "There is?"

"I am going to enjoy showing you. But no more this morning. This is new to you, and your body will be sore if we overdo it. Just let me hold you in my arms. I like having you close to me, feeling the warmth of your body against mine."

"I like it too, Cain."

THEY FOLLOWED THE same routine each night and morning for the entire week. By the end of the week, they'd received confirmation that guardianship of her sisters had been officially transferred to Cain. He now controlled their trust accounts and them.

Hen did not view it as control, but rather as freeing her and her sisters from their awful cousin and his wicked wife.

A great weight was now off her shoulders. Her sisters were safe, and that meant everything to her.

All the emotions she had been holding back now came flooding to the fore. As the dam she'd built inside of her burst, tears of relief spilled out.

Cain was there to wrap her in his arms. "Hen, love. They can't ever hurt any of you again."

"I know. I was so worried. I cannot wait to tell Phoebe and Chloe."

Since they had accomplished all they'd hoped to achieve while in London, she and Cain were now ready to return to Moonstone Landing. The journey would take several days by carriage. This was a topic Hen needed to raise with him, especially since Prudence would be traveling with them.

Her cousin, who had returned to Malvern House yesterday, was now out shopping for some gifts for Hen's sisters. Hen had remained behind, since she and Cain had gone shopping for them days earlier.

She was glad for the privacy, since she had an important topic to broach with him.

He was in his study, reading over some documents concerning his Malvern holdings. "May I interrupt you for a moment?"

"Of course, Hen. I am never too busy for you." He set aside the papers and came around his desk to stand beside her. "Shall I close the door? You look troubled. Is something wrong?"

"I should have raised the matter sooner, but now knowing Prudence will be with us on our journey home…it is about the sleeping arrangements. She will know something is wrong if you and I take separate rooms."

"Ah, that bothers you?" The door clicked softly as he shut it behind them.

"Not for myself. I just don't want her asking questions. Everything shows on my face. It is none of her business what goes on between us, but I am afraid of giving something away."

He crossed his arms over his chest and regarded her thoughtfully. "What you are asking is to sleep with me. No, Hen. It will be worse if my dreams are haunted and you wake with a bruise on your face. Everyone at the inn will see it and think I beat you. But I have given this problem some consideration as well."

"Of course—I should have known."

"You'll share a room with Prudence. She is a woman alone, and since we are traveling without lady's maid or valet, I think it is best for you to share a room with her." He arched an eyebrow when she did not immediately respond. "I thought it was a good plan. Do you not like it?"

She groaned. "What I don't like is being away from you. But it is sensible. Completely logical and will not raise any suspicions."

He tucked a finger under her chin and raised her gaze to his to give her a light kiss. "I know you are disappointed, love. But this is the safest way. We'll see how it goes once we've settled in at St. Austell Grange. You cannot rush this. I still have bad dreams, you know I do, since you've heard them."

She frowned. "Have you had them every night? There was a

night or two all seemed quiet, but I wasn't certain. It could have just been me sleeping too soundly to awaken."

"Yes, love. You were sleeping too soundly. I've had them every night. But they aren't as severe as they have been in the past, and that is a marked improvement. However, we are not testing anything out while traveling. Nor will we push ourselves into anything once we are back home."

She smiled at him. "Moonstone Landing is home, isn't it? It felt like that to me and my sisters immediately upon our arrival."

He shook his head. "No, Hen. Let me modify that statement. It is a beautiful village, and St. Austell Grange is a grand manor. But *you* are my home. You hold my heart."

She walked into his outstretched arms. "You make it impossible for me to ever be irritated with you. It is most frustrating, you know."

"Give me a kiss, love. We are still too new in the marriage to squabble. Just wait until we have children. They will give us headaches galore."

"Children…" She shook her head and laughed. "You are thinking ahead again. Is this how your mind always works? Never just in the moment?"

"The only time I am ever in the moment is when I am in bed with you. I can think of nothing but you. As for everything else? My brain does not shut off. Yes, this is how I look at everything. Like a chessboard. Knowing where I need to be and figuring out how best to arrive there. I have to see the entire game before me and let it play out in my head. This is how I have always been, even as a child."

"Fascinating. You were probably able to outsmart your parents and the entire Malvern staff by the time you were the age of three."

He shook his head and emitted a hearty chuckle. "Just because I knew how a game would play out does not mean I always won. Nor does it mean my game was clever. I often thought up stupid things and regretted the consequences. Never anything really serious. Mostly stupid boy things, like knocking a beehive out of a tree and then realizing I had miscalculated and could not outrun that angry swarm."

"Oh no."

"Well, I did manage to escape them by diving into a nearby pond and holding my breath underwater for as long as possible," he continued. "I saved myself, but ruined a pair of brand-new boots. Then there was the time I decided to test whether a trellis would hold me up as I climbed up to my bedroom window in the wee hours of the morning. I was only fifteen, stinking drunk, and did not want my parents knowing I had been out carousing. Of course, casting up my accounts on my bedroom carpet was a dead giveaway. So was the fact that my clothes reeked of stale perfume. Nor was my mother happy that I destroyed her beautiful roses as I climbed the trellis."

She had been smiling with mirth, but now eyed him in confusion. "Roses have thorns."

He nodded. "Fortunately, I was too drunk to feel them gouging my skin. However, they tore up my hands so badly, they had to be cleansed and bandaged. Shall I go on with more of my idiotic boyhood misadventures?"

"Well, you've managed to survive them all." She could not suppress her giggles. "I think my sisters and I were angels compared to you. We rarely gave my parents cause to worry."

"That's because you are sweet girls. The sort idiot boys like me need to marry in order to keep us out of trouble. Are we all right, Hen?"

"Yes, of course. I'll share quarters at the coaching inns with Prudence, and hug my pillow pretending it is you if ever I get lonely." She reached up on tiptoes and gave him a kiss. "I'll leave you to your work."

"No, love. I'm just finishing up. Is there anything you'd like to do on your last day here?"

"Well, the weather is lovely. I've already said my farewells to Lord and Lady Ashbrook. We could take a stroll in the park. In fact, I think we ought to stop by the home of your friend, the Marquess of Burness, and see if he'd like to join us with his little nieces. I can watch them while the two of you talk. Perhaps we can stop for ices at Gunter's afterward."

"Well, look at you." He shook his head and chuckled. "Who's planning ahead now? I like that idea. Give me ten minutes to send off my last note and I'll be ready."

She nodded. "I'll have the carriage summoned in the meanwhile."

The plan turned out to be a good one, for Lady Stockwell was hosting a small dinner party that evening for her husband's fellow bank directors and needed the girls distracted. Hen knew she also needed the marquess out of her hair because he was still behaving like an unruly child.

His nieces and Cain coaxed him to leave the house and join them.

"Yes, Uncle Cormac, we shall have ever so much fun together," the eldest girl, Ella, said, looking up at him with her big, innocent eyes and pleading in her sweetest voice.

"I've looked after my sisters for years," Hen assured him. "It will be nothing for me to look after your nieces."

The marquess cast Hen a wry smile. "Well, let's hope you don't regret it."

"Oh, I have the easier job. Cain is the one who is charged with looking after you, for you are the one who growls at the world and has no intention of behaving."

He took her teasing in good nature. "I can be nice when I want to be." He knelt and tickled Ella. "Right, duckling?"

The younger sister, Imogen, jumped on him. "Me too! Me, too!"

He soon had his nieces running around him and shrieking as he playfully grabbed at them and roared like a lion. No wonder their poor mother always looked so frazzled. He probably took a bit of wicked delight in upending his household.

Both girls were now leaping on him as he knelt on one bended knee to hug them. "All right. You win, my ducklings! I surrender."

The five of them climbed into Cain's open carriage and headed to the park. The marquess maintained a look of amused detachment as the girls bounced in their seats and squealed in excitement. He'd agreed to come out for them, but mostly for Cain. Their friendship was as deep as could possibly be, and Hen imagined this was the marquess's way of letting Cain know he would walk through fire for him.

Of course, they were not going to do anything more than take a ride in the park. But Hen knew he was in turmoil beneath his casual exterior, for Cain was the same way, and she recognized the subtle hints.

They rode slowly through the park and then took another turn around it. This time, Cain and his friend stepped down and walked on ahead of them in order to speak in private. Hen had expected this would happen and was ready to entertain the girls while the men discussed their own weighty matters.

She ordered the carriage brought to a halt near an area where other children were playing. Some boys were floating their boats in a small pond. A few children were flying their kites. Most were merely running around on the finely manicured lawn while watched by their hawk-eyed nannies.

Hen realized she was out of place, for there were very few parents here with their children. But she knew how to take care of young ones as well as any nanny and wasn't in the least daunted. Perhaps she had a bit of the little girl left in her, because she enjoyed running around with Ella and Imogen, squealing as loudly as they did while they chased each other in circles and finally fell dizzily onto the soft grass.

The three of them were out of breath from laughing by the time they returned to the carriage.

The men were waiting for them, genuine smiles on their faces as the trio approached. Cain helped the girls scamper up and then circled his hands about Hen's waist and helped her in. He settled beside her. "Your cheeks are pink, love."

The girls giggled. "You called her what our papa calls our mama. Love," Ella said. "And then he gives her smoochy kisses."

Cormac climbed in and settled the little one, Imogen, on his lap. She looked up at him with worshipful eyes. "What is it, little duckling?" he asked.

"I'm sad."

He glanced at Hen, obviously pleading for assistance.

She reached over and took Imogen's hand. "I thought we were having a nice time. We'll be going for ices next. Why are you sad, sweetling?"

"Because Uncle Cormac doesn't have a lady to love or kiss."

Cormac cleared his throat. "I have plenty of ladies for that, Imogen. Don't be sad for me."

She nodded. "But Papa says they are all horrible."

Hen could not contain her snort of laughter.

Cormac laughed, too. "He is right, they are all horrible. But I'll find the nicest lady one day. Don't be sad for me, little duckling. She is out there. I'm just not looking for her at the moment."

They rode on to Gunter's.

While Hen helped the girls choose their ices, the men settled in their seats at one of the desirable corner tables, their backs to the wall so they had a view of the entire parlor. The pair looked every inch the powerful lords, and caught the notice of everyone in the place. Several elegant lords and ladies came up to them and engaged the men in conversation.

Hen looked after the girls and made certain most of their ices went into their mouths instead of ending up on their chins or down the front of their pretty frocks.

She had just finished moistening her handkerchief to wipe the stickiness off their hands when Lady Alexandra appeared with two of her friends, equally unpleasant ladies. The one called Lady Seline seemed to have a history with Cormac. Hen could sense the icy tension between them and the cruelty in her regard.

These were beautiful women, but so haughty and disdainful, she did not see how anyone could tolerate them.

"Well, is this not a quaint domestic scene? Are you bored to tears yet, darling?" Alexandra said, addressing Cain and sparing not even a glance for Hen. "Come visit me tonight if you find married life too tedious."

She then turned to Cormac. "And you, Burness? You are choosing them rather young these days, are you not?"

Hen saw the anger rise in Cormac. If he were a teakettle, the steam would be pouring from his ears. Hen gripped the edge of the table, afraid the marquess would say something awful in front of his nieces.

Cain was also furious and about to get to his feet when Imogen looked up at Lady Alexandra and said in all her beautiful innocence, "Uncle Cormac, is that one of the horrible ladies?"

Both he and Cain were momentarily speechless, and then grins broke wide on their faces. "Yes, my little duckling. She is. And so are her friends."

Her eyes were still wide and innocent as she said, "I thought so."

Lady Alexandra and her friends strode off in a huff.

Cormac lifted Imogen onto his lap and gave her a kiss on the cheek. "You are priceless."

Ella hopped on his lap and demanded a kiss, too.

Hen's heart did a little flip, for this man was at his best with these girls. But she could tell by the look in his eyes that he was not yet ready to settle down. He was angry, and anything could set him off…save for his precious nieces.

Perhaps Cain was the same, a powder keg of a man whose fuse might be lit by anything at any time, and this was what he feared most. He did not want Hen near him should it go off. He could control himself while awake but did not trust himself while in sleep.

After finishing their ices, they dropped Cormac and the girls back at the Burness townhouse, and returned to Malvern House.

They said no more about the incident at Gunter's, instead listening to Prudence as she told them of her shopping finds. But once they had all retired for the evening, Cain opened the door between their rooms and settled on the bed beside Hen, stretching his large frame next to her.

She had changed into her nightgown, but he was dressed in shirt and trousers. Although the shirt was undone and fell open on his chest, she did not think he meant to couple with her tonight. That he was also frowning lightly was another indication he did not intend to touch her. "What's wrong, my love?" she asked.

"I'm sorry about Alexandra."

Hen couldn't help but grin. "That horrible lady, as Imogen called her? She was rude and haughty, everything awful in a person. I was afraid you were going to bodily toss her out of Gunter's."

"I wanted to. More to get her away from an enraged Cormac. He would never strike a woman, but I wasn't sure what else he might do. It is one thing to taunt him, but to bring his nieces into it was a foolish and dangerous thing. This is what Lady Alexandra is all about, laying hurt, misery, and condescension on others. I didn't want Cormac rising to the bait and scaring the little girls."

"Well, Imogen saved you both."

He laughed. "She did at that."

She propped herself on one elbow and turned to face him. "You are still troubled."

"More kicking myself for ever attaching myself to someone like her. Oh, I knew I was never going to propose to her. But I wonder if ever I was that insufferably haughty and unfeeling toward others. I wonder if my father saw that behavior in me and was disappointed."

She nestled against him and sighed as he wrapped his arms around her. "He loved you and saw you for the fine man you are. It is evident in his letters."

"I hope so."

"I'm going to miss this when we travel."

He nodded. "So will I. But we'll be back at the Grange soon enough. Hen, do you want your sisters to come live with us? There's certainly plenty of room for them."

"I thought about that, too. But I'll let them decide. We all adored living at Moonstone Cottage, and I'm not sure they'll want to leave it. They'll be all right if they decide to stay. Mr. and Mrs. Hawke will look after them."

"Yes, I expect they will manage. But how will you feel being without them?"

Chapter Seventeen

HEN'S SISTERS RAN out of their cottage the moment they heard Cain's carriage rumble through the gate. They were obviously excited, hopping up and down as the driver brought the team of horses to a halt in front of their home.

Hen could not subdue her joy either. She poked her head out the window and waved to her sisters.

Cain helped her down first, and then Prudence, and the pair almost trampled him in their enthusiasm to greet Phoebe and Chloe.

Prudence, although invited to take up residence with him and Hen at the Grange, had declined. "Ask me again in another month," she said when asked. "You don't need a widowed cousin underfoot before you've had the chance to settle in yourselves."

So they had stopped at Moonstone Cottage to drop her off and for Hen to see her sisters, who were now smothering her with kisses and both trying to embrace her at the same time. She was tugged in two directions but did not seem to mind at all, since she was laughing and just as eager to embrace them.

Her sisters began tossing questions at her, giving her no time to answer before they peppered her with more. "Mr. Weston told us you were married," Chloe said. "Is this true? And is Wicked Willis no longer our guardian? Are we saved?"

"Yes, yes. We are all of us saved. Cain is now your guardian."

They rushed to hug him. "You did it!" Chloe said. "How can we ever repay you for all you've done for us?"

He glanced over at Hen and cast her a tender smile. "I got Hen in the bargain. It is the best reward any man can have."

Chloe squealed. "We knew it. Did I not tell you, Phoebe? He simply had to love her!"

Phoebe was all smiles.

They finally made their way into the house, still chattering all at once.

Cain declined when Phoebe asked if they would stay for tea. "Come up to the Grange and have tea with us this afternoon."

Prudence nodded. "Yes, we'll do that. Right now, I am eager to change out of these dusty travel clothes. Phoebe, I assume I am to have the same guest chamber as on my earlier visit?"

"Yes, we have it freshened and ready for you." Phoebe then turned to Hen in dismay. "I just realized! You'll be moving your things to the Grange."

Hen placed a comforting arm around her sister. "Yes, but not today. We'll get around to it over the next few days. There's no rush. I have what I need in the clothes I took to London. We also wanted to talk to you and Chloe about moving to the Grange with us."

Chloe shook her head. "No, Hen. We couldn't impose on you like that."

Phoebe agreed. "We discussed the possibility while you were away. We're very comfortable here, and you are right next door if we ever need anything. We'll see you every day, so it really will be very much the same…even if it does feel terribly upsetting for us right now."

Cain had expected Phoebe and Chloe would decline to move, at least for the present time. It seemed everyone thought a newly married duke and duchess ought to be on their own to acclimate to married life. Perhaps this was true for most couples, but not for him and Hen.

He'd felt the rightness of their match within moments of

meeting her. They did not need to get used to each other so much as learn not to ache whenever they were apart.

He could feel Hen's disappointment as they left the cottage and climbed back into the carriage, for this separation from her sisters was hitting her hard.

Cain settled beside her and took her hand. "The offer is always open for them. We'll make sure they understand we will always welcome them."

She cast him a wistful smile. "Their minds are set. I think I knew it all along."

"Sorry, love. As their guardian, I could require them to live with us."

"No, I don't want to force them. They love Moonstone Cottage so much and are very happy there."

He nodded. "Will you be all right?"

"Yes, more than all right. I'm excited to start married life with you. I know my sisters will manage without me, and as Phoebe said, I'll be seeing them every day. We'll take Chloe in when Phoebe marries, but she's a few years off from that yet."

He and Hen received an effusive greeting upon arriving at St. Austell Grange. The staff lined up to formally meet his new duchess, and Hen did him proud, just as he knew she would.

Weston stood beside the door, waiting his turn to welcome them home.

Cain saw him glance around as though hoping Prudence would be with them. "We've invited the Killigrew sisters and their cousin to tea this afternoon. You're invited, too. Be patient, Weston. You'll see her then."

Weston grinned. "Am I that obvious? Don't answer. I'll leave you and Duchess Henley to settle in. I've left documents on your desk for your review, but nothing that cannot wait until tomorrow."

Footmen carried their trunks upstairs, and Cain's cook had refreshments sent up for them. Baths were also ordered.

He made sure Hen was comfortably settled in her adjoining

duchess's quarters before he went into his bedchamber and attended to himself. Well, he did not attend to himself so much as have his valet fuss over him and a brace of footmen walk in and out while bringing up the tub and water, the last of his trunks, and a tray of tempting delights prepared by his efficient cook.

The door between his chamber and Hen's was closed for the moment, but he could hear his housekeeper and maids fussing over her. Hen was fairly independent and not the sort to enjoy being cosseted, but all fine ladies were expected to have a lady's maid, and his staff would be offended if she did not choose one from among them for the role.

He knew Hen would take care of the matter without his need to mention it. Although her manner was warm and unaffected, she had a strong sense of duty and knew what was expected of a duchess.

She took her responsibilities seriously, probably had a hundred ideas whirling in her head about the running of the household—something he would gladly cede to her—and whatever charities or projects she thought needed attention.

They were similar in their desire to make a difference in the lives of others, for he never took his title as something that came only with privileges and little responsibility.

He eased back in his bath and allowed the warm water to soak into his bones.

Yes, life with Hen would never be dull or ordinary.

CAIN WAS NOT surprised when within a month of their return to Moonstone Landing, Hen had organized and flawlessly pulled off a garden tea party on the grounds of the Grange for the entire village, now to be turned into an annual affair. She had also organized a wedding breakfast to celebrate the marriage of his estate manager, Charles Weston, to Hen's cousin, Prudence. In between, she had hosted several charity affairs to promote the cause of widows, orphans, retired soldiers, a new church roof, and wild ponies.

They were now going on three months home, and the cooler October air had replaced the hot summer breezes. The sunlight hours were also growing shorter, so Cain made certain to send a carriage out at sunset to collect Hen whenever she visited her sisters at Moonstone Cottage, which she did daily.

"Who do you plan on saving next?" Cain teased that night, entering her bedchamber through their adjoining door and taking her in his arms, as had also become their nightly ritual.

She smiled up at him. "You, of course."

"Me?" He'd thought at some point the starlight gleam in her eyes would fade, but it hadn't. And he never tired of looking at her, for there was something so alive about her features that he always found something new in her expressions to fascinate him.

"Yes, my love. I think it is time we set aside your barricades. It pains me, Cain. I cannot bear it when you leave me to retire to your own chamber."

He raked a hand through his hair. "Hen..."

She emitted a ragged sigh. "I know I am asking much of you. If you are not ready yet, I will understand. I suppose I can put my efforts toward saving dolphins, puffins, and sea turtles. I've made quite a bit of progress saving wild ponies. But I would rather save you. Are you still having those terrifying dreams?"

"Yes, although they are much less ferocious. There was a night or two I wasn't even certain I'd had them."

"I thought you seemed more at peace with yourself lately. What do you say? Do you think you are ready?"

He kissed her full on the mouth. "Hen...what if I hurt you?"

"You won't. I think you are ready. Truly, Cain. I wish you would trust my judgment."

Pain tore through him. "You know I trust you with my heart, with my life, with all my being."

"Then please, my love. Sleep with me tonight. Let us have no more doors between us."

Why was she pushing him now?

What if it was too soon?

More pangs of anguish shot through him. "I would give anything to wake to you in the morning, to feel your sweet, warm body curled against me."

"So would I. It is time for you to stop punishing yourself, to stop blaming yourself for all the wrongs you could not prevent. No one is holding you responsible for the horrors of war. Forgive yourself for not being able to save the world. You need to be a husband to me now." She cast him an achingly gentle smile and held out her hand to him.

He laughed, but it was mirthless laughter as he lifted her in his arms and carried her to the bed, setting her down in the middle of it. "All right." He glanced around her bedchamber, wanting to run away. But their nightly separation truly distressed her, so he could not ignore her plea. "I'll give it a try. Be warned, Hen. The demons are not gone from my soul."

"I know, but much of their rage has gone out of you," she insisted. "Because you have given your life purpose. The good you do for others, the hope and enthusiasm you inspire. These count for something."

He shook his head. "You are the one who provides hope and inspiration. This is your strength. Look at how many people you have helped in the short while you have been my duchess."

"I can accomplish much *because* I am your duchess. You gave me this opportunity and have supported me every step of the way."

He still held her in his arms. "You once said love can conquer all problems."

She kissed him on the cheek. "It can."

"I heard you the other day when you were making your speech at the village hall about those wild ponies you are trying to save."

"You heard me? I did not realize you were there."

"I stayed outside and listened beside one of the open windows. I knew I would be a distraction to everyone if I walked in. But I heard your speech, so filled with passion and conviction. I saw how you swayed the audience and how much they believed in you." He sank onto the mattress beside her. "I love you, Hen. I believe in you, too. I always have. I also believe in the strength of these feelings we have for each other."

"This is why I know you will never hurt me, not even while in sleep," she said. "You recognize me. I am in your blood and in the air you breathe. You know my scent. My body. This is how deeply you are aware of me."

He emitted an agonized sigh and rubbed a hand along his face. "All right. Let's try this. I'll never forgive myself if I hurt you."

She cast him a stubborn look. "You won't hurt me."

Perhaps she was right, not only about how deeply she had become embedded in his soul, but about his own progress in overcoming his anger. He had come to realize the past could not be undone. The friends lost in battle would never return. Their loss would always be unfair. But if all he held on to was anger, rage, and frustration, then he would be doing them a great dishonor. Their sacrifice would have been for nothing.

"Thank you, my love," he said.

Her eyes captured the glow of candlelight from the tapers around his room.

They spoke no more as he kissed her.

She fell asleep in his arms.

He took longer, perhaps needing to fight off the last vestiges of doubt.

But he loved her so deeply.

She was right. How could he ever hurt her?

However, the demons of doubt overcame him as he began to drift off to sleep. He quietly tossed off his covers and moved to his own bedchamber. In a way it was cheating, for he awoke just before dawn and then returned to Hen's bed in time to watch her stir awake come morning.

She was not quite arisen yet, merely purring as she curled up beside him, her eyes closed and lips slightly parted. Her cheeks were pink and her hair was in a glorious tumble.

His heart tightened.

He'd wanted so badly to make it through the night without being plagued by the torments of hell.

But not tonight. He was still too uncertain.

Perhaps next week he would try again.

But he had made some progress, having left the door open between their chambers. It was a start, and although that feeling of suffocation had gripped him sometime during the night, the dream had been mild and passed quickly.

He kissed her when she began to insistently burrow against him, seeking the warmth of his body. She mumbled something unintelligible, so he thought she might be awake enough to hold a conversation. "Good morning, love."

She sat up and opened her eyes, an eyebrow tipped in question when she realized they were together in bed. "Did it work?"

He told her the truth.

"I see." She could not mask her disappointment. "Will you try again tonight?"

He shook his head. "No, love. I will do no more than keep the door open between us. I am no longer worried about climbing out of my bed to hurt you. And I will stay with you until you fall asleep, as I have been doing these past nights. If I pass a few more peaceful nights in this fashion, then next week I will try again."

She was clearly disappointed but agreed and cast him a delicate smile that lit up the room. "All right. Small steps."

He immediately thought of his father's words. *You need to meet this girl who sparkles with silver light.*

He returned her smile with a tender one of his own. "How did you sleep?"

"Quite soundly. I did not even realize you had left my bed in the night. Thank you for telling me the truth, even though it is not what I had hoped to hear. But we will get there, I know we will."

"Then you are all right, Hen?"

She nodded. "Always."

ANOTHER WEEK WENT by, and he did feel as though they were making progress, for the door between their bedchambers remained open, and he had actually fallen asleep holding her in his arms a time or two. Yet he'd quickly awoken and left her side to return to his own bed.

He did the same the following week.

As they faced another night apart, Hen cast him a lost puppy stare that shot straight to his heart. "All right. We try again tomorrow night." It was important for him to work harder and take this next step of spending the entire night by her side.

He retired to his own bedchamber and had been lying alone in his bed for several hours, lost in thought, when Hen suddenly cried out, "Cain! Oh no. Cain!"

He sprang out of bed, his heart pounding as he forced himself to alertness, for it was the wee hours of the morning. Why was she crying out? She sounded in pain. He raced to her side. "Hen, love. What's wrong?"

She was clutching her stomach and crying. "I think I am losing the baby."

"What?" He quickly lit the candle by her bedside to cast light upon her while he set aside the covers to see what was happening. His brain had yet to wrap around what she'd just told him until he saw the crimson stain of blood on her sheets.

His heart stopped. His head began to reel. "Love, you're bleeding."

He frantically tugged on the bellpull, calling for Mrs. Chiltern and his head butler, Manton, and probably rousing the entire household in his urgency. "Get Dr. Hewitt here right away," he told Manton, who had run up dressed only in his nightclothes.

"At once, Your Grace! Dear heaven!" He ran off faster than Cain had ever seen him move.

Cain then turned to Mrs. Chiltern, who had almost collided with Manton in the doorway. She had also rushed up, sparing a moment to toss a robe over her nightgown. Her mobcap was askew and she had clips in her hair.

"Bring me clean cloths, fresh water," Cain ordered her. "As fast as you can, Mrs. Chiltern. Wake whoever you need to assist you. I'll want you to stay with my wife until the doctor arrives. Blessed saints, do you have any idea what to do in the meanwhile?"

"Yes, Your Grace. Please do not fret."

Hen put a calming hand on his forearm when he reached over to grasp her hand. "I am all right. It is the child leaving my body. It happens, my love."

But he was devastated. "How far along do you think you were?"

"No more than two months, if that. I was going to wait another week before I shared the news with you because I still had my doubts. It is all happening so fast. I'm so sorry, Cain."

"Don't ever apologize to me. This is not your fault." But no wonder she had wanted him to share her bed and had been making an issue of it all week long. What would have happened if the door between them had been shut so he could not hear her soft cries?

She needed him to be a husband to her in every sense. He resolved then and there never to fail her again.

He stayed by her side, refusing to leave or let go of her even while the doctor examined her or while Mrs. Chiltern washed her and put a clean nightgown on her.

Once things calmed, Cain carried Hen into his bed, since she could not remain in hers with all the blood on the sheets. She claimed it looked worse than it was and she was in no physical pain, but this did not mollify him at all.

It was almost dawn by the time they were finally alone and Hen comfortably settled in his bed. She was too overset to fall back to sleep, so he carefully settled her on his lap. "I will never leave you alone again, love," he said, wrapping her in his arms. "From this night forward, we sleep together. Every night for the rest of our lives."

She put her arms around him and hugged him tightly. "This is all I ever wanted, to sleep next to my big golden bear."

He gave a pained laugh. "As I will enjoy waking to my starlight. Have I mentioned you have the most beautiful eyes?" He kissed her. "And have I told you how much I love you? We shall try for a child again whenever you are ready. But first, you must let that exquisite body of yours heal. I want your promise, Hen. We must not rush this, and I do not ever want you to feel pressured. I will wait until you are ready. I will wait for you forever. I love you and I am not going anywhere."

She finally fell asleep in his arms.

He was true to his word.

They shared a bed from that day forward.

Despite all his concerns, her prediction had proved true.

He slept in peace knowing she was by his side. The warmth of her body sweetly curled against him, the touch of her hand upon his chest. Her soft breath against his neck. All of these little things brought him a peace he had lost during the war years and thought he would never regain.

She was embedded in his soul.

She was his balm, and he could never harm her.

Epilogue

Moonstone Landing
February 1816

WHEN THE CLOCK on the mantel of his study chimed one o'clock, Cain realized he had gotten lost in the pile of documents atop his desk and was probably keeping Hen awake, since she always waited up until he joined her in bed.

He had expected her to be drowsing off or perhaps reading a book while in wait for him, but he never expected to find her crying. She was not the weepy sort, and the last time he'd found her crying was that awful night four months ago when she miscarried.

He groaned. "Hen, your tears are torturing me. What's wrong, love?"

"Nothing is wrong." She threw her arms around him when he sank onto the mattress beside her.

"Hen?"

She buried her face against his neck. "Do you like my body?"

"What a question to ask," he remarked with a light laugh. "It is exquisite, as you well know, because I can never keep my hands off you. Have I not told you often enough? It is perfect and divine. Why are you so overset?"

"My body will not be all that exquisite much longer. Soon,

there will be a lot of me."

He tipped her chin up and stared at her, unable to speak for the tug to his heart. "Hen?"

"In about seven months there will be a little something else. I hope you know what I am talking about."

Warmth flooded through him.

Joy overwhelmed him.

No wonder Hen had seemed to be putting on weight and yet eating less. This also explained her sudden sensitivity to everything and why she had been clinging to him tightly every night this past week.

What a dolt he was not to suspect her condition.

She needed him more than ever now.

He was ready, not only to be a proper husband, but a devoted father as well.

"It is early days yet, Cain. It may be a false alarm. But I am almost two months late in my courses, and that has never happened to me. I am ridiculously punctual. Have you noticed the subtle changes to my body?"

He nodded. "Great fool that I am, I merely thought you were putting on a little weight. I liked it. You seemed to glow."

"It is too soon to make any announcement. I dare not even tell my sisters yet."

"There's no rush, love. Although I'm sure they will suspect."

"I wanted to tell you last night, but you were so busy poring over your estate documents and I did not want to distract you. Also…I am scared we'll lose this one, too."

"Hen, whether we do or not is in the Good Lord's hands. Whatever happens, we are in this together." He caressed her cheek. "Together at every step. Whatever happens. No blame ever cast. There is nothing you can ever do to disappoint me. You simply don't have it in you to be other than warm and compassionate. I love you beyond anything imaginable."

He meant those words to the depths of his soul, for he had fled to Moonstone Landing to heal his wounds.

He had found his miracle cure in Hen.

A lifetime of paying her back would not be enough to express his gratitude for the happiness she had brought into his life.

He told her so, and let out a breath when she graced him with one of her dazzling smiles.

The wind was howling outside their window, and there was snow on the ground. The nights were colder and bleaker now, far colder than the miserable October night when they had lost their first babe. Something had changed in him that night. He could not explain it, nor did he quite understand his subsequent transformation, but despite their sadness, a great weight had also lifted off him. He knew in that moment he had conquered his demons. Those violent dreams would never terrorize him again because Hen needed him to be her safe harbor, her anchor no matter how rocky their plight.

Since then, he had been a proper husband to her and would always be.

On that October night, he had given her an oath. "I shall stay with you every night for the rest of our lives."

He'd kept that vow and always would.

"Hen, love. Are you feeling a little better now?"

She nodded and cast him a look of aching tenderness. "Yes. I'm all right, truly. I just needed to get that good cry out of me. I love you so much, Cain."

He kissed her on the lips. "We are each other's comfort and the peace to each other's soul."

Now smiling, her tears no longer falling, she placed a hand to his heart and brought his hand to rest on hers. "Even our hearts beat together, as though we are one."

He cast her a wicked grin. "Love, if you keep my hand on your lovely, swollen breast much longer, I am going to do something quite naughty with it, and by extension, with you."

She laughed. "I am trying to be sentimental and romantic. We have just had a miraculous breakthrough. Are you not happy? Imagine, we are going to have a little golden bear just like his father."

"Or a little girl with eyes of starlight, just like her mother." He did not think his heart could hold so much love, but he was wrong. It was expanding by leaps and bounds to take in the news of their growing family.

This time truly felt different.

AND IT WAS.

Hen stayed healthy throughout her term.

The months flew by, winter coming to an end, then spring, and now August was drawing to a close, and with it summer. Hen delivered twins, a boy and a girl. The midwife had swathed the babies, who were now asleep in the adjoining duchess's bedchamber that Hen now only used for tending to her personal grooming and dressing, for Cain's bed was the one they always shared.

He was eager for another peek at his children—Lord, his beautiful children—who were under the supervision of the capable midwife, but he was not going to disturb them until he heard their little squawks.

Hen slept with him in his bedchamber, as she had every night since last October. She looked exhausted, utterly drained, but so delicate and enchanting that he could not take his eyes off her. The hours while she agonized in delivery had been sheer terror for him.

He'd worried about losing her, feeling so helpless to prevent it. Everyone knew of the dangers of childbirth. This was a common enough occurrence and his greatest dread. But she was strong and persevered.

He now held her in his arms, achingly aware of her still-delicate condition. "Are you happy, Hen?"

"Yes, love. What beautiful babies we have."

"They are, indeed. But no one is more beautiful than you."

He had put his faith in the strength of their love and conquered his night terrors. They had not completely gone away, but were leashed now. He was in control of them, but only because Hen put his heart at peace.

He awoke shortly after daybreak the following morning to an overcast August sky. The drapes had been left open, so he lay in bed beside Hen and watched the warm but blustery wind push gathering storm clouds across the cove.

He quietly left the bed and walked over to the window and its scenic overlook onto the cove. The grayness of the day did not bother him. As far as he was concerned, it was the best and brightest day he had ever seen.

He heard not a peep from their babies in the adjoining room. Of course, the door was closed, so he was not likely to hear anything unless they were wailing. He would check on them shortly, for he was eager to hold those two little bundles.

He was a father.

Their father.

Nothing was going to temper his joy today.

He turned to gaze at Hen, who was still nestled in his bed and sleeping soundly.

Yes, demons conquered.

Vanquished.

Pounded to dust.

He turned back to the window and watched the tide roll out of the cove. The waters were more roiled than usual because of the oncoming storm. There was no sun to glisten upon the aquamarine waves, and yet…what was that glow?

"Cain," Hen said in a whisper, joining him by the window.

"Love, you should not be out of bed."

"I'm fine. You know I am sturdier than I look." He thought of her, how she had come to him that first day, a lost mermaid almost swept out to sea. "Oh, the tide is low."

"We'll have rain today." He wrapped his arms around her and drew her up against him so that her back leaned against his chest.

"It certainly looks like it, but I don't mind. Do you see the moonstones shining beneath the surface of the water? Look closely, Cain."

He kissed the top of her head. "I do. They're beautiful. I never noticed them before. Is this why the village is called Moonstone Landing? And why your ghost sea captain called his house Moonstone Cottage?"

"Yes, but do you know what those moonstones represent?"

He shook his head. "I haven't heard that lore. But you are grinning like a kitten fallen into a tub of cream, so I think there must be something sentimental and romantic to the story you are about to tell me."

She cast him a beautiful smile. "How brightly do you see them?"

"They're very bright. Like sparkling gemstones. Almost blinding in their brightness. All right, tell me. What do they signify?"

She turned in his arms and reached up on tiptoes to kiss him on the lips. "True love, my handsome golden bear. For only those who truly love can see them with such clarity and brilliance."

He laughed. "Then I am found out. I shall never win an argument with you or ever be able to deny you anything now that you are aware how much I need and love you."

"I knew it all along, but it is nice to have the lore confirm it. I hope my sisters get their moonstones, too. As for me, I can also see them with equal clarity and brilliance. So I think we shall be a pathetic pair, always thinking of the other and wanting to make the other happy."

"Is that so bad?"

"Not at all." She huddled against him and remarked on his warm skin. "But I am cold. I think you had better take me back to bed."

"With pleasure, my love," he said with a soft growl.

He looked forward to waking to her smile and the noisy wails of their children every day for the rest of their lives.

The End

Also by Meara Platt

FARTHINGALE SERIES
My Fair Lily
The Duke I'm Going To Marry
Rules For Reforming A Rake
A Midsummer's Kiss
The Viscount's Rose
Earl Of Hearts
The Viscount and the Vicar's Daughter
A Duke For Adela
If You Wished For Me
Never Dare A Duke
Capturing The Heart Of A Cameron

BOOK OF LOVE SERIES
The Look of Love
The Touch of Love
The Taste of Love
The Song of Love
The Scent of Love
The Kiss of Love
The Chance of Love
The Gift of Love
The Heart of Love
The Hope of Love (novella)
The Promise of Love
The Wonder of Love
The Journey of Love
The Treasure of Love
The Dance of Love
The Miracle of Love
The Dream of Love (novella)
The Remembrance of Love (novella)
All I Want For Christmas (novella)

MOONSTONE LANDING
Moonstone Landing (novella)
Moonstone Angel (novella)
The Moonstone Duke
The Moonstone Marquess
The Moonstone Major

DARK GARDENS SERIES
Garden of Shadows
Garden of Light
Garden of Dragons
Garden of Destiny
Garden of Angels

LYON'S DEN
The Lyon's Surprise
Kiss of the Lyon
Lyon in the Rough

THE BRAYDENS
A Match Made In Duty
Earl of Westcliff
Fortune's Dragon
Earl of Kinross
Earl of Alnwick
Aislin
Gennalyn
Pearls of Fire
A Rescued Heart
Tempting Taffy

DeWOLFE PACK ANGELS SERIES
Nobody's Angel
Kiss An Angel
Bhrodi's Angel

About the Author

Meara Platt is a USA Today bestselling author and an award winning, Amazon UK All-star. Her favorite place in all the world is England's Lake District, which may not come as a surprise since many of her stories are set in that idyllic landscape, including her award winning, fantasy romance Dark Gardens series. If you'd like to learn more about the ancient Fae prophecy that is about to unfold in the Dark Gardens series, as well as Meara's lighthearted, international bestselling Regency romances in the Farthingale series and Book of Love series, or her more emotional Braydens series, please visit Meara's website at www.mearaplatt.com.

Printed in the USA
CPSIA information can be obtained
at www.ICGtesting.com
CBHW061037040824
R15448600001B/R154486PG12554CBX00025B/49